'Let me stay longer.

'I do so want to know you better.'

'Do you, Chloe?' His dark eyes were intent, his mouth somehow softer than usual. His voice was making her feel odd. 'That is good, for it is what I want also.'

Pasha gave her a hungry look that made her tremble. She remembered the magic of that dance on board ship, and for the first time began to understand what she had discovered in his arms. This was the passion she had seen portrayed on the cinema screen—but for real! A feeling of intense excitement mixed with a hint of danger ran through her. This was real! She was beneath desert stars with her own Sheikh and he was about to kiss her...

Anne Herries lives in Cambridge but spends part of the winter in Spain, where she and her husband stay in a pretty resort nestled amid the hills that run from Malaga to Gibraltar. Gazing over a sparkling blue ocean, watching the sunbeams dance like silver confetti on the restless waves, Anne loves to dream up her stories of laughter, tears and romantic lovers.

Recent titles by the same author:

THE ABDUCTED BRIDE
CAPTIVE OF THE HAREM

and in the Regency series
The Steepwood Scandal:

LORD RAVENSDEN'S MARRIAGE
COUNTERFEIT EARL

THE SHEIKH

Anne Herries

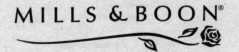

First published in Great Britain 2002
Harlequin Mills & Boon Limited,
Eton House, 18-24 Paradise Road, Richmond, Surrey TW9 1SR

© Anne Herries 2002

ISBN 0 263 83495 6

Set in Times Roman 10½ on 12 pt.
04-0203-81216

Printed and bound in Spain
by Litografia Rosés S.A., Barcelona

THE SHEIKH

Chapter One

'So that's my news,' Chloe said, trying hard not to show her excitement too much. 'I'm off to Morocco next week, and I don't know when I shall be back...'

'You are so lucky!' Justine cried as she stared enviously at her cousin. 'All I've managed to find is a job at the local library—and that's after years at college.' She pouted her rouged mouth at Chloe and adopted what she fondly thought of as an artistic pose.

Chloe Randall tried to look suitably sympathetic as Justine bemoaned her lack of success in finding a really exciting job, but her mouth wouldn't stop smiling.

She had a soft, pretty mouth, which was free of the lip rouge her cousin liked to wear, and her straight, fair, collar-length hair was worn brushed back from her face and held in place by a scarf. Justine's hair had been cut recently into a style favoured by some of the stars of the silent screen, and was short at the back with longer sides. She was also very daringly wearing red lipstick!

They both looked what they were, young girls of good family emerging from the restrictions of their education and beginning to flex their wings in the sun of freedom like little butterflies. It was 1925, the terrible war that had blighted the lives of the generation before them seemed almost a distant memory, and life appeared made for having fun and enjoying oneself.

'It was sheer luck,' Chloe said for perhaps the tenth time that evening, and got up to wind the gramophone once more and play her favourite recording of Paul Robeson one last time. 'I do love this. It was wonderful actually seeing him on stage when Daddy took me.'

'Oh, don't play it again yet,' Justine begged. 'I've got a new jazz record I want to put on in a minute. Sit down and talk to me. Tell me about what happened—how you came to meet this professor...'

'As I was saying, it was luck.' Chloe left the gramophone and sat cross-legged on the floor on a pile of 'harem cushions', which were another one of Justine's fads and popular just at the moment with all the Bright Young Things. 'I happened to be in the research department of the museum when he came in. He was carrying an umbrella, several parcels and a bag of oranges. The paper was wet because it had been raining hard, and his oranges went all over the floor.'

Justine giggled as she pictured the scene. Although she tried very hard to be sophisticated, she was still an innocent at heart, a little starstruck, which came of going to the cinema as much as she possibly could, and being thoroughly spoiled by her indulgent and wealthy parents.

In that she was luckier than Chloe, who had lost her mother to a painful illness while she was away at school, and whose father always seemed rather a cold man to Justine, though she would never have voiced her thoughts aloud out of loyalty to her cousin.

'What did you say his name was—the professor?'

'Hicks—Charles Hicks,' Chloe said and flicked a stray wisp of hair from her eyes. 'The thing is, I helped pick up his oranges and naturally we got talking—and it appears that he knew my father from way back. Apparently, he was at my christening but lost touch with Daddy when he went out to Egypt soon after that. Naturally, I invited him to dinner…'

'And that's when he asked you if you would like to accompany him on a trip to Morocco.' Justine stared at her with a mixture of envy and disbelief.

'To help with some research,' Chloe agreed, her mouth refusing to stay in a straight line. 'Just now, he's working on a book about various nomadic tribes—particularly the Bedouin and Berber peoples. He has already done most of his research on the Bedouins, who inhabit much of northern Africa, and now he wants to do a study of the Berbers—so that he can compare them, apparently. He's also interested in the religious customs and intends to visit a lot of places considered holy—if he can get permission, that is. It's all very clever and beyond me, but interesting, don't you think?'

She laughed as she saw Justine's blank look. Obviously her cousin didn't agree, but then Justine's interests were mostly clothes, dancing, and going to the cinema, as were most young women's these days.

'When Daddy told him that I was interested in Arabic literature, he thought I would be the ideal person to help—especially as I took shorthand as one of my skills.'

'You jumped at the chance, of course.' Justine

sighed. 'I wish I could find someone to give me a free holiday abroad.'

'I wish you could come with us,' Chloe said regretfully. 'But Professor Hicks is paying all my expenses so I can't very well ask if my cousin can come too. I doubt if he really needs help with his research at all, but Daddy told him I'd just finished college and was looking for work while I did my own research. He was quite impressed with my ambition—that's how he put it. Something about admiring a girl who wasn't prepared to settle for marriage straight away.'

'Well, I suppose that's what most of us do—get married and have babies,' Justine said with some regret. 'You're the exception, Chloe. I went to college because my father wanted me to, and you were already there so it was fun. But Mummy expects me to do the season, and I expect I'll get engaged—if I can find someone who looks like *him*…'

Justine reached for a copy of the magazine she had discovered at the library that morning. It had a full-page picture of the actor Rudolph Valentino inside and was advertising his latest film.

'We must see this before you go away,' Justine said and sighed over the picture of the screen idol. 'I've seen all his films over and over again, but I love *The Sheikh* the most. They say he's planning to make a sequel to it soon.'

'Oh, he's just wonderful,' Chloe agreed and crossed her legs. She was wearing a short skirt, which her grandmother, Lady Margaret Hatton, thought was shockingly indecent, and fine silk stockings.

'Marvellous,' Justine said and reached for the silver cigarette box on the table beside her, offering it to

Chloe, who shook her head. 'Oh, of course, you don't. Mummy hates it if I smoke when she's in the room, but Daddy doesn't mind. He says there are worse things than a woman smoking, and he smokes too much himself. I take after him; at least, that's what Mummy always says whenever she's annoyed with me.' Her laugh was tinkling and infectious.

Chloe smiled affectionately at her. Justine was bright and pretty, and always saying things she really didn't mean, because she thought it was clever. It was fashionable to behave in the slightly outrageous way she did amongst her friends, and Chloe knew that her cousin wasn't really wild at all underneath. She would fall in love, get married and live in a beautiful house in the country somewhere with occasional visits to town, and no doubt be very happy. Her parents spoiled her all the time, which was very nice. Chloe could have done with a little of that spoiling herself, but she knew she wasn't likely to get it from her father.

He had always been a reserved man, but since her mother's death he had withdrawn more and more into his own world, leaving Chloe to fend for herself. If it hadn't been for Justine, of whom she was very fond, Chloe thought that she might have been rather lonely.

Her grandmother rarely left her home in the north of England these days, and her health was not good. She preferred not to have visitors, though she asked to see her granddaughter once a year, and remembered to send her a birthday card.

'I expect you'll like being married,' she said to Justine. 'When you find the right person.'

'But don't you want to marry?' Justine looked at her curiously.

'In time, I suppose—but not yet.'

Chloe wanted something more of life than her mother had had being Peter Randall's wife. She knew that a life similar to that of her own or even Justine's mother, who had a busy social schedule, would not suit her. She wasn't sure what she was looking for, but an independent observer might have seen that she needed affection.

'Smoking is all right if you like it,' Chloe said as her cousin selected one from the box. 'It makes me choke and I don't enjoy the taste.'

'Oh, well...the taste is something you get used to.'

Justine wasn't going to admit that she only did it because her Bohemian friends said it was smart. She had to be a part of the crowd if she wanted to be invited to all the best parties. She looked at the magazine on her lap and sighed again.

'Do you ever wonder what it would be like to meet a real Sheikh, Chloe? Would he be at all like Valentino, do you think?'

'Lord, I shouldn't think so for a moment,' Chloe replied and giggled. She was giggling as much at her cousin, who was taking a delicate puff of smoke through her elegant cigarette holder, as at the suggestion, but she didn't let Justine know that. 'He would probably be fat, greasy and smell absolutely awful.'

'Oh, don't,' Justine begged, tipping back her head in the manner of Gloria Swanson on screen. 'Please don't shatter my illusions. I'll have you know I dream of meeting Valentino...I see him bending down to swoop me up in his arms and carry me off to his tent in the desert.' She gave a delicious little shiver at the thought.

'You and a million other women,' Chloe said and

smiled. She too had imagined herself in similar situations to those endured by the slave girl played by the actress Agnes Ayres, but in her heart she knew she wasn't likely to meet someone who looked and behaved as the film star did on screen. 'But I agree that it would be romantic to meet Rudolph Valentino... Just imagine if someone asked you to star with him in a film.'

'Oh, I would die for the chance,' Justine said and laughed. 'I still think it would be romantic to be carried off by a Sheikh to his tent beneath the desert stars...'

'You might not like it when you got there,' Chloe said. 'I think it would be better to stick to the film version—much safer.'

She had often thought how exciting it would be to act in a Hollywood film, and her mouth curved as she imagined being asked to play the slave girl in a film similar to *The Sheikh*. Of course it was just a silly dream, and she had never told anyone, even Justine, of her foolish thoughts.

'Well, I shall have to be content with my library job until Prince Charming comes to sweep me off my feet,' Justine said, shrugging her elegant shoulders. 'At least you have an exciting holiday to look forward to.'

'It isn't just a holiday,' Chloe said. 'Professor Hicks is a dear, kind man, but I dare say he will expect me to work for my privileges.'

'It's a pity he's so old,' Justine said. She pulled a face of disappointment. 'Older than your father. But you never know, you might meet someone exciting on your trip, Chloe. Perhaps he will be dark and handsome and carry you off to his casbah—'

'I doubt that very much,' Chloe said, but it didn't stop her dreaming. In her heart she was as romantic as Justine, though she tried hard not to be. Her father had always told her to keep a clear mind on things and judge the situation before she made any decisions. Chloe knew that it was best not to dream or to expect too much, because that only led to disappointment.

'Act on impulse and you may live to regret it,' had been Mr Peter Randall's maxim all his life. It was a very sensible, safe way to look at things, but could be a little dull, Chloe had discovered. Sometimes she thought it might be exciting to do something mad and totally irresponsible for once in her life.

'Well, we can all dream,' Justine said and got up to put on a new dance record she had bought. 'Come on, Chloe—try this…'

Chloe jumped to her feet, laughing as Justine began to demonstrate one of the latest dance crazes. She was always trying something new, which was perhaps why Chloe found it fun to be with her.

'Oh, I do wish you could come with us,' she sighed. 'But I suppose it's no good wishing for the moon.'

'Mummy would never agree anyway,' Justine said. 'She is determined to marry me off to someone very rich and very dull.'

Chloe shook her head. 'Well, the very rich part wouldn't be so bad, Justine. Poor Daddy has found it difficult to manage since the war. He invested in a company that failed and it reduced his income almost by half. That's why I was so pleased to get a job almost straight away.'

'Well, I wouldn't mind the money,' Justine agreed.

'I can see myself in furs and jewels. Summer on the French Riviera and winter in Biarritz...'

'Yes,' Chloe agreed. 'And if he has lots of it, Justine, perhaps he won't be so very dull after all.'

It was all so exciting and glamorous, being seen off by her friends on board a luxury cruise ship. On deck the atmosphere was just like a big party, with champagne corks popping, people laughing and streamers flowing. Everyone seemed to have friends who had come to wish them 'Bon Voyage', and Chloe was pleased that her father and Justine had insisted on making the journey to Southampton with her.

She had noticed that most of the other guests on board seemed very wealthy, the women dressed in elegant clothes with furs draped over their shoulders, and the men quietly confident though often wearing sober suits. Perhaps that was why she noticed *him* almost immediately, because he stood out from the others. His suit was a light fawn colour and obviously expensive, and his shoes were handmade leather, his shirt the kind that came from Savile Row.

'That's the horn telling us it's time to go ashore,' Chloe's father said and kissed her. 'Take care of yourself, my dear. Have a good time and be as useful as you can to Charles. Above all, do as he tells you and behave yourself. I want to be proud of my daughter and it was very good of Charles to give you this job.'

'Yes, of course, Daddy,' Chloe said and hugged him. 'Take care of yourself.' He nodded and released himself firmly from her embrace.

'I shall just go and say goodbye to Charles.'

'Yes, you must.'

'You girls must say your goodbyes quickly,' Mr

Randall warned as he went off, leaving them at the rails together.

'Oh, damn,' Justine said. 'I suppose we shall have to go ashore.' She pulled a face. 'I do so wish I was coming with you.' She kissed Chloe. 'Don't do anything I wouldn't—and don't run off with a Sheikh!' She threw out her arms dramatically as she spoke, accidentally striking a man standing just behind her.

'Be careful, young woman!'

In her exuberance, Justine had knocked the man's arm, causing him to jerk and spill champagne over his suit. It was the man Chloe had noticed earlier being seen off by a party of friends, all of whom were dressed as elegantly as he was, and one of them a rather beautiful young woman. He was glaring at Justine furiously, and she was clearly embarrassed, which made Chloe jump to her cousin's defence.

'It was rather foolish to bring your drink into a crowd like this, don't you think?' she said. 'Justine didn't mean any harm.'

'No, of course not,' Justine said and smiled at him winningly, her cheeks a fiery red. 'I'm terribly sorry. I hope I haven't done any real harm?'

'The suit is probably ruined, but it is of no consequence,' he said and turned away.

'What a rude man!' Chloe said as he moved further down the rail; the crowd was thinning out now as people began to leave. 'It was his own fault for getting so close to you.'

'I expected he wanted to wave to his friends on shore,' Justine said. 'Oh, lord, I must go or they will take me with you...'

They hugged and Justine ran off to join the last few stragglers going ashore. Chloe laughed as her friend held on to her hat and tried to wave all at the same time, then she turned to look for her travelling companions. Catching sight of Professor Hicks and his secretary, Miss Amelia Ramsbottom, she raised her arm to signal to them. As she did so, she heard a muffled exclamation and swung round to see that she had succeeded in tipping the remainder of that glass of champagne over the man Justine had upset earlier.

'I see you are determined to ruin this suit,' he said, and just for a moment she thought there was a glimmer of humour in his eyes. 'Did I do something to annoy you?'

Chloe bit her lip. She was tempted to snap at him, but they were going to be on the same ship for a while and there was no point in creating an unpleasant atmosphere as they were bound to meet from time to time.

'I am sorry,' she said, trying for composure. 'Can it be cleaned on board? I shall be happy to pay the bill.'

'It is of no consequence,' he repeated, but this time he smiled. Chloe realised that he was quite attractive when his features relaxed from the harshness they had assumed earlier. His hair was black, cut short and slicked back from his forehead, and his eyes were almost as dark as his hair. He spoke with a cultured English accent, but somehow she did not think he was entirely English. His features were too strong, too— would exotic be the right word? She wasn't sure. He frowned at her. 'Is there something wrong?'

Chloe realised that she had been staring and blushed. 'No—forgive me. I must join my friends.'

She left him abruptly, her heart racing. There was something a little unnerving about him, something that made her uneasy. There was an arrogance about him, and something she couldn't quite place—a feeling that beneath the surface this man was not quite what he seemed. He certainly wasn't at all like most of the men she knew.

At college she'd met serious-minded professors, the brothers, cousins or fathers of her friends and fellow students. They were all much alike, gentlemen and sons of gentlemen. Some had been nicer than others, of course, but they had all behaved properly, treating her with the respect due to a young woman of good family.

At times Chloe had almost wished they wouldn't be quite so respectful, but she knew she wasn't the kind of girl that drove men wild with passion. She wasn't pert and pretty like Justine, and she didn't realise that her quiet, thoughtful manner was in itself very attractive—or that she was rather lovely in her own way.

'Oh, there you are, my dear,' Charles Hicks greeted her with a smile as she went up to him. 'We were just wondering where you had got to, weren't we, Amelia?'

The professor and his secretary, who was of a similar age to himself, had seen many such send-offs on board ship, and had chosen to stay well back from the crowd flooding the rails. They were both dressed in sober tweed suits, which seemed quite unsuitable for the occasion to Chloe.

'Oh, Chloe was saying goodbye to her friend,' Amelia Ramsbottom said. 'You can't expect her to spend all her time with us, Charles. She's young and this is her first time on board ship. She ought to enjoy herself while she can.' Chloe was aware of a slight hostility in the professor's secretary, and suspected she might be a little jealous of her. Amelia had been travelling with him for years and must wonder why he had invited a young woman to accompany them this time. Chloe had wondered herself at first, but she suspected it was merely kindness on the part of her father's old friend. He was a successful man, and could afford to indulge his whims, and no doubt he had been aware that money was a little tight in the Randall household.

'It is certainly all very exciting,' Chloe said. 'But I want to help Professor Hicks as much as I can.'

'I shan't need you all the time,' he said. 'You must enjoy the voyage, my dear. I may ask you to take some dictation for me. Amelia types all my work beautifully, but I go too fast for her when I dictate. Your shorthand should be a big help to me.'

'I'm going to my cabin,' Amelia announced. 'If I were you, Chloe, I should do the same. You may find yourself feeling a little unwell once we get properly underway.'

Charles Hicks watched her go. She was a small, thin woman with greying hair and a prim manner. 'I fear Amelia is not a good traveller on board, Chloe. She has been a loyal companion for many years, but I really believe she would prefer to stay in England. I think this may also be my last adventure.'

'Oh, that would be a shame, sir.'

'Please don't call me sir—Charles. You must call me Charles.' His faded blue eyes twinkled at her. He was still a good-looking man though into his senior years. 'I am sixty-nine, Chloe. I think I shall be content to settle once I have completed this trip. I spent many years in Egypt, as you know, and I have been into the desert on numerous occasions—but I am still looking for a lost city…' He laughed as she looked at him. 'Something as wonderful as Petra that would make my name…but I dare say I shall never find it.'

Chloe smiled her understanding. She knew about Petra—in Greek it meant 'city of rock' and was an ancient city of Arabia, situated between the Dead Sea and the Gulf of Aqabah, near the intersection of important caravan routes from Gaza to the Mediterranean. It had once been a flourishing city, but then it fell into decay and had been lost, rediscovered in the nineteenth century by a Swiss explorer.

'I expect many people would like to discover something as wonderful as Petra,' she said. 'As you know, my own interest is in discovering beautiful poetry that has been ignored for a long time. Of course, I don't read Arabic, though I can recognise certain words, but I have done some research and I have been fortunate enough to find some wonderful translations into French and English, which I am collecting together for a book I hope to publish one day.'

'Yes, so your father told me. I find that interesting. You must show me your work another day, Chloe— but now I think we should follow Amelia's lead and find our cabins.'

Chloe had been given an inside cabin, which was disappointing in a way, because it would have been pleasant to look out at the sea and the sky. However, she knew that they were more expensive, and she didn't intend to spend much time in her cabin anyway.

She had wondered how long it would take her to find her sea legs, but soon discovered that she was unaffected by the slight swell of the sea. It might be different if they hit rough weather, but for the moment she was feeling fine and enjoying herself.

Amelia did not join them for dinner that evening, which Chloe thought a shame since there was a festive air as everyone was greeted by the captain when they entered the dining room. Chloe and the professor hadn't been invited to the most important table that evening, but the other passengers at their own table seemed very friendly and she enjoyed being introduced and talking to all of them.

'Is this your first voyage?' a rather plump lady called Mrs Vermont asked. 'I am a seasoned traveller, of course, but my niece Jane is with me for the first time. You two girls will be company for each other. Now, isn't it lucky that you are both here?'

Jane Vermont seemed rather a silly girl to Chloe, but they were of a similar age so she smiled and agreed. It would be impossible to avoid the Vermonts and she would need someone to talk to. Most of the other passengers seemed to be much older, which was a little disappointing.

'What are you going to do after dinner?' Jane asked her. 'There's masses of entertainment—a dance, the live show and they are running a film this evening. I would like to see it, but Aunt Vera doesn't want to go.'

'It depends,' Chloe said cautiously. 'What are they showing?'

'I'm not sure—shall we ask the captain later?'

Chloe thought the captain would have more important things to occupy his time, and surely there were enough stewards to ask anyway. Jane was look-

ing towards the top table, smiling and waving, obviously wanting to be noticed.

Chloe glanced that way herself and saw that one
of the favoured guests was the man she had bumped
into earlier. He was wearing a very elegant black dinner suit and a pristine white shirt with a black bow
tie. As she looked at him, he seemed to become aware
of her and lifted his glass to her in a salute.

'Who is that perfectly divine man?' Jane asked immediately. 'He's so handsome—just like Rudolph
Valentino, dark and mysterious and sort of threaten-
ing.' She gave an artificial shiver. 'Do you know
him?'

'No—we met briefly on deck earlier, but we
weren't introduced,' Chloe said and looked down.
The smoked salmon she was eating had suddenly become very interesting and she kept her eyes firmly
fixed on her plate. Her heart was behaving very stu-
pidly, and she was afraid that her cheeks might be
flushed.

'Well, he seems very interested in you,' Jane said
and giggled. 'I wish he would look at me like
that…smouldering, that's the word.' She smiled at
him, but to her discomfiture got nothing but a blank
stare. 'Did you know that there is a film crew on
board? They are American, I hear.'

'A film crew?' Chloe looked at her, her attention
caught. 'I had no idea—are there any famous actors
or actresses with them?'

'No—I think they probably flew to wherever
they're going. The director is with the crew, though.
I think he wants to take some shots on board for some
reason. They say he's looking for a star for his new

picture.' She preened her fluffy dark hair. 'Do you think I look a bit like Mary Pickford, Chloe?'

Chloe didn't think she looked at all like the famous star everyone called the 'World's Sweetheart', but she was embarrassed to say so straight out.

'Well, perhaps a little bit,' she said. 'Your hair is the same as hers was in her last film.'

She saw that Jane was pleased, and it was obvious that she had chosen to wear her hair that way in order to look as much like the star as possible.

She really was a bit silly, Chloe thought, and wished her cousin had been on the ship with them, but it was no use sighing over something she couldn't have. She glanced briefly towards the table, and saw that *he* was lighting a cigarette for a woman sitting to his left. She was a very beautiful woman, expensively dressed and very sure of herself as she smiled into his eyes.

Chloe looked away again quickly. She wasn't in that sort of league, and couldn't compete with a woman like that—not that she wanted to, of course.

'Do say you will come and watch the picture with me,' Jane said as people began to make a move from their tables a little later. 'I just asked one of the stewards and he said it was Valentino's latest picture. I am longing to see it.'

'I saw that before I came away,' Chloe said, but then as Jane's face fell. 'Oh, well, I suppose I wouldn't mind seeing it again.'

'You two young things get off,' Mrs Vermont said indulgently. 'I'll sit here and keep the professor company for a while.'

Chloe caught the look of dismay in his eyes before he managed to hide it and smiled inwardly.

'Do you mind?' she asked him. 'Or is there some work you would like me to do for you this evening?'

He looked tempted, but shook his head. 'I am not such an ogre as to make you work on your first evening, Chloe. No, my dear, you run along and enjoy yourself.'

Jane was full of the film as they left the small theatre afterwards. She went on and on about the star of the film being so handsome and exciting, until Chloe thought she would scream.

'I really ought to go now,' she said. 'I must see if Miss Ramsbottom needs anything before I go to my own cabin.'

In her haste to escape her chattering companion, Chloe took the next turning, which she imagined to be the corridor leading to her own and Miss Ramsbottom's cabins. However, when she got to the end and found that it led into yet another corridor leading in a different direction, she realised that she had come the wrong way.

As she turned to retrace her steps, she saw someone coming towards her and hesitated, wondering if there was some way to avoid another meeting. It would look foolish if she went back the way she knew led only to the staterooms, so she really had no choice but to stand her ground.

'Ah, so we meet again,' he said and looked amused. 'I really think we should introduce ourselves, Miss…?'

Chloe hesitated, then took a deep breath. This was ridiculous!

'Chloe Randall,' she said and offered her hand. 'I am travelling with Miss Amelia Ramsbottom and Professor Charles Hicks—and I seem to have taken a wrong turning.'

'Very easy to do,' he said, and took her hand, holding it for a moment before releasing it. 'I am Armand…Philip Armand…and if you would care to tell me the number of the cabin you seek, I should be delighted to help you find your way, Miss Randall.'

Chloe was trying to make up her mind what nationality he was. His surname sounded a bit French, but she didn't think he looked French—and he had hesitated for a moment, almost as if the name he had given her was not his own. But surely he wouldn't lie—why should he?

'I—it is nice to meet you,' Chloe replied formally and then felt silly. 'My cabin is number fifty-two and Miss Ramsbottom's is fifty-nine. I was going to call on her and see how she was feeling before I went to bed. She wasn't well earlier.'

'Bed so early?' His brows rose, a curl of amusement on his lips. He was very much the sophisticated man of the world, and made Chloe aware of how young and naïve she must seem. She knew that her clothes were too young for her, and nowhere near as elegant as the other women on board were wearing. 'You shouldn't think of such a thing while on board ship, Miss Randall. A young girl like you should be dancing the night away with a handsome partner.'

Chloe knew he was mocking her. She hadn't seen any handsome young men on board—and the few older ones who fitted his description would be dancing with someone more interesting than little Chloe Randall.

'I assure you that I have no intention of dancing with anyone, Mr Armand,' she said. 'It has been a long day and I am tired. If you could please direct me to my cabin, I shall not trouble you longer. Especially if there is someone waiting for you...'

Now why had she said that? It sounded as if she were interested—and she wasn't! Not in the least.

'Unfortunately there is no one I care to dance with either,' he replied, smiling oddly. 'My fiancée was forced to remain in London. However, I should be happy to have you as a partner if you do feel tempted to dance another evening—when you are not so tired.'

To her annoyance, Chloe found herself blushing again. How was it that he was able to make her feel like a stupid schoolgirl? She was about to ask him for directions again when she saw a steward come out of one of the cabins, and turned to him quickly.

'Certainly, I can show you the way, miss,' he replied to her hasty question. 'I am going that way now. Please follow me. Goodnight, Mr Armand.'

So he had not been lying about the name after all, Chloe thought as she nodded to him and followed the steward. Philip Armand shot her an amused glance and walked on down the corridor to where Chloe knew the staterooms were situated. They were much larger than her cabin, and had an opening so that the fortunate guest could step outside in privacy and take the air. She had been told that there was also a sitting room and two large bedrooms, and felt a little envious of the passengers who could afford such luxury.

But she was lucky to be here at all! Chloe reminded herself. She would never even have had the chance to travel abroad like this if it had not been for the generosity of Charles Hicks.

She knocked at Amelia's door and was asked to enter. When she went in, she saw that the poor

woman was lying flat on her back and looked most
unwell.

'Can I do anything for you?' she asked, and Amelia
shook her head. 'Would you like me to call the doctor
to you?'

'Thank you, no,' Amelia replied. 'The steward has
already given me something to help settle me. It was
good of you to ask, Chloe—but all I want is to be
left in peace. I shall be all right in a day or so.'

'I'm sorry to have disturbed you,' Chloe said and
closed the door quietly as she left.

She was thoughtful as she went into her own cabin.
Who was Mr Armand, and why had she had the dis-
tinct impression he was lying when he gave her his
name?

There was really no reason why he should lie to
her—or none that she knew of. Perhaps he was travelling under a false name? Yet why should he be?
Was he a spy or something underhand like that—a
gangster, perhaps?

Chloe didn't visit the cinema regularly for nothing!
And yet he didn't look anything like the pictures
she'd seen of gangsters in the movies.

She considered what he did look like, and decided
he was rather like a picture she had seen in a newspaper of a foreign prince a few weeks earlier. No, not
a prince…but she was sure it was something of the
sort. She couldn't quite place the article, but she
thought it had something to do with politics…or was
it big business? She wasn't certain, and gave it up.

It surely didn't matter, because she wasn't likely to
have much to do with him. He would probably avoid
her like the plague in future, especially if he happened
to have a glass in his hand.

Chloe smiled as she remembered his face when Justine had tipped half that champagne over him. He had been rather put out at the time, but on the second occasion he had seemed as if he had begun to see the funny side of it—and he had been perfectly pleasant this evening, even if she did suspect that he had enjoyed mocking her.

She yawned as she began to undress. She really was sleepy, and she had become irritated by Jane Vermont's meaningless chatter. It would be too bad if she was forced to put up with that for the whole of the voyage, and once again she regretted that her cousin had not been able to come on the trip with them.

Sighing, she went to bed and fell asleep almost instantly, dreaming of the film she had just seen, but at some time during her dream the face of the Sheikh changed, becoming that of someone she had just met.

'You are a beautiful, dangerous woman,' he told her as he looked deeply into her eyes. 'I shall have to take you to my casbah and lock you away.'

Waking briefly, Chloe remembered where she had seen that article, then went back to sleep and forgot all about it again...

Chapter Two

He stood watching the dancers for a moment, his features as hard as the Atlas Mountains, which banded the plains where his ancestors had roamed for centuries, moving relentlessly through deserts and fertile regions on the caravan routes from Gaza to the Barbary Coast. Pasha Ibn Hasim, otherwise known as Philip Armand—or even on occasions Philippe—watched as the girl danced with her elderly employer, a frown on his face that was generally considered strong rather than handsome.

At first he had thought she must be the professor's niece or his mistress, for he had watched her saying goodbye to her father and friend that day in Southampton. Pasha was not certain why she had aroused his interest, except that she had something in her manner that brought back memories of another girl—his half-sister Lysette.

Lysette's mother was a woman of French–Algerian extraction, and had married Sheikh Hasim Ibn Ali after they met when the Sheikh was in Paris following the death of his first wife.

Pasha's own mother had been the favourite daughter of an English gentleman, but she had a French grandmother. It was his great-grandmother's maiden name that Pasha sometimes took when he wished to travel to countries and cities where his relationship to a certain prince might cause his life to be threatened. It was easier when he did not wish to make his visit official to use the English passport he had obtained in that name.

His uncle, Prince Hassan, had arranged for him to be given an English education at Harrow and Cambridge after Pasha's father was assassinated. Lysette had gone to America with her mother—and it was there that she had died in a car accident only a few months previously.

Once again Pasha's features hardened as he thought of the beautiful sister he had adored. Although they had met infrequently after their father's violent death, Lysette had been a warm, loving friend. Her needless death had shocked and then angered him as he began to suspect that it might not have been the accident that it was supposed to have been.

The doctors who examined her at the time of her death had told Pasha that she was carrying a child. That alone would have been enough to make Pasha vow to punish the man who had ruined her—but the suspicion that she had been killed because she was carrying a child filled him with a bitter anger.

Pasha would not spare the man who had destroyed Lysette if he could be certain of where the guilt lay, but as yet the agents he had set to work for him in America had come up with little in the way of proof. No matter! He was wealthy enough to pursue his enemy to the bitter end, which for Pasha meant a fitting punishment—but for the moment he had equally important concerns.

His visit to Morocco was dual purpose in that he intended to mix business with pleasure. He had family he had not seen in years, whom he intended to visit—but there were other secret reasons for his journey.

The whole region of the Middle East had become volatile of late. Oil was becoming an increasingly valuable commodity, and the Sheikhs of the various small states were jostling for power and territory. Land that had once been merely poor grazing ground could now be worth millions of dollars. His uncle, Prince Hassan, was the ruler of one such state and a powerful man, but he had equally powerful enemies. If he were not to die at the hands of an assassin, too, his family and friends must be vigilant.

A recent plot had been foiled thanks to something Pasha had learned in London from someone at the Foreign Office. The British were keen to support Prince Hassan, who had always been very pro-British and was a valuable ally in the shifting sands of a difficult political situation. And it was another such hint that had brought Philip Armand to this ship.

After the attempt to murder his uncle had been foiled, two men had been captured and persuaded to talk—but a third had escaped. Forbes, his contact at the Foreign Office, had told Pasha that according to his sources the culprit might be found in Marrakesh.

'We can't touch him, because the French wouldn't stand for British interference—besides, he's sheltering with a man of some political influence out there,' Forbes had said.

'But I may be able to achieve what you cannot?' Pasha's mouth had curved in a wry smile, which hid his true feelings. Clearly Forbes imagined that he would take a thing like political assassination in his stride. Pasha believed that there were certain circumstances that might lead him to kill, for the way of his people was an eye for an eye and a part of him responded to that. And yet there was another side that found what was, after all, little better than cold-blooded murder abhorrent. But he knew that his uncle's life must be protected, not just because of the family tie, but for stability in the region. 'Tell me, my friend—what is the British position in all this?'

'Officially, we cannot meddle in the politics of the Arab world—but between you and me, Abdullah Ibn Hassan has been a thorn in our side for too long. We suspect him of sabotage as well as murder.'

'Then you would be happy if someone arranged for him to be eliminated?' He raised his brows as the icy trickle started at the nape of his neck. This thing that was being asked of him gave him a nasty taste in the mouth, and yet he knew that he might be forced to comply—unless there was another way? He would have to give the matter a great deal of thought.

'Unofficially, we should be delighted—but this conversation never took place.'

'Of course not.' Pasha smiled. 'I am merely taking a little trip for business and family reasons.'

'Family out there too, have you?' Forbes asked. 'I thought your family were more from Algeria...or Syria?'

'My father's people were the true Bedouin,' Pasha replied, pride tempered with amusement in his eyes. 'That means they never settled in one place for more than a few months. I have uncles and cousins all over Morocco, Algeria—and, yes, one of my own homes is in Syria. The Bedouin knew no boundary—we simply wandered where we chose along the caravan routes.'

Forbes nodded. 'You're so damned English most of the time it's hard to remember you were born out there.'

'In my father's *casbah*,' Pasha said. 'I believe I was conceived in a tent under desert stars, but my mother wanted a Western doctor to attend the birth.'

Forbes nodded. 'Helen Rendlesham was a beauty by all accounts—and brave. The Sheikh must have been devastated when she died so suddenly.'

'Blood poisoning,' Pasha said. 'She was helping one of her women assemble a sewing machine she had imported to help them learn new skills—and she cut her hand on the rusty underside of a metal plate. No one imagined it would kill her.'

'Septicaemia,' Forbes said. 'It killed an awful lot of men in the last war. We're only just beginning to make the medical advances we need here. It must have been hopeless in the desert—your father couldn't have got her to a hospital in time.'

'It was a tragedy and nearly broke his heart.' Pasha frowned. 'I was but a child then and I cried for a long time after she died…'

He had wept a few bitter tears for Lysette too, but he was a man now and this new grief had settled into a hard anger that lived with him night and day. For weeks he had retired into himself, hardly noticing what happened around him…but a young girl had startled him out of the black mood that had possessed him.

He saw her dancing again, and thought of asking her to be his partner when the next dance began—

and then a man walked into the ballroom: a man that aroused distrust and hatred in Pasha's heart. He turned and left abruptly as the bitterness mounted in his throat like gall—the dance would keep until another time.

Chloe caught glimpses of Philip Armand over the next few days. She had thought he might ask her to dance one evening, but he hadn't and for some reason they didn't meet anywhere else. It crossed her mind that he might have been avoiding her, but she didn't let it bother her. There was so much to do on board that she was always busy, and she found herself dividing her time between taking dictation from Professor Hicks and attending all the various functions with Jane Vermont.

Chloe much preferred the time she spent working for the professor to the hours she was obliged to be with Jane Vermont. He really was a clever man and he knew an awful lot about the history of the region they were going to visit over a period of several weeks.

'It may even run into a few months,' the professor told her. 'We shall disembark at Cetua, Chloe, and make our way to Fez and to Marrakesh, as well as other places of interest I want to visit. I hope you are prepared for a long stay—though, if at any time you want to leave us, I shall make arrangements to get you on a ship going home.'

'Thank you,' Chloe said. She was grateful for his kindness, but felt sure it was unnecessary. 'But I'm really looking forward to this trip. I am confident I shan't want to leave until you and Amelia are ready to come too, but I know you would look after me if I had to return for any reason.'

Chloe was learning a lot about the nomadic peoples of the Middle East as she took dictation and then transcribed her own notes in a fair hand so that Amelia could type them up into manuscript form on the battered portable typewriter that accompanied her everywhere.

Amelia had recovered her health and her spirits after a couple of days at sea, and seemed friendlier towards Chloe as the cruise progressed. She encouraged her to go on the shore trips at the various ports the ship called during the leisurely voyage, telling her that she ought to make the most of her chances to see a little bit of France and Spain while she could.

'I've been on most of these trips over the years,' she told Chloe. 'I was in Egypt with Charles for several years, and we have been all over that whole region. All the regions bordering the Sahara—apart from those to the west. That is why Charles wants to visit Morocco again. He has been there before, of course, but not right to the Western Desert. He is most meticulous, you know, and will collate far more information than he could ever actually put into his books.' She smiled in a self-congratulatory way. 'Of course I am the one who does the cutting when the publisher demands at least fifty thousand less words.'

'You must be of invaluable help to Professor Hicks.'

'Yes, I believe I am—though what he will do when this last book is finished…if it is his last book, of course.' Her expression showed that she thought it unlikely.

Chloe listened but offered few comments. She

found it all fascinating, including the trips she made ashore to Spanish and Portuguese ports, then to Gibraltar. They were nearing the end of their voyage now, for Cetua was a Spanish port at the edge of Morocco and only just across the water from Gibraltar.

'Oh, are you leaving us at Cetua?' Mrs Vermont asked. 'Jane will be so disappointed. You must keep in touch, Chloe dear, and perhaps come to stay with us when you return to England.'

'That is very kind of you,' Chloe said. 'But I am not sure when we shall be returning. It may not be until next year.'

She had gone up on deck to escape Jane's chattering on the morning of her last day on board the ship, when she was approached by a man who she knew to be the one Jane believed to be a film director. She had previously only nodded to him in passing—probably because he had seemed to prefer to keep his distance.

'Good morning, Miss Randall—it is Miss Randall, isn't it?'

'Yes…' Chloe caught the faint twang of an American accent. 'Someone told me you were Brent Harwood, but somehow we haven't been introduced.'

He nodded and smiled. 'You've been told I am a Hollywood director and you are wondering if it's true?' Chloe nodded herself. 'Well, I can assure you it is. I do not enjoy being hounded by starstruck young women, Miss Randall—that is why I keep a distance. But I have noticed you. You have a certain poise—a way of holding your head that is most attractive. Have you ever considered becoming an actress?'

Chloe's heart missed a beat. How many times had she dreamed of something like this? But somehow, now that it was happening, she didn't quite believe it, and imagined that he was merely flattering her. Though she couldn't see why he should.

'Oh, I don't suppose I could do it,' she said. 'I'm not sure I have any talent.'

'Talent is something that is not always required,' he said. 'A star is made on the cutting-room floor, Miss Randall.' He smiled at her a little wolfishly, and she thought he might be a vain man—but perhaps he was entitled to be if he was good at what he did. He could obviously be charming when he chose, but he had acquired a reputation on board for being off-hand with anyone who approached him. What she'd heard had put Chloe off him, but now she responded to his smile. 'What I had in mind was in the nature of—'

Chloe wasn't destined to discover what he was about to say, because Jane came bounding up to them like an eager puppy.

'Oh, good, I've found you at last,' she cried, fluttering her eyelashes flirtatiously at Brent Harwood. She gave him a coy look. 'It's lovely to see you again, Mr Harwood. It's amazing how we do keep bumping into each other.'

Her giggle made Chloe cringe, especially as she saw the way Brent Harwood reacted. His face took on an expression of extreme annoyance, which was quickly covered by what Chloe realised was a false smile.

'Yes, isn't it?' he agreed and inclined his head to Chloe. 'Another time, perhaps?'

Chloe sighed as he walked away. She doubted very much that she would get a second chance to talk to him. Whatever he had to say could not have been important or he would have asked her to meet him in private somewhere. Not that it mattered, she supposed. Jane thought him terribly attractive with his dark blond hair and blue eyes, but Chloe wasn't sure she either liked or trusted him. That smile he had turned on for Jane had been completely false.

'Isn't he just too divine?' Jane asked. 'You must tell me—what was he saying to you just now?'

'Oh, he was only passing the time of day,' Chloe said, refusing to be drawn. 'Nothing interesting.'

'We've spoken several times,' Jane said and preened herself. 'He told me that I should take acting lessons and that he thought I would be perfect as a slave girl in one of his films.'

'And what did Mrs Vermont think of that?'

'Oh, I haven't told her,' Jane replied and giggled. 'Daddy would never let me do it anyway. He wants me to get married. There's an awfully boring man at home who asked me, and I've come away to think it over.' Her face brightened. 'We're losing several passengers at Cetua and taking some more on. Who knows what will happen before I get home?'

'I hope you find someone you like,' Chloe said.

'Oh, I suppose I like Henry well enough,' Jane replied. 'He just isn't very exciting—not in the way *he* is, for instance.' She touched Chloe's arm and gestured with excitement at a man who was coming towards them.

Chloe saw that it was Philip Armand. She had noticed before that he seemed to take his stroll at about this time each morning, seldom speaking to the other passengers. He was clearly a man who preferred his own company, and she expected him to walk straight past her, but to her surprise he stopped.

'It is a pleasant morning, Miss Randall.'

'Yes, Mr Armand. Very pleasant.'

Jane fluttered her eyelashes at him, but received only a nod as a curt acknowledgement. She blushed and looked uncomfortable, making Chloe annoyed on her behalf. Jane might be tiresome sometimes, but there was no need to be rude to her!

'Oh, I must speak to Mrs Bond,' Jane said catching sight of a passenger she knew well. 'Excuse me…'

Chloe glared at Philip Armand. 'You've frightened her away. Would it have hurt to smile at her?'

'I have no time for foolish girls, or for false smiles. Besides, had I encouraged her she would have made a nuisance of herself.'

'Then I wonder you have time to speak to me?' Chloe tipped her head defiantly.

'I did not imagine you were foolish, Miss Randall—though you do seem to keep company with some remarkably silly young ladies.'

'Justine isn't silly! That was an accident,' Chloe cried and then realised she had betrayed herself. 'Yes, I admit that Jane is a little silly at times—but there was no need to hurt her feelings.'

'You are perfectly right. I was thinking of something else and did not realise I was giving offence.'

'Well, you did.' Chloe was determined not to spare him.

'Then I must make some recompense. Do you both attend the dance this evening?' Chloe nodded. 'Then I shall ask both you and Miss Vermont for a dance—will that suffice?'

'I dare say Jane will think so if you smile at her.'

He laughed, his face easing into softer lines that brought out the charm she had suspected might be there, hidden away behind his frowns.

'So, I must smile as I go as a lamb to the slaughter? Very well, Miss Randall—I shall obey your command.'

Chloe shook her head, but her annoyance had faded. 'You should do so because it pleases you.'

'Ah—but I find little to please me,' he said. 'Except when I am in company I enjoy—as now.'

'You have not chosen to seek my company before this,' Chloe blurted out and then wished she hadn't when she saw the gleam in his eyes. Now he was laughing at her again! And she had asked for it, she thought ruefully. He seemed to bring out the worst in her.

'I was not sure you would wish for it,' he replied. 'You seem to make friends easily, Miss Randall. But I learned from Professor Hicks that you are leaving the ship at Cetua, and as I also leave tomorrow I wanted to offer my services. If I can be of any help to you and your companions with travelling arrangements or accommodation, I should be delighted to do so.'

'You are kind to think of us,' Chloe said, feeling surprised that he had bothered. 'The professor is an experienced traveller and I expect he has already decided on his itinerary, but it was good of you to ask.'

Philip Armand inclined his head. 'I am sure you are right, Miss Randall—but should you need assistance I would be happy to oblige.' He looked at her oddly. 'Now, I shall allow you to rejoin your friends—until this evening.'

Chloe watched as he walked away. What an extraordinary man he was—sure of himself, almost arrogant and yet undoubtedly attractive. She found herself torn two ways and was not sure whether she liked or disliked him.

She still could not make up her mind that evening, even though he was completely charming as he danced with both Jane and her aunt. He might have been a different man, Chloe thought, watching him, and wondered at the change.

She had danced with several men that evening, most of them staid, older men, pleasant but a little dull, when he finally approached her.

'Am I forgiven now?' he asked as he led her into the throng of dancers. It was a tango, and in Chloe's opinion one of the most thrilling of the newer dances. And it took skill to execute the exciting steps, especially when the gentleman bent his partner backwards.

'You should be asking Jane, not me,' she said and looked at him a little naughtily. 'Did you know that the Kaiser forbade his troops to dance the tango, because it might affect their moral fibre?'

'Undoubtedly that was why they lost the war,' he replied promptly and made her laugh. It was usually only Justine who responded to her humour so swiftly. 'Ah, so I am forgiven after all…'

'Only if you can dance this as beautifully as I hope.' She gave him a bewitching smile. Something flashed in Mr Armand's eyes and as his hand reached out for hers she felt a tingle rather like an electric shock. For one moment she felt mesmerised as she gazed into his eyes, her lips parting in a little gasp of surprise as she glimpsed the passion beneath the mask he habitually wore. This man was very different from the cool, polite stranger she had encountered from time to time on the ship and she sensed something slightly dangerous. Her heart began to race wildly, and as he placed his hand at her waist she felt close to swooning. Her teasing had somehow roused a tiger!

'Oh, I shall certainly be on my mettle now,' he said, and swept her into the dance with a flourish.

Chloe had never danced like this in her life. He was in control, in tune with the melody and with her, guiding her effortlessly through the intricate steps. It felt as if her feet hardly touched the floor, and she was floating with the music and the power and magnetism of her partner. Her whole body seemed to throb with a strange new feeling—a recklessness that she did not recognise but dimly realised might be desire.

What was she thinking? Had she lost her senses completely? It must be the evocative rhythm of the music that was making her feel this way—and yet as his hand slid against the satin softness of her bare arm she knew it was far more to do with the man himself.

'Oh…' she breathed as the music finally died and after a brief moment, when his eyes seemed to burn into her soul, he released her. 'What a pity. I should have liked to go on dancing forever.'

'Then I shall consider myself forgiven,' he said. His gaze strayed across the room to where Jane Vermont was talking at Brent Harwood, and the warmth died from his eyes. 'I see your foolish friend is making up to that American. If I were you I should warn her to be careful. Apart from the fact that he makes ridiculous films, I know that he is not to be trusted.'

Chloe felt the withdrawal in him and was hurt.

How could he change so suddenly after that magical dance? For that brief time they had seemed almost indivisible and now he was miles away from her again—but perhaps it had only been her who had felt the magic. She immediately threw up a screen to hide her foolish sensitivity.

'Why don't you like his films?'

'I believe he intends to make something rather similar to the picture that Valentino caused such a stir with three, or perhaps it was four, years back—*The Sheikh.* I imagine you may have seen it?'

'Yes—seven times,' Chloe said, half-defensive, half-angry. 'I loved it!'

A wry smile touched Philip Armand's mouth. 'Valentino is a remarkable actor. He made what was a very foolish plot seem almost believable. Unfortunately, it has provoked a rash of copycat films, which are an insult to the Bedouin way of life. You should know that, Miss Randall. Professor Hicks certainly agrees.'

'Yes…well, of course I know it isn't really the way things are. But surely that doesn't matter? As a film it was romantic and fun…and surely its purpose was to entertain?'

'As you say.' He inclined his head as he escorted her to near where her friends were standing. A tiny nerve was flicking in his cheek and she sensed that she must have upset him. But why should it bother him that an American film director was intent on making a copy of the kind of picture that had made Rudolph Valentino famous?

Chloe found that she couldn't get Philip Armand out of her mind as she prepared for bed that last evening on board ship. He was certainly the kind of man Justine would consider romantic and her foolish heart had been led astray during their dance. For a moment she had thought that there was something special between them, something rare and intense, something that if lost might never be found again…but of course that was ridiculous. They were merely strangers meeting briefly, their lives soon to diverge, never to meet again.

She would be ridiculous to imagine otherwise, of course she would. After all, he had mentioned a fiancée, hadn't he? Feeling the sharp sting of jealousy at the thought of the unknown fiancée, Chloe tried to dismiss him from her mind. She was being so silly to imagine that he had anything but a passing interest in her. She really must stop letting her imagination run wild. The truth was that she had found him intriguing from the start—but what was it about him that made her think she ought to know more of him than she did?

She was sure that she had seen his picture in the paper, had almost captured the article the other night. Her brow furrowed in concentration as she tried to recall whatever it was that hovered at the back of her mind, then all at once she went cold as she remembered. Of course! He had been with another man…a man wearing the flowing robes and headdress of a Sheikh! Of course…it had been an article about an assassination attempt. She could almost remember it now. There had been an attempt on the life of an important ruler of one of the oil-producing countries on the Arabian Peninsula. And Philip Armand was a cousin or something of the man pictured with him in the paper. Yet she didn't think he had called himself by that name. It was more like Hassan…or Pasha. Or had that been the ruler's name?

Chloe couldn't be certain, and he had looked very different in the picture because he too had been wearing the robes of a Sheikh. Surely she must be mistaken? Yet if she was right, it would explain why he was so annoyed to find himself travelling with an American film director who made films that he clearly believed misrepresented the Bedouin way of life.

Even so, that didn't quite explain his attitude towards Brent Harwood. There had been real anger in him as he spoke of the man…an underlying menace that she sensed must have a cause. It had seemed almost a personal thing…

Chloe dismissed her thoughts—she shouldn't worry about something that was of no real concern to her. She wanted a good night's sleep so as to be ready for the following day.

'Oh, do please keep in touch,' Jane begged as she said goodbye the next morning. 'It has been so nice having you as a friend, Chloe. I wish you were staying for the whole of the cruise. But I suppose you can't wait to get off to wherever it is you're going.'

Chloe promised she would write and tell Jane where they went and what they saw.

'It may be ages before I can post a letter,' she said. 'We are going to be travelling to the more remote villages as soon as the professor can arrange transport. We are on a research trip, not a holiday. I have to take dictation and help the professor find what he is looking for—which could mean lots of reading and walking.'

'You poor thing,' Jane said, looking at her in horror. She had never worked in her life and hoped she never would. 'I hope it won't be too terrible for you. Aunt Vera says that some of these places can be very primitive. Do be careful what you eat, Chloe. My aunt was awfully ill once when she stayed in Morocco.'

'Miss Ramsbottom carries a lot of emergency kit,' Chloe assured her. 'My friends know all about travelling in the region so we should be safe enough.'

'Well, goodbye—and do keep in touch.'

There were several people leaving the ship that morning. Chloe saw Brent Harwood with the other members of the film crew, all of whom she knew only by sight. None of them had been particularly talkative, though apparently they had taken a few shots of the captain and his crew.

She noticed Philip Armand—or whatever his name really was—being met by a man who saluted him and took the briefcase he was carrying off to what looked like an expensive French car. He glanced back at the ship just before he got into the back seat, inclining his head to her but not smiling. She thought he looked angry again, and wondered what had upset him this time.

What a very odd man he was! He could be so charming and friendly when he chose, and the next withdrawn, as cold as ice. She wondered what made a man like that, and decided that he must have an awful lot on his mind.

'Well, here we are then,' Professor Hicks said to her. 'All your goodbyes finished, Chloe?'

'Yes, of course.' She smiled at him. 'I'm looking forward to our adventure.'

'Adventure?' He nodded and looked pleased. 'Yes, I suppose it is a kind of adventure. Some of my research can seem dull, especially to a young woman like yourself, I dare say—but meeting people and seeing new places is always exciting.'

Chloe and Amelia Ramsbottom sat at the back of the rather crowded bus that was to take them to their hotel. It was quite new and provided by one of the Spanish-built hotels that had begun to appear in the last few years.

'When we first came here there were no buses and hardly any cars,' Amelia confided to her as the bus reached its capacity load and lurched off down the bumpy road. 'I remember we hired a kind of dogcart pulled by one tired old horse—and in Morocco we had to ride on donkeys. Camels when we went into the desert, of course.'

'How brave you were to accompany the professor on his early trips,' Chloe said. 'Of course things have changed a lot since the war, haven't they?'

'Oh, yes, a great deal, everyone is beginning to catch on to the idea of foreign travel. I dare say it will be as popular for ordinary people to holiday in places like Spain and Portugal as it has been for the rich on the French Riviera one day.'

'Do you think we shall travel by camel this time?'

'I certainly hope not,' Amelia said. 'Charles will have a vehicle of some sort. Do you drive at all, Chloe?'

'Yes, though I haven't had much experience. I couldn't afford a car, but Daddy did arrange for me to learn. He thought it might come in useful.'

'I dare say it might. The professor drives, but I'm afraid I don't.'

Chloe was excited by what she saw as they drove along a very bumpy, dusty road. The sky was a clear, cloudless blue, which seemed to make the brilliant white of the houses seem even brighter, and the flowers spilling out from gardens, pots and hanging boxes were a riot of colour. There was a definite style to the arches and domes, giving it the flavour of the East that she had expected, for even though it was a Spanish protectorate Cetua still had that Moorish feel.

Now and then she caught sight of beautiful villas and gardens behind high walls and wondered about the people who lived there, but there were also small houses that seemed to be made of either stone or mud bricks and some looked to be in danger of tumbling down. They passed children standing by the roadside, many of whom were barefooted and dressed in little better than rags. There were also beggars with sores or missing limbs, traders who held up their wares as the bus passed, and men leading a string of camels into town.

The bus made slow progress through the town itself, which was crowded with carts, donkeys, people and motor vehicles. Chloe hadn't been sure what to expect, but the modern ways of the West seemed to have begun to influence this ancient world and the hotel they were taken to had been built since the war.

From the hot, dirty street they entered a cool courtyard, which was paved with a beautiful mosaic of jewel-coloured tiles, and had a fountain playing in its centre. Terracotta pots held a variety of fleshy green plants with spiky leaves or trailing fronds, and two large palm trees stood at either side of the lobby entrance.

Inside it was a mixture of Moorish taste with some Art Deco influences in the furnishings. They were greeted politely by the hotel manager himself, but the language Chloe thought was being used most often was not Spanish, as she had expected, but French. She was glad that she had taken it to a higher level at school. However, it was not long before she became aware of a heated argument, taking place in English between a rather pretty young woman and one of the desk clerks.

'But it is absolutely impossible for me to manage in that perfectly dreadful little room!' the woman cried in a sharp voice. 'Brent promised me a suite and I really must have it.'

'But, Angela darling, they don't have a suite available,' a man dressed in a crumpled white suit was telling her. He looked hot and there were beads of sweat on his forehead. Clearly he was at a loss what to do in the circumstances. 'Brent has the only one and he—'

'Then he must give it to me,' she said and pulled a face. 'I only came to this awful country because he promised me it would all be lovely and that I could have everything I wanted.'

Chloe was unable to hear any more of the argument, because a smiling, white-robed porter was picking up her bags and beckoning her to follow. She did so, though she was curious about the woman, whose face seemed familiar. She was almost certain she was a film star. Oh, why couldn't she think of her name? He had called her Angela… Yes, of course, that was it! Angela Russell. She had been in several silent films, most of them supposedly set in exotic locations.

'What on earth was that fuss about just now?' Amelia asked as they paused at the end of the landing.

'Oh, I think that was Angela Russell, the film star,' Chloe said. 'I've seen some of her films, though I don't think she has made one for a while—at least I haven't seen it. She seemed to be upset about the room they have given her. I think she wanted a suite or something.'

Amelia gave a snort of disgust.

'This hotel is a palace compared to some we've stayed in. A woman like that has no business travelling at all if she is going to make a fuss over every little thing. One has to expect some discomfort when one leaves home.'

Chloe smiled, but thought that everyone couldn't be as confident as the intrepid Miss Ramsbottom. She had thought the filmstar rather lovely and had sympathised if she didn't like her room.

Her own room seemed perfectly comfortable when she was shown into it a moment or so later. Although the furniture was basic, with just a narrow single bed, a chest of drawers and a wardrobe, it was clean and adequate for her needs, and the bathroom was only just down the hall.

'Mine is just the same as yours,' Amelia said when she popped in to collect Chloe on her way downstairs. 'Nice and cosy, all perfectly comfortable.'

'Yes, it is fine,' Chloe said as they went out and walked down the stairs towards the dining room. 'But we are not staying here long, are we?'

'We shall make this hotel our base,' Professor Hicks answered her question as he caught up to them. 'Most of our luggage will remain here, but we shall drive out to the various towns and villages, Chloe. And we may need to stay over sometimes so we always keep an overnight bag in the vehicle.'

As they were shown to their table, Chloe noticed that the actress was complaining again. She was with the man who had been trying to pacify her earlier, and now Brent Harwood was also with them. Chloe couldn't help overhearing what the actress was saying, because her voice was so loud and shrill.

'It's perfectly ghastly,' she said. 'If I eat this stuff I shall be ill again—and goodness knows when we shall be able to start shooting...'

'Send it back and order something else,' Brent replied, looking faintly annoyed but obviously trying not to show it. 'Nothing is too good for you, Angela.'

Chloe had ordered a dish of lamb cooked with vegetables and rice, which she found delicious. She wondered if anything would ever satisfy the actress, who was clearly pampered and used to getting her own way.

Chloe had finished her main course and was pondering whether to have a pudding when she saw a man being conducted to a table behind a potted palm; it was secluded and hidden from view from most of the dining area, and had remained empty until now.

So Philip Armand was staying here too, she thought, and blushed as he looked at her across the room, giving her a curt nod. She had been staring again—but she knew that there was a new hotel on the other side of town that was far more luxurious than this one, so why wasn't he staying there? There must be nicer places to eat! She couldn't imagine why he had chosen to stay here—unless he was trying to avoid someone? It would, she supposed, be easier to lose himself amongst the latest influx of tourists here than in more exotic restaurants.

Was she letting her imagination run wild again? He had always seemed a mysterious character and her active mind began once again to weave all kinds of impossible plots, which she hastened to dismiss as he frowned in her direction. He had noticed her interest and would think her as bad as Jane Vermont, and imagine she had been trying to catch his attention. And she wasn't! Her cheeks felt warm as she recalled her foolish thoughts after that dance. It had just been the magic of the dance, of course. He wasn't interested in her and she wasn't sure she even liked him…well, not really. She certainly wasn't in love with him. Being in love was fun and feeling happy all the time, or that's how she'd always thought it would be—all that this man made her feel was agitated, on edge! Bother him!

'Do you want a pudding?' Professor Hicks asked, causing her to look at him and forget the irritating Mr Armand. 'Only I thought you might want to make the most of this afternoon. Get out and have a look round—do a little shopping in the bazaar, perhaps? I shall want to leave early tomorrow.'

'Yes, I think I shall,' she said, putting down her napkin. 'If you are sure you don't need me this afternoon?'

'I am going to be arranging transport,' he replied. 'No, my dear, you get off and enjoy yourself.'

'Would you like to come, Amelia?' Chloe asked.

'No, thank you, Chloe,' the older woman replied. 'I shall have a little rest in the hotel gardens. Enjoy yourself—but wear something on your arms, and keep your head covered—and don't go too far from the main streets. We don't want you disappearing on your first day—do we, my dear? I dare say your father would never forgive us.'

'Whatever do you mean?' Chloe was astonished. 'Why should I disappear?'

'She means that you are a very pretty girl,' the professor explained with a smile. 'And I assure you, it wouldn't be unknown out here for a pretty girl walking alone to be snatched by unscrupulous men. But as long as you stick to the busy main streets you should be all right.'

'White slavery?' Chloe asked. 'I thought that was something out of Hollywood films.'

'Not at all,' Amelia said. 'I can assure you it does happen. Some years ago when we were in Egypt, a man tried to buy me for six camels from the professor. Now would you believe that?' She looked a little coy and laughed oddly.

'Yes, and I had a devil of a job shaking him off,' Charles said with a rueful look. 'I had almost forgotten that, Amelia. You were an exceptionally handsome woman in those days, my dear. One tends to forget with the passing of the years…'

Chloe noticed the swiftly hidden look of pain in Angela's eyes and realised that she was in love with him—had probably been in love with him all her life. But of course he had never noticed. He had been wrapped up in his work and it had probably never occurred to him that his secretary had that kind of feeling towards him.

That brief but revealing look made Chloe feel sympathy towards the older woman, and she determined not to mind if Amelia was grumpy sometimes.

'I promise I won't do anything silly,' she said. 'Besides, this is a Spanish protectorate. We aren't in Morocco yet. I'm sure I shall be perfectly safe…'

Chapter Three

It was the first time Chloe had been out alone in a foreign city. Jane and Mrs Vermont had always been with her on the excursions planned and guided by one of the ship's crew, but now she was completely alone and it felt a little odd.

Chloe was glad she had taken Amelia's advice to cover her arms and her hair. After being stared at by both men and women as if she were some sort of curiosity, Chloe was almost ready to return to the hotel within a few minutes of leaving it. However, she was determined not to let an attack of nerves betray her, and she forced herself to walk as far as the bazaar she had noticed on their way to the hotel.

Once she had conquered her initial feeling of uncertainty, she began to relax and enjoy herself. It was all so very different and exotic—the people with their dark skins and flowing robes, and the children who clamoured for coins as she passed. She had been warned not to give them money, and resisted the temptation, even though their little faces were very appealing. She was fascinated by the Moorish architecture, and the glimpses of paved courtyards behind high gates was intriguing, the colours brilliant.

The bazaar was crowded with people, the merchants at the doors of their shops calling out to entice passers-by to enter. Chloe took her time, lingering over a profusion of beautifully worked soft leather goods, long silky scarves, sandals, beaten brass and little wooden tables that had either brass or silver inlaid into their surfaces. Sensibly, she had brought only a little money with her, for the professor had advised against large sums in case of theft. She did have enough to buy a leather bag she liked, and was able to conduct a bargaining session with the merchant in French.

Satisfied that she had secured a good deal for herself Chloe handed over a few coins, then, as she left the shop, found herself besieged by other shopkeepers extolling their own wares as she made her way back to the bazaar entrance.

'No, thank you,' she said as they clawed at her arm and chattered away in a language that was strange to her. 'I have no money to buy anything else.'

Discovering that they would not take no for an answer, Chloe broke away and started to run. She turned to her right as she left the bazaar, realising only after her panic had begun to ease that she had mistaken her way and left by the wrong entrance.

She was not in the main street she knew but a narrow alleyway between houses built close together. It seemed darker all of a sudden, and she looked up at a sky that was leaden with clouds, thinking that it might rain at any moment. She realised that she had spent longer in the bazaar than she had intended, and that the evening had pulled in much more quickly than she had anticipated.

Anxious to return to the hotel before the rain came, Chloe turned to retrace her steps. She must find the main street so that she could get her bearings, but she wasn't sure which way to turn.

It was only after a few minutes of wandering that she sensed she was being followed. She glanced over her shoulder and saw two men dressed in long white tunics walking towards her; they appeared to be looking at her excitedly and she was suddenly afraid. Supposing Amelia's warning had not been as ridiculous as it had sounded back at the hotel? Supposing the men were intent on kidnapping her?

Her heart began to pound rapidly, and, seeing the main street at the end of the alley she had just turned into, she began to run. Fear took over as she heard one of the men call out to her and knew that they had begun to pursue her.

Oh, why hadn't she returned to the hotel at the beginning? She had been aware of intense interest almost immediately, but pride had forbidden her to give in to her anxiety. Wild thoughts of being sold into a harem filled her mind, but she was nearly at the main street now and surely she would be safe then?

They were catching up to her! She redoubled her efforts and catapulted out into the street, colliding with a man walking past.

'Oh, I am so...Mr Armand!' Chloe cried as the relief swept over her. 'Those men are chasing me. I think they are trying to kidnap me.'

'I doubt it,' he replied, turning to fire rapid questions at the two men in a language Chloe had never heard before. Some sort of argument seemed to ensue before the men looked at her and made what was clearly an apology. Philip Armand's expression was definitely amused as he looked at her. 'It seems to be a case of mistaken identity, Miss Randall. They had heard that a beautiful American actress was staying at a hotel near here—and since you are beautiful and looked as if you might be American, they wanted your autograph.'

'My autograph?' Chloe stared at him in disbelief, and then at the men, who were shuffling their feet and looking shamefaced. 'But why did they chase me? I was frightened.'

'I have explained and they are very sorry, but they had seen films where fans pursue their idols in America and they did not think it was wrong.' He spoke to the men, and they mumbled another apology before turning and walking off in a dejected manner. 'They were excited by the thought of meeting an American actress—they would probably have asked you to take them to America, for they have heard it is a rich country. It isn't often someone famous comes their way. They are simple people, Miss Randall. I told them you had forgiven them—I hope that was right? You did not wish to press charges?'

'Of course not!' Chloe was feeling foolish by this time. 'I—I suppose I let my imagination run away with me.'

'Perhaps you have seen too many Hollywood films?' he suggested and she blushed as she caught the mockery in his look. 'I do assure you that my people do not often abduct young women these days.'

'Your people?' She stared at him. 'So I was right.

I thought Armand wasn't your real name. I saw a picture of you in the paper once…'

'Yes, that was a mistake,' he said and frowned. 'I should never have allowed it. If you recognised me, others might—'

'Oh, I didn't—not at once. It was only when you spoke of the Bedouin way of life…' She blushed again as his eyes narrowed. 'I don't suppose most people would have taken much notice of the article. It was only because I was interested…' She faltered as he frowned again. 'Not in politics. I have an interest in Arabic literature…poems, to be exact. You quoted something from Umar Ibn Abi Rabia, whose work was disapproved of by more pious scholars. That was what caught my eye.'

'Ah, yes, the love poems.' His brows lifted. 'I would hardly have thought you a scholar of Arabic, Miss Randall?'

'I am not, of course. I wish I could claim to be that clever. I can recognise a few words here and there—but there are some wonderful poems and other forms of literature that have been translated into English and French. I am making a collection. One day, I may inquire if anyone would like to publish them as a book. You see, I think other people might like them if they were readily available—especially some of the love poems. They are so beautiful…'

Her cheeks were on fire as she finished. He looked amused but also approving, and something about him at that moment was making her stomach tie itself in knots. She was finding it a little difficult to breathe—foolish girl!

'Yes, they are,' he agreed. 'And it is a shame that so much of merit languishes unread for want of interest. Some of the most beautiful prose and poetry were originally written in Arabic—there is a sensuality about the language that flows from the tongue.'

And about his mouth! How attractive he was when he looked at her like that.

Chloe checked her unruly thoughts. What on earth was going through her mind? She was an incurable romantic!

'I have often wished that I could read the original but, as I said before, I am not clever enough.'

'That is because no one has taught you,' he said, and there was a look in his eyes that sent an odd little tingle down her spine. 'Perhaps you will tell me more of what you have discovered as we walk back to the hotel, Miss Randall?' His dark eyes met hers in a challenge.

'You know of the *Rubaiyat,* of course.'

'Oh, yes, I know some of it by heart…' She faltered as his brows quirked, and then closed her eyes. 'It begins… "Wake! For the sun, who scattered into flight…"'

'"The Stars before him from the Field of Night,
    Drive Night along with them from Heav'n and strikes
    The Sultan's turret with a Shaft of Light."'

'Oh, yes,' she breathed as he stopped and arched his brows at her. 'I thought I must be the only one who had learned that verse. Most people only seem to know the bit about the cup of wine and thou.'

'But you are different,' he suggested. 'You intrigue me, Miss Randall. Tell me more.'

Chloe looked shyly at him. 'I've never talked about

my work before. Daddy calls it my little hobby, and my friends don't understand why I find the study of Arabic literature interesting. Justine says there are already too many English poets to bother with something in an impossible language that no one can understand.'

'Justine is your exuberant friend from the ship?'

'Yes. I am sorry that she ruined your suit—and that I made it worse.'

'I am not sure that once something is ruined you can make it worse.'

'You're laughing at me!' Chloe accused.

'Yes, and it is very unkind of me,' he replied with a twist of his mouth—a mouth she again realised was very attractive. 'But it is good to laugh sometimes. Believe me, I have not wanted to laugh for a long time.'

'May I ask why?'

'Someone I cared for died.'

'Oh, I see—I am very sorry. I know that hurts. I was devastated when my mother died.'

He nodded, but did not elaborate. Clearly his grief was private, and still too raw to be discussed.

'May I ask your real name?'

'You could not remember—even though you saw the newspaper article?'

'No. I thought it might be Hassan—or Pasha?'

'It is Pasha,' he said. 'Pasha Ibn Hasim—can you be trusted to keep that to yourself, Miss Randall? I would prefer that it did not become common knowledge at the hotel—or anywhere.'

'Yes, of course—if you wish,' she said and frowned. 'I expect you have a good reason for using a false name.'

'Armand is my maternal great-grandmother's name. She was French—and her father was called Philippe. I have a British passport in that name so it is not entirely false.'

'Oh...' Chloe felt her cheeks getting warm again. 'I didn't mean to imply anything.'

'You did, of course, but no matter. I do have very good reasons for travelling under an assumed name. My father was assassinated in Algeria when I was a child of nine years. My uncle sent me to England to be educated because he believed I would be safer in a foreign country—and, as my mother was English, I had relations there.'

'Your father was... I am so sorry! I had no idea.' Chloe was appalled. She had never heard anything so dreadful and it had completely shocked her. 'That's why...I mean, I shan't say a word about what you've told me to anyone. Are you an important Sheikh or something?'

Pasha laughed. 'Not important in the way you mean, merely wealthy. However, someone in my family is very important.'

'Please don't tell me any more,' she said. 'I don't think I ought to know. In case I inadvertently say something I shouldn't.'

'I had no intention of telling you anything that might compromise his safety—or your own.'

Chloe's eyes were wide with wonder. 'You really are important, aren't you? You must be if your... friend might be in danger through something I might accidentally learn from you.'

Pasha didn't answer and she felt that he had withdrawn from her once more, but she no longer wondered at it or that he should look so stern at times.

He had a great deal on his shoulders, and his life could not be easy. She saw that they had almost reached the hotel, and turned to him.

'Thank you for helping me. I can manage now.' She hesitated. 'In case we don't meet again—good luck.' And then without knowing why she did it, she leaned towards him and softly kissed his cheek. 'Stay alive, Pasha Ibn Hasim. Goodbye.'

Chloe turned quickly away before he could answer, running into the hotel without looking back. She had acted impulsively and was already regretting what he must see as very forward behaviour.

She had no idea why she had done it, except that the little he had told her made her feel he might be in danger himself, and for some reason she couldn't begin to explain, she couldn't bear for him to be assassinated like his father.

Chloe looked for Pasha at dinner that evening, but he wasn't in the hotel dining room. Nor was the film crew, and Amelia told them that she had earlier seen the actress and Brent Harwood being called for in a large, expensive car.

'I think they have been invited to dine with some local bigwig,' she said. 'There's quite a buzz going round over this film they are making. Apparently, it's going to be shot mainly in Morocco, but they are doing some of the scenes here at the hotel—and they think it will make them famous.'

'The manager hopes it will bring new visitors to his hotel,' the professor said. 'Can't see it myself—never been to one of those films in my life and don't care to. Give me a good German-made film—or the French make some decent artistic stuff.'

'Daddy won't go to a German film on principle,' Chloe said. 'Because of the war. But Justine and I went to one—it was rather macabre and frightening. We didn't like it.'

'I dare say you young things would prefer an Elinor Glyn script,' Amelia said. 'Personally, I don't think you can beat Charlie Chaplin. He is the master of comedy.'

'Now I don't mind watching that fellow,' the professor said. 'He is quite amusing…' He beamed at them. 'Do you feel up to taking a little dictation this evening, Chloe? Or would you like to get an early night before we start in the morning?'

'Oh, of course I don't mind taking some dictation,' Chloe assured him. 'That is why I am here.'

'Then we'll find a quiet corner in the gardens,' he said. 'I spotted a little shelter where we can sit and be undisturbed. I'll go up and fetch my notebook and meet you in a few minutes.'

'I'll be in the garden,' Chloe agreed. 'I think I know where you mean—I'm sure I do, near the palm trees in the corner…'

'Yes, that's right, my dear.' He nodded to her and went off.

'I think I shall have some coffee in the lounge and settle with a book,' Amelia said. 'You don't need me for anything, Chloe?'

'No, thank you,' Chloe said and left her, wandering out through the hotel to the back gardens, which were rather attractive and quite large for a hotel. She stopped to sniff at a pretty yellow rose, and then became aware of raised voices coming from behind a large flowering bush. It sounded as though two men were arguing, but she was unable to understand because they spoke in a language she did not recognise.

And then one of them mentioned a name she had heard for the first time that afternoon…*Pasha Ibn Hasim!* Chloe strained to catch more of what was being said and she thought she heard the word *Hassan*…and then again Pasha's name. Oh, how she wished she knew what they were saying! It was so frustrating to know that they were talking about someone she knew but not to be able to understand, and then one of them said something in French, and she knew they were talking about an attempt at murder.

Chloe's blood ran cold. Surely she must have heard wrongly? She wished they would continue to speak in French, but they had returned to the first language, which she found unintelligible.

'Ah, there you are, my dear! I am sorry to keep you waiting.'

The professor's words startled her, and she swung round to see him approaching. The men had abruptly stopped speaking, and as her employer joined Chloe, they came from behind the bushes, glancing at her as they began to stroll off in the direction of the hotel.

Chloe felt her mouth go dry as she saw the expression of menace in one of the men's eyes. He said something in a low voice to his companion, but he shook his head and frowned. Obviously the second man was of the opinion that they were in no danger, as a foreign woman wouldn't have understood what they were saying.

And she hadn't, of course—except for the names and that one sentence in French. She probably had it all wrong, of course she did! And yet Pasha had told her that his father had been assassinated…

Chloe's thoughts were confused, but had to be dismissed as the professor found his little shelter and asked her to sit down so that they could begin. Chloe took the notebook she always carried from her bag and smiled at him, indicating that she was ready to begin.

Even if those men had been plotting something, there was nothing she could do for the moment. Pasha had not been at dinner, and she did not know how to contact him—though she would leave a note for him at the desk before she went up to her room.

Chloe asked for an envelope at the foyer, and was given one by an obliging desk clerk. She slipped her note inside, and wrote Philip Armand on the envelope, handing it in with a request that it be given to Mr Armand when he returned.

'Certainly, Miss Randall. Is there anything else I may do for you?'

'No, thank you—just make sure that Mr Armand gets the envelope.'

Alone in her room, Chloe thought over what she had heard earlier. She couldn't be sure that it was significant—and she had made that clear in her letter. Pasha would probably think she was letting her imagination work overtime again, but at least she had done what she could.

She found it difficult to sleep at first, and lay tossing from one side to the other as her mind went over and over the events of the day, but eventually she fell into an uneasy sleep. She dreamed of a tent in the desert and a handsome, slightly dangerous Sheikh.

The professor wanted an early start, and there was hardly anyone in the dining room when they had their breakfast. Chloe inquired at the desk and was told that Mr Armand had been given her letter when he came in the previous evening, but that there was no reply.

She felt a little disappointed, but decided that it would be foolish to have looked for a reply. As she had half-expected, he probably thought that she had imagined the whole incident.

'Are you ready, Chloe my dear?'

The professor was calling to her, and she hurried to his side. They were beginning their trip in truth now, for they were to enter Morocco and would make their way to various villages. The first important destination on the professor's itinerary was Fez, and after that Marrakesh.

The car he had hired for their use was quite a large tourer, and more comfortable than Chloe had imagined, with a soft top that came down so that they could enjoy a breeze as they drove on fine days.

Looking back at the hotel as the professor drove away, Chloe saw Pasha come out of the main entrance, but she didn't wave to him, even though she knew he had seen her. It would probably be the last time she would see him and that thought left her feeling a little low, though she didn't know why it should.

'Marrakesh was founded in 1062,' the professor told Chloe as they looked out of the window of the house they had taken just outside the city for a few days. Situated on a hillside, it had a good view over the city itself. 'It was a centre of the caravan trade for centuries, and is just as important commercially today.'

'It looks exciting,' Chloe said. 'Amelia was telling

me that it was the capital of the sultans, and there are many old buildings and mosques that are interesting to see.'

'Yes—though, unfortunately, neither of you will be allowed inside,' the professor said. 'I was disappointed in Fez not to be able to even approach the mosque of Mula Idris, but the shrine is considered so sacred that non-Muslims may not approach its entrance. However, I dare say there are many fine buildings here that you will be allowed to look at, at least from the outside.'

They had been travelling for three weeks now, and Chloe had discovered that the professor was indefatigable when it came to visiting places he wished to see. She was glad that they were going to stay put for a few days, because she wanted to catch up on some correspondence.

'Did you need me for dictation this afternoon?' she asked. 'I thought I might stay here and wash my hair.'

Charles seemed to realise that he was asking a lot, and looked contrite. 'You must forgive me, Chloe. I have worked you both hard these past few weeks,' he said. 'That's why I thought we would take the house for a few days rather than stay in hotels. You should be comfortable here, Chloe. And, no, I don't need you this afternoon. I shall go into the city myself, but you may stay here and relax for a few hours.'

'Yes, I should enjoy that,' she said. 'I saw a pleasant garden just down the road from us, and I think I might take a walk there once I've washed my hair—let it dry in the sun.'

'And I shall stay here and prepare a meal for us all,' Amelia said. 'It will make a pleasant change to the bread, cheese and fruit we've lived on for the last few days.'

They had preferred to live on food they bought in the local markets rather than eating at the various small inns they passed on their travels. The roads were long and dusty, and they carried a supply of boiled water with them, because Amelia said one couldn't be too careful about these things.

Chloe had found the travelling interesting, but hard going at times and she marvelled at the resilience of her companions, who seemed to take it all in their stride. Of course they were used to it, but she had not liked some of the rooms she had been forced to sleep in, and had thought longingly once or twice of the comfortable bedroom she had left behind in Cetua.

They had brought sufficient clothing with them to manage, though it meant washing out undies and blouses at night, and they often could not be ironed.

Chloe walked down the hillside to the garden she had seen as the professor drove to their house. It opened out on to the road and, since there were no notices saying that it was private and no fences, she assumed that it was open to the public.

The house they had hired had only a back yard, which was not particularly nice to sit in. Chloe thought that she would enjoy relaxing in this pretty garden with its palm trees, flowers and—yes, to her delight she saw that there were fountains and a little ornamental stream.

She wandered by the stream, which wended its way in and out of delightful shrubs and flower beds, until she came to a wooden seat and decided to sit there for a while with the book she had brought with her.

Her hair was almost dry, and she could feel it blowing in the slight breeze that had sprung up.

However, the seat was hard and she found it uncomfortable, so she sat down on the dry grass, and, after reading for a while, lay down and closed her eyes. It was so peaceful here in this beautiful place and she had not been able to relax like this for ages…

'It would be unwise to fall asleep in the hot sun.'

The man's voice startled her and she opened her eyes, sitting up in alarm as she saw someone standing there. She shaded her eyes against the sun, and then gasped as she realised that she knew him.

'Pasha…or should I say Mr Armand?' she said, wondering for a moment if she was dreaming again. He had featured in her dreams rather too often of late. 'Forgive me, I'm not sure…'

He came to her and squatted down on the grass beside her. 'My name is Pasha,' he said. 'In the hotel I wished to be known as someone else—but we are quite safe here. This is the home of my cousin, Ahmad Al-Hadra.'

'Your cousin's home?' Chloe stared at him, her cheeks growing warm as she realised what that meant. 'Then I am trespassing. I'm sorry. I saw the garden and thought it was for public use…there were no fences or notices.'

'My cousin prefers it that way. He says that the traveller is always welcome to his home—providing, of course, that he comes in peace.'

'Oh, I come in peace,' Chloe said and laughed. 'What a wonderful man your cousin must be—to allow others the beauty of a garden like this is so unselfish.'

'It is his culture—his tradition, if you like,' Pasha

said. 'When our people were travellers, we always made strangers welcome at the oasis—food and water were given freely to those who came as friends.'

'And those who did not?'

'Ah—that is another story, and not one to be told on such a lovely afternoon.' He offered her his hand, helping her to rise. 'Would you care to meet my cousin, Miss Randall?'

'Oh…yes, if that's all right,' Chloe said. 'I mean— do I look respectable? We've been travelling for ages, and I washed my hair this afternoon. It probably looks a fright, and my clothes are creased.'

'Sashimi will be delighted to lend you a comb if you need one,' he said. 'She is my cousin's wife and much your age, I imagine—how old are you, Miss Randall? Nineteen…twenty?'

'I'm twenty-two,' Chloe replied. 'Everyone says I look younger—which means I am naïve, I suppose.'

'Not at all,' he replied with a smile that set her heart racing. 'Innocent would probably be a better word to describe you. You have a funny little lost look in your eyes sometimes, Miss Randall…which is actually quite charming.'

'Oh…' She arched her brows at him. 'I am not sure whether I ought to take that as a compliment or not.'

'I assure you it was meant as one.'

Chloe did not reply, because he had led her a little further through the bushes and now the house was in view. It was a long, low building with arched door-ways and windows, and there were mosaics of vibrant hues on parts of the courtyard walls, though the rest of it was painted a brilliant white. Terracotta pots spilled over with flowers, and there was a cane table and chairs set out beneath a yellow umbrella.

Chloe could see that a man and woman were near the table, and as they approached they stood up and looked inquiringly towards them.

'Now what have you found?' the woman asked in French. 'Who have you brought to see us, Pasha?'

'Miss Randall—this is my very dear Sashimi,' Pasha said. 'She is of French–Algerian birth and a cousin to my stepmother Mariam—who lives in America. Sashimi, I should like you to meet Miss Chloe Randall. I discovered her sleeping in your garden, but I have had the honour of meeting her before. We travelled out from England together on the ship.'

'Ah—then it is fate,' Sashimi said in English and inclined her head. 'It was written that you should come to our garden, Miss Randall—or may I call you Chloe?'

'I should be delighted if you would call me Chloe. And I am happy to be here—though I must apologise for trespassing in your wonderful garden.'

'It was written as Sashimi said.' Ahmad spoke for the first time and smiled. 'Such things do not happen unless Allah wills it—and so you bring a blessing to our home, Chloe. We are happy that you are here. You will stay and have tea with us?' He clapped his hands and a man in simple white robes came out, inclining his head as the order was given.

Chloe looked at Sashimi. 'I think I must look very untidy...'

'You would like to freshen yourself before we have tea?' She smiled and nodded. 'Please come with me, Chloe.'

Chloe followed her into the house, which was tiled with cool mosaics and furnished very simply with dark wood furniture in the hallway through which they passed. But it was very different in Sashimi's private rooms, which were light and airy, the furniture of French design and very elegant, the drapes white and filmy, blowing slightly in the breeze from the open windows.

'Here are combs...perfume...' Sashimi indicated the dressing table. 'Through there the bathroom...please use whatever you need. I shall be outside when you are ready to rejoin us...unless there is more you need?'

'Nothing more, thank you.' Chloe went through into the bathroom, which was styled in what was obviously an Art Deco design and very modern. The bath and basins were green, and the floor was black and white, with a geometrical pattern that was echoed in the tiles on the wall. Everything had a French style, but combined with a vaguely Moorish flavour that gave it a unique charm.

It was the first time Chloe had been in a private home in Morocco, and it was clearly the home of people who were if not wealthy at least well off. She ran a little water into the basin and splashed her face, which had caught the sun a little when she had lain on the grass, then she used a brush she found on the shelf to tame her hair into something resembling its usual style. She noticed that it had grown longer than she usually wore it, and the sun had lightened the ends a little. Brushing it back behind her ears, she decided that she looked reasonably tidy and decided to go back outside.

She heard Sashimi's laughter as she approached the door leading to the patio. 'You are a terrible liar, Pasha,' she cried. 'But I shall not tease you. Your little English miss is delightful...delightful...'

Sashimi turned as Chloe emerged from the cool of the interior into the heat of the late afternoon sun.

'Ah, there you are—you were quick,' she said, her eyes noting that Chloe had not taken advantage of her invitation to use the various cosmetics that had been on offer. 'But you need no artifice to make you beautiful.'

'You make her blush, Sashimi,' Ahmad said and Chloe noticed that her face dimmed for a moment, as though she resented something. Chloe wasn't sure what. 'Do not tease our guest. Please sit here by me, Chloe. Tell me how it is that you find yourself here in this place today.'

'Thank you,' Chloe said as he pulled out a chair for her next to him. 'Perhaps Pasha has told you that I am travelling with Professor Hicks and Miss Amelia Ramsbottom?' She paused and he nodded his head in agreement. 'We have been travelling almost non-stop since we left Cetua three weeks ago. We had planned to return to our hotel, but the professor was caught up in his work and we just kept on driving from place to place. It has been difficult to wash or iron clothes— which is why I look so crumpled today.'

He inclined his head but made no remark. 'I have heard of Professor Hicks's work. I believe he is a remarkable man. Do you think he would give us the pleasure of his company at dinner one evening— yourself and Miss Ramsbottom included, of course?'

'I am sure he would enjoy that very much,' Chloe replied. 'We are staying just up the hill—in those houses at the very top, number five, I think it is.'

'Then I shall call tomorrow and make the arrangements,' Ahmad said. He glanced at Pasha. 'Unless you would care to do so, cousin?'

'I am a guest in your house,' Pasha replied and his cousin nodded. 'Where do you plan to go next, Miss Randall?'

'The professor often doesn't make up his mind until the morning he is ready to leave,' Chloe said. 'We have been working our way along the coast, and have visited Fez and Rabat as well as many other places of interest, and when we leave Marrakesh I think we are going to visit Agadir—and we should end up at a village near the Western Sahara, I believe. The professor intends to take a trip into the desert as a highlight to our visit to Morocco—and after that we shall make our way home.'

'Have you been to the mountains?' Pasha asked. 'I think you would enjoy that, Chloe.'

She smiled as he said her name. Always before it had been Miss Randall, but Sashimi had done away with formality.

'You must see something of the city while you are here,' Sashimi said. 'And I don't mean just the buildings. Let me take you to the homes of some of my friends, Chloe—and you would like to see where I buy my clothes, I am sure.'

'Well, yes…' Chloe had taken to the friendly darkhaired girl. Sashimi was very lovely and her outfit was beautiful. She was dressed in what looked like French clothes, and although her skirts were longer than were worn in the West at the moment, they were very feminine and modern and not at all what Chloe would have expected of a Muslim wife. 'If the professor can spare me for a while, I should love to.'

Sashimi looked pleased. 'I am sure he will spare you to me for at least one day,' she said and it was clear that she was accustomed to getting her own way—at least most of the time. 'I shall ask him when he dines with us, and I am sure he cannot refuse.'

'You think no one can refuse you, Sashimi,' her husband said with an amused smile, and again Chloe noticed some change in his wife's expression. It was just a flicker in her eyes, nothing more, but it made Chloe wonder. 'As you see, Chloe, my wife is much indulged. It is the way with us, I am afraid. We tend to spoil our women.'

'Chloe has seen too many Hollywood films,' Pasha said, teasing her. 'She thinks we keep our women in harems and never let them out.'

'Of course I don't,' Chloe said. 'But I have noticed that many of the ordinary women wear heavy veils when they go to the markets. You don't do that, Sashimi?'

Sashimi went into a peal of delighted laughter. 'I wear a scarf over my head when I go out in the streets—but I would never wear the veil.'

'You see how I spoil her?' Ahmad said and smiled at his wife. 'But she observes the customs when necessary. However, we are often in Paris and London—or New York. I do not see any reason for my wife to be any different from the other beautiful women you see in those cities.'

'But Ahmad is enlightened,' Pasha said with a frown. 'There are many amongst our people who still believe a woman should go veiled in public. Particularly amongst those who have not received the benefit of education as have Sashimi and my cousin.'

'Yes, I see,' Chloe said, enjoying the easy camaraderie she had found here. 'I usually cover my arms and wear a scarf over my hair as a mark of respect, especially when we are visiting sites of interest that take us anywhere near a mosque. Today, I thought no one would see me.'

'It was written that you should find us,' Sashimi said. 'And now we shall have our tea…or would you prefer sherbet as the women often do, Chloe?'

Since she had already seen that the tea was served in tall glasses with ice and mint, Chloe asked for tea. She knew that it was a delicious drink and very refreshing taken this way, as were the little almond cakes offered with it. Before she knew where she was, she noticed that an hour had slipped away.

'I should be getting back,' she said. 'Or my friends will begin to wonder where I am.'

'I shall walk with you,' Pasha said. He rose as she did, and Chloe found that the prospect of a little time alone with him was very pleasing.

'I liked your cousin and his wife,' she said as they walked back through the gardens. 'Do you have many relations here?'

'Oh, a few,' he replied. 'They are scattered all over—from Morocco to Algiers and the Persian Gulf…' He raised his brows at her. 'Why do you ask?'

'Merely idle curiosity,' she replied. 'I was surprised, that's all. I thought you said your people travelled all over the place?'

'In the old times they never ceased to travel and a tent was all the home they knew, but life has changed for the Bedouin as for others in this modern world of ours, Chloe. Many of my people have acquired wealth, and they choose to live in permanent homes built of stone or brick—but, as you heard my cousin say, they still travel frequently. Now it is more often to cities like Paris or London than the old caravan routes, though there are some that remain true to the old ways.'

'It is so interesting to hear you talk.' Chloe nodded her head. 'Yes, that fits with the professor's research. He thinks it a shame that—' She stopped speaking as they neared the house at which she was staying. 'It looks as if the professor has company.'

A large, expensive car had drawn up outside, and as Chloe paused she saw a man get out. She gave a little exclamation of surprise.

'Isn't that…Brent Harwood the film director? You remember, he was on the ship with us.'

'Yes, I believe it is.' Chloe turned to look at Pasha as he spoke. His face had taken on its harsh expression and his eyes were icy cold. He had withdrawn from her again, just as if the pleasant interlude they had spent together had never been. 'I think you must excuse me; I must leave you to your friend now. Goodnight.'

'But…' Chloe stared after him as he began to stride off back down the hill. Now what was wrong? He had implied that Brent Harwood was her friend, but that was ridiculous. Why should he think that? She had spoken to him only once on the ship, and that had not been at her instigation.

She hesitated, half-inclined to go after Pasha and ask him what was wrong, but then she decided against it. His moods were so unpredictable… She felt as if a shadow had fallen over her—and it had been such an enjoyable afternoon! Chloe felt irritated. Why had he gone off in such a manner?

And she hadn't even had a chance to ask him about the conversation she'd overheard in the hotel gardens the night before she and the professor left Cetua. She had forgotten it for a while, and she had meant to ask him as they walked. It was a nuisance, because she still didn't know whether or not it had been important.

She felt still more annoyed as she went inside. Why had the professor brought Brent Harwood back to the house—and what on earth did he want? The last time she had seen him had been in the hotel in Cetua, and she had not expected to see him ever again...

Chapter Four

'I'm not sure I understand what you mean?' Chloe
stared at Charles Hicks in dismay. Surely he was not
really suggesting what he seemed to be saying? 'But
I thought we had planned to stay here for at least a
week?'

'Yes, that was my original idea,' the professor
agreed and beamed at her. 'But when I met Mr Harwood and he came up with this idea—well, I thought
it was too good to turn down.'

'It would be such a help to me,' Brent Harwood
said, turning his charm on Chloe as if sensing her
reluctance. 'Angela simply refuses to do the desert
scenes and I was at a complete loss—and then I happened to meet the professor and I remembered you.'

'You are asking me to be a stand-in for Angela
Russell?' Chloe was disbelieving. 'But I don't even
look like her…'

'You could do once our make-up artist has finished
with you, enough for our purposes anyway,' he said.
'I noticed a faint likeness when I was on the ship. It's
more a mannerism than a look. I had intended to ask
you if you would do some stand-in work for us then—

but we were interrupted by that rather silly young woman.'

'Jane Vermont,' Chloe said and frowned at him. 'I'm not sure…'

Despite her doubts, she was tempted. After all, she had dreamed of being in the movies and she would never be offered another chance.

'It is such an opportunity for me,' Charles Hicks said. 'Mr Harwood is flying to the edge of the desert and he has offered to take us with him. It will save days of driving, Chloe dear, but it's really up to you.'

He was looking at her in a way that made her feel she would be selfish to turn the offer down. She thought regretfully of the invitations from Pasha's cousins that would have to be refused, but there was a tiny seed of excitement stirring inside her. After all, she didn't have to like the director to act in his film, did she?

'Well, if you think I can do it…'

'I knew you would agree,' Charles said. 'I said so, didn't I, Harwood? Amelia thought you wouldn't, but I was sure you would see what an excellent opportunity this is for us.'

'If you don't mind, I think I might stay here,' Amelia said, surprising them. 'I am feeling a little tired, Charles. And I have been to the desert on several occasions…'

'Feeling a bit under the weather, Amelia?' Charles nodded his understanding. 'Well, I am sure we all sympathise with that—and I have taken the house for the week. Yes, stay here by all means, my dear. If you need to take the house on longer, you must do so, of course—but I should have seen enough by that time and I shall rejoin you here.'

'If you are sure you don't mind?'

Chloe looked at her, thinking that she did seem rather tired.

She was still concerned and spoke privately to Amelia before they all went to bed that evening.

'Are you ill? Would you rather I stayed here with you?'

'No, of course not, Chloe dear. I am not ill, just a little weary—and to tell the truth I do not care for the idea of flying… Besides, Charles would not be pleased if you changed your mind now. I have never told him that I am nervous of flying.'

'Oh, I see.' Chloe felt relieved. 'Yes, it can be a little frightening the first time. Daddy took me on a flight to Paris for my twenty-first birthday. It was quite exciting once I had got over my nerves.'

'Yes, I expect so,' Amelia agreed. 'But I don't think I shall change my mind. Besides, I don't like that man very much.' She gave Chloe an odd look. 'Be careful of him, my dear. I don't trust him.'

'To be honest, I am not sure I do, either,' Chloe said and laughed. 'He can be charming, of course, but there's something…' She shrugged. 'I don't have to like him to act in his film, do I?'

'No, of course not. That will be quite exciting for you, Chloe.'

'Yes, I think it might,' she agreed. 'I did so love Rudolph Valentino's film…and this ought to be a bit like it, don't you think?'

'Perhaps…' Amelia looked doubtful. 'It will please Charles, anyway. Mr Harwood promised that he could use his plane to take trips into the desert…apparently there's a ruined fort he particularly wants to see.'

'Oh, well, then I can understand why it is so important to him,' Chloe said. 'Someone was going to call at the house to invite us all to dinner tomorrow. If I leave a letter…would you give it to him?'

'Yes, of course, my dear.' Amelia looked at her curiously. 'Friends of yours, Chloe?'

'Do you remember Mr Armand from the ship?'

'Armand…?' Amelia nodded. 'Vaguely. He was rather a reserved man, wasn't he? I am not sure that I spoke to him, though he may have nodded in passing. I believe Charles had an interesting conversation with him once.'

'Yes, he was rather reserved then—though we spoke a few times. He helped me in Cetua, when I thought some men were following me.' Chloe blushed as Amelia looked at her in surprise. 'They thought I was a famous actress and wanted my autograph. Well, anyway, Mr Al-Hadra is a cousin of his. I met them this afternoon and had tea…' She explained about the garden and the way she had been made welcome. 'So I don't want to just go off without some kind of explanation.'

'Certainly not,' Amelia said and looked approving. 'They were generous and hospitable, Chloe. The least you can do is to write a note of explanation. I shall be happy to give it to Mr Al-Hadra if he calls.'

Chloe thanked her and went to bed with an easier mind. She was still disappointed not to be able to visit her new friends again, because she had been looking forward to getting to know them better—but she couldn't help feeling a little excited about the prospect of being in a Hollywood film. She wondered what the actor who was playing the Sheikh would look like.

Her dreams were of the desert once more and of being in a tent, and the man who came to her in those dreams looked like Pasha Ibn Hasim.

Chloe had to agree that the flight to the village at the edge of the western Sahara had saved them days of travelling over dusty roads, and was very much more comfortable. The plane Brent Harwood had hired was in fact similar to the one Chloe had flown in on that trip to Paris with her father, and she marvelled that anyone should hire it for their personal use. But Brent Harwood was obviously rich, and when they arrived at their destination they were taken not to the small and probably dirty hotel Chloe had expected they might find in such a remote place, but to the rather large and palatial home of a rich Moroccan.

Chloe was shown to a bedroom with a veranda that opened out on to private gardens, with a little fountain and shady walks. It seemed almost unbelievable that something like this could exist at the edge of what were miles of inhospitable desert.

Chloe knew that only a small population of Bedouin and Berber peoples managed to scrape a subsistence living from rearing sheep, goats and camels in the area, which was hot, dry and arid. Once the Bedouin tribes had been warriors of the caravan routes but these days, the professor had told her, many of them found only a poor living from the area that was cultivated.

'Of course they may find minerals or oil here one day,' he had told Chloe. 'And that might change things—but it would still be difficult to exploit because of the shortage of water.'

Chloe wondered what Pasha would have to say about all this, and whether he also had relatives living in this part of Morocco. She had addressed her letter to Sashimi, feeling that it might be the correct thing to do—and could only hope that she had not offended her new friends. Perhaps when they returned to Marrakesh she might visit them again one day.

'I think Angela might have changed her mind about coming if she'd realised what this was like,' Brent observed when Chloe and the professor joined him in one of the huge reception rooms that evening. 'It's certainly better than anything else we've been offered in this country. I hope you are satisfied with your room, Chloe?'

'It's very nice,' she said. 'Much better than the hotel—but I know that the homes of wealthy Moroccans can be very attractive.' She blushed as he stared at her. 'I was invited to take tea with some people I met—and it was very pleasant.'

'Well, you've been luckier than we have,' Brent said, looking annoyed. 'It cost me an arm and a leg to get this place, because they were reluctant to hire it to us—and then Angela said she was ill and wouldn't come. But I guess we can manage without her. I can shoot all the desert stuff with you—we'll take it from back view or side and make it slightly indistinct.'

'How do you do that?'

'Oh, we have special lenses for different effects,' he told her. 'All you have to do is smile and look pretty—or act as if you're scared when the Sheikh scoops you up on his horse and rides off into the desert with you. But don't worry, you don't need to

know any of this. I'll be telling you what to do all
the time. It doesn't call for any real acting. We'll do
all the close-ups in the studio when we get back
home.'

'Couldn't you have shot it all in America?' Chloe
asked. 'I mean—you didn't really have to come all
this way, did you?'

His eyes narrowed as he looked at her. 'I wanted
to make the background authentic—and I've got some
pretty good stuff in the can. Besides, I had personal
reasons for coming out here…'

His expression told Chloe that he was not very
pleased by her asking questions. He obviously expected blind obedience from his actors and actresses.
Clearly, he didn't expect her to think, merely to do
as she was told.

Her opinion of him hadn't improved on closer ac-
quaintance, Chloe thought, and she felt a little re-
gretful at having agreed to go along with the suggestion that she help with stand-in work.

However, when she was introduced before dinner
to the actors and actresses who were making the film,
she found herself caught up in the excitement. The
leading actor—a man called Duke Earl, which was a
name that caused Chloe to giggle inside—wasn't
quite as handsome or compelling as Valentino, but he
was certainly attractive and should cause a few female
hearts to flutter when the film was released. There
were three other male actors, who introduced themselves as Kendal, Harry and Joe, and each played several parts, for which they told her they wore different
wigs and make up. Also two actresses, who were
playing slave girls, but both had walk-on parts as

waitresses and various other characters in the earlier part of the film.

'Brent uses a lot of extras,' an actress called Belle told her. 'It's cheaper that way—stars cost a lot of money. We only get paid a fraction of what Angela and Duke are getting for this.'

'I suppose it's always like that,' Chloe said. 'Brent didn't actually say he was paying me anything—but he did say he would provide some decent clothes for me to wear. Most of mine were left back at the hotel in Cetua.'

'Oh, we've got plenty of stuff in costume,' Belle said. 'The crew came down ahead of us. I'll take you over in the morning and you can sort something out.'

'It's all exciting, isn't it?' Chloe said. 'What is the film going to be called? I don't want to miss it when it comes out.'

'I think the title at the moment is something like *Desert Lover,*' Belle said. 'But they change that all the time. Don't worry, Chloe. If you give me your address at home I'll write and let you know. It's no use relying on Brent for anything. He'll forget you the minute he's got what he wants from you, so be very careful and don't believe a half of what he tells you. He would promise anything to get his own way.'

Chloe was a little startled by the other girl's frank words. 'Well, I wasn't expecting to become a star.'

'Don't worry, Angela won't let you,' Belle said. 'I wouldn't mind betting that when she finds out someone is taking her place she'll high-tail it down here as fast as she can.'

'Oh.' Chloe thought this over and realised that her trip might have been in vain. 'Well, I hope she doesn't come too soon. I want to see how everything is done.'

'You'll get bored after a couple of days,' Belle told her. 'It's mostly standing around until they want you—then an hour of action and then it's back to waiting again.'

Chloe digested this in silence. She wondered if Belle was trying to discourage her, but the other actors all said something similar when she talked to them. Apparently, the director was in charge and they all hung around waiting for him to tell them what to do—which sounded a little boring to Chloe.

'Do we get to see any of what has already been filmed?' she asked, but the reply was a firm no. The film was put together when Brent Harwood got back to his studio in Hollywood, and much of it would end up on the cutting-room floor.

Chloe thought it all over as she looked out of her room at the sky before retiring for the night. The stars were out over the desert and she felt an odd yearning to go there…not with all the camera crew and actors, but alone. Then she dismissed the idea as nonsense. She had never been to the desert and she wouldn't have the faintest idea of how to survive there…and it wasn't likely that a Sheikh would come along and take her back to his *casbah*.

She was beginning to realise that her dreams were far from reality, and that there was nothing particularly romantic about making a film.

Despite her thoughts before she went to bed, Chloe once again dreamed of being in a tent. This time when she woke she remembered quite clearly who had been with her in her rather naughty dream, and blushed for shame. She was thankful that Pasha could not guess that he had featured in her dreams so often of late— and that no one could know the nature of the dreams she had experienced so vividly the previous night. Oh, why did he linger in her mind all the time?

It was ridiculous to let herself think of him so often. Her common sense told her that Pasha would have forgotten her by now. He would have been annoyed that she had broken her appointment with his cousin—but then he would dismiss her as being unworthy of his notice.

She must forget him or she would never settle to anything! She was about to discover the exciting world behind the films she enjoyed so much, and it would be foolish to let a man who could never be anything to her spoil the experience.

The camera crew had been out the day before and set up tents for the actors to use while they were waiting around. Everyone was dressed in the costume of the Bedouin, and Chloe noticed that there were some locals dressed in similar costume mixing with the crew.

She presumed they were the extras, and the tents being used were meant to represent the Bedouin camp portrayed in the film. Brent seemed to be concentrating on taking shots of the camp for most of the morning, and the extras were encouraged to walk around with water skins tucked under their arms, and look as if they were going about their normal business. Camels had been brought to the location, and some of the men led them across the set from time to time.

There was a lot of shouting and gesturing going on, but otherwise very little action as far as Chloe could see. She was beginning to think that Belle was right, when at last she was told that she was wanted in make up.

'Well, Brent says you've got to look like Angela,' the girl said to her as she was asked to sit down in a canvas chair in the tent provided for make up and costume. 'It's a pity—you've got better skin than she has and your face is younger, fresher. You would look better without this, but we'd better do as the master says.'

She lowered a silvery-blonde, curly wig on to Chloe's head, and then added a jewelled headband, which Chloe saw to her disappointment was cheap glass and gilt metal and looked tawdry.

'Oh, it doesn't look like that on film,' she said, glancing at herself in the mirror. 'Do I need all that make up, Jilly?'

'Yes—the lighting would make you look washed out otherwise,' Jilly said and laughed. 'Nothing is natural and normal when we're filming. It's all make believe, fantasy stuff. You'll never see a movie in the same way again, Chloe.'

'No, I shan't…' Chloe was faintly disappointed. She watched as her appearance was transformed, feeling slightly embarrassed as she was handed the filmy costume that had been provided. 'You can see right through this skirt.'

'You need these.' Jilly handed her some flesh-coloured tights. 'Sorry, darling. I didn't think to tell you. Forgot you weren't one of us.'

Chloe felt a little better as she retired behind the screen and slipped on the tights before changing into the costume. She came out feeling awkward, and blushed as she looked at herself in the mirror.

'That isn't me.'

'It's the slave girl the Sheikh wants for himself even though she belongs to another man,' Jilly said. 'You look really good, Chloe. You've got a much better figure than Angela. I wonder if Brent has thought about that. You make her look plump...'

Chloe didn't reply. She was feeling very nervous, and when someone came to tell her that Brent was ready for her she felt like running off and hiding. How could she go out there looking like this? Her father would be horrified if he saw her—and she thought Justine would have a fit of the giggles. She had never imagined it would be like this!

'Come on,' Belle said to her. 'He's on the warpath this afternoon—don't make him wait or we'll all suffer.'

Chloe walked out of the tent feeling as if she wanted to die. Everyone was looking at her and she was terribly embarrassed. She had never worn anything this revealing in her life! They must think she looked a fright or they wouldn't be staring at her.

'Chloe...' Brent came to her, laying his hand on her bare arm. 'You look great. Just great. Don't be nervous.' He was staring at her, a thoughtful expression on his face. 'I was going to shoot a scene from the back, where you walk across the set carrying a water bag...but I've changed my mind.'

Chloe was overwhelmed with relief. 'Shall I go back and change out of this, then?'

'What are you talking about? I'm going to have a look at you through the camera. Just stand by that tent there...and look at me, then do exactly as I tell you.'

Chloe nodded, feeling confused. Why did he want

to take shots of her face? Hadn't he said they couldn't take close-ups? But perhaps he was going to use her as an extra slave girl? She felt a bit nervous as she took up the position he had indicated and put up a hand to brush a strand of hair away from her face.

'That's great!' Brent called. He was behind his camera looking at her. 'Do that again, Chloe...put your hand up and brush your hair back. Sigh and look as if you're hot and tired.'

That was easy enough, she was hot and tired—and fed up with sitting around all day. She suited her actions to her thoughts and Brent yelled excitedly.

'That's it! That's just what I wanted, Chloe. Now walk towards me...come on...slowly now. Remember, you're hot and tired and your heart is breaking...'

Chloe obeyed him. She wished he would finish whatever he was doing and take the shots he really wanted so that she could get out of this ridiculous costume.

'That's great,' Brent said. 'Now turn to look towards the edge of the camp...towards your right. Someone is coming...he is the man you love but he shouldn't be here, and you know he is in danger...look shocked...upset...'

Chloe turned her head and then her heart stood still. A man *was* standing at the edge of the camp looking at her, and the expression on his face was so angry and disgusted that she was terrified. Shock waves ran over her, and she felt sick with shame that he had seen her like this. What must he be thinking of her?

'That's wonderful, darling,' Brent said. 'Now turn and run back into the tent as if you are in distress.'

Chloe was only too happy to obey that instruction. She had felt dreadful out there in her tawdry finery and skimpy costume. She had seen the look in his eyes, and knew that he despised her for taking part in a film he would think cheap and insulting to his people.

'Back so soon?' Jilly asked. 'That was quick. Has Brent finished with you? He usually keeps his stand-ins hanging about for ages.'

'I don't know if he has finished,' Chloe said. 'But I have. I can't do this, Jilly. I should never have agreed to try.'

She walked to the dressing table and picked up a cloth, beginning to wipe the make up from her face. It smeared all over, so she picked up some face cream and rubbed it in, scrubbing at her mouth and cheeks until most of the heavy rouge had gone. Then she tore off the wig and threw it on the table, heading for the screen as someone came in.

'They want you again,' Belle said. She stared at Chloe's face in surprise. 'What have you done…you can't pose for the camera without make up.'

'I'm not going to,' Chloe said. 'You can tell Mr Harwood that I am very sorry, but he will have to get someone else to stand in for Angela. I'm going back to the house.'

'But you can't do that,' Belle cried. 'Brent is wild with excitement. He thinks he's discovered a new star. He's talking about writing in a part for you.'

'I'm not interested,' Chloe said and went behind the screen to take off the costume and put on the dress she had discarded earlier. Even that was a flimsy affair she had borrowed from the costume department and wasn't something she would have chosen for herself.

When she went outside, it was to discover that

some kind of an argument was going on. Brent was shouting at one of the crew.

'I thought I told you no spectators? It doesn't matter who they are—keep them away from the set while we're filming—' He broke off to look at Chloe, his look darkening as he saw she was no longer wearing her costume. 'Why are you dressed like that? I wanted to take some more shots of you.'

'I've changed my mind,' Chloe said. 'I don't want to be in your film, thank you. You can get someone else to stand in for Angela.'

'Look, Chloe…darling…' he said, coming over to her. 'That's all finished. I was a fool to think you could be Angela's stand-in. You've got a much better figure and the camera loves your face. I want you to let me teach you how to act. You could be the next Mary Pickford.'

Chloe stared at him uncertainly. There was no sign of Pasha now. She had no idea why he had been there earlier, but he had obviously seen all he needed to and left. He had thought her an immature child before this, and would now be certain that she was beyond redemption—besides, why should she care what he thought of her?

Why had he come here? It couldn't have had anything to do with her or he would have come to find her. Oh, she was being so foolish. What did any of it matter?

The sight of Pasha and the look in his eyes had made her panic, but she realised now that she might have overreacted. She hadn't felt comfortable in that ridiculous costume, but Mary Pickford didn't wear things like that. She played much more believable roles, the kind of thing that Chloe would feel comfortable with, and she was always dressed in lovely clothes.

'I felt silly wearing that costume.'

'And it didn't do you justice,' Brent agreed. 'I am sure the costume department can find you something better...if you would just consent to try again.'

'I'm not sure...'

'Not today,' he said. 'Look, why don't you go back to the house and have a nice cool bath and a rest, Chloe? You've had a long day, and you think it will always be like that, but you're wrong. I made a mistake keeping you hanging about all morning—but it won't be that way in future. I know how to take care of my stars.'

Chloe hesitated. She still wasn't sure that this business was for her, but surely she ought to give him a chance to explain what he meant. It had been a boring, tiring day, but she sometimes found dictation tiring and, on occasions, it could be a little dull. There were other things about being a film star that might be much more fun.

'Well, I suppose I could think about it.'

'Yes, you could,' Brent said, smiling at her. 'This is entirely my fault, darling. Just go back to the house and rest—and this evening we'll talk.'

Chloe nodded. She walked towards one of the cars that had been provided for transporting the actors backwards and forwards to the location, and a driver opened the door for her. He grinned at her, and she wondered what he thought was amusing, but didn't bother to ask.

'The boss must be keen,' he remarked as he got into the front of the car. 'He doesn't usually react that way when one of his girls plays up.'

Chloe frowned but didn't ask what he meant by *one of his girls*. She wasn't one of Brent Harwood's girls in any sense of the word, and she wasn't even sure she wanted to be a star—but she did need time to think about it before she made up her mind.

She wished that Amelia Ramsbottom had been with them, because it would have been nice to ask her advice. She wasn't sure she could talk to the professor about this...but she might try. Taking a stand-in part for a few days was very different from being made into a star...if that was possible. Could someone make a star—or did it just happen? She supposed Brent would tell her that evening.

Chloe was shocked to discover that the professor had gone off to visit a ruined fort in the desert and would not be back for a couple of days. His brief note said that he was sure she would have more fun filming with her friends than she would have got from visiting some ruins with him, and that she was to relax and enjoy herself. He would return by the end of the week at the latest, and then they would go back to Marrakesh together.

Chloe frowned over the note. She wished the professor had mentioned his intention the previous night, and felt almost as if she had been abandoned. Of course, he couldn't have known that she would become disillusioned with her new job so quickly, but he might at least have told her what was in his mind.

Since she had no one to talk to, Chloe took a long cool bath and then dressed in a pretty frock that she had borrowed from Belle. It was sleeveless, red and had a low waist and a short flirty skirt, and it made

Chloe look a bit like the film star Brent was saying she could be if she tried.

She wound a filmy pink scarf about her hair, and used a tiny flick of lipstick, dabbing some perfume she had bought in one of the bazaars behind her ears. Her sandals were high heeled and a soft gold leather, something she had also borrowed for the few days she stayed here and unlike the more sensible ones she usually wore.

Brent looked at her approvingly as she joined the others for dinner that evening. He inquired where the professor was, nodding as she told him that Charles had gone off to visit a fort in the desert.

'Apparently the guide was available and he seized the chance. He thought I would be too busy to want to go with him.'

'A pretty girl like you doesn't want to be bothered with boring old men like that,' Brent said, smiling at her in a way Chloe found slightly unnerving. 'I think we can find something better for you to do, darling.'

The word *darling* grated on Chloe's ears, but she made an effort to smile at him. She was stuck here for the next week and she supposed she ought to at least try to do what she had promised.

'I'm sorry I threw a tantrum this afternoon,' she said to him after dinner was finished and they had gone out into the garden because Brent wanted to talk to her alone. 'It's just that…I felt a little silly in that costume. It looked so tawdry. Not at all the way it does on the films.'

Brent nodded his understanding. 'Yes, I know how it seems—but think of all the films you've seen, Chloe. We may have to do things that seem strange to you, but that's the way films are made—the finished product is very different.'

'Yes, I expect so.' She felt a bit foolish now. 'I think being a film star might be quite exciting—and I will have another try tomorrow.'

'I knew you would,' he said and smiled at her. 'Besides, I've already got a team of writers working on a part for you. You're not going to be a slave girl, Chloe…so you won't have to wear that costume.'

'I won't—but I thought you wanted me as a stand-in for Angela?'

'That was the idea, but I've decided to cut her part to a minimum—she doesn't look that good on screen any more. We'll change the direction of the story. She can be killed off and the hero will go back to a French woman he met in Algiers…' Brent was obviously excited now. 'It's a fantastic plot, Chloe. He falls in love with this woman he meets in a nightclub—but she betrays him so he goes back to the desert to think about his life, and that's where the slave girl bit comes in—but then she is killed and he returns to his true love, who has regretted the quarrel and wants him back.'

'Well, it is certainly different…' Chloe looked at him uncertainly. 'What kind of clothes would I wear?'

'Oh, very slinky dresses that cling to that fantastic figure of yours, Chloe. Why have you kept it hidden under those awful clothes until now?' His eyes went over her. 'You look better this evening—but you wait until I dress you properly. When I take you back to America with me I'll have you dressed by the best designers…and your hair. We'll have that lightened just a little and maybe just a hint of a wave—and keep growing it. We'll use wigs for the film, but your hair suits you longer...' His voice had become softer, almost like a cat purring. 'You're a very beautiful woman, Chloe.'

Chloe wasn't sure she liked the sound of all this. He seemed to think he was going to take over her life.

'I'm not sure about coming back to America with you—' she began, but stopped as Brent suddenly grabbed her by the arms, his fingers digging into her flesh. 'What are you doing? You're hurting me!'

'You're so damned beautiful,' he grated. 'Surely you know I'm mad about you, Chloe? Don't think I'm going to use you for one film and then forget you. I'm going to make you a huge star. You will be famous...men will fall in love with you, and women will envy you. You'll have fabulous clothes and jewels...I'll cover your body in furs...' His voice took on a husky note. 'I didn't realise until today what a beautiful body you had...'

Chloe reacted instinctively as she heard that note. No, she didn't want this. She didn't want him to talk to her like this. It was all wrong! She pulled back from him, but he gripped hard, pulling her against him as he brought his head down and took possession of her mouth. She made a protest of disgust, then jerked back and pushed him away from her.

'How dare you! What do you think I am?'

'A woman who wants to be a star—and knows that favours have to be paid for,' he replied with a sneer. 'You didn't think it all came for free, did you, Chloe?'

'You—you disgust me!' Chloe stared at him in revulsion. 'If you imagine I shall let you touch me—'

'I want to do more than just touch you,' he said

and then grabbed her, whispering words she had never heard before against her ear. Words that were so horrible that they made her feel sick with disgust.

She wrenched away from him again, striking him across the face. 'I think you are foul,' she said. 'I wouldn't let you do that to me for all the money in the world and I don't want to be one of your stars, thank you.'

'Bitch,' he snarled and reached out to grab her again.

Chloe gave a little scream of fear and ran away from him. She was frightened and distressed, and wished that either the professor or Amelia was around so that she could go to them for help. What was she going to do? She couldn't stay here in case he came after her again. She just couldn't!

He might try to attack her again…he might try to do some of those awful things he had whispered to her before she'd struck him across the face. The thought made her feel sick, sending little shudders running through her. She had to get away from this place—but where could she go?

If only the professor were here! But the fort he had gone to couldn't be that far away, surely? He had given her the name and a little diagram. It was in her bag in her room.

She ran along the hallway to her own room, half-fearing that Brent would come after her, and locked the door while she gathered her things together, thrusting what she could into her large shoulder bag. The professor had drawn her a rough map, to show her where he was going. It seemed to be in more or less a straight line once you left the village. There was certain to be a little encampment nearby. Surely it would be easy enough to find?

She ran back along the hall to the front entrance, and heard Brent talking to Belle in the room just beyond the hall. He was asking if she'd seen Chloe—obviously intending to come in search of her. And she could imagine what he would do if he found her!

She couldn't stay here in this house another night. It was impossible! She would leave and in the morning she would hire someone to drive her out to the fort, but for tonight…she must find somewhere to stay. She wouldn't feel safe until she was somewhere that Brent Harwood couldn't reach.

She went outside into the cool of the night air. Pausing for a moment, she noticed one of the cars used by the crew. The driver was nowhere to be seen, but he had left the engine running and the door open. Chloe hesitated, then threw her bag on to the passenger seat and got in. She slammed the door to and was just driving off when she heard a shout from the house.

She opened the window and shouted that she would return the car when she had finished with it, then drove off into the darkness.

It was a nuisance that she had been seen. If she went to the only inn in the village and asked for a room, Brent might follow her there.

Why not start her journey tonight? A brief glance at the petrol gauge seemed to indicate there was a full tank, which should surely see her through. She had no real idea of how far the fort was, but there was certain to be somewhere she could buy more petrol, wasn't there? Boys selling cans of petrol had besieged them everywhere they stopped on their journey so she was sure to see someone before long.

There was a bright moon and stars over the desert and she wasn't afraid to go there alone. She had felt the pull of its mystery the previous night, and wished that she could be out there alone.

She had her map, what else could she need? It was less than a day's journey, according to the professor, so she could be there within a few hours—and it was much cooler at night. She could complete at least half the journey before the sun came up. Chloe felt much better at once. Yes, it made sense to leave now. She might even be with the professor for breakfast.

She was sure to see someone selling fruit and water as she passed the little outcrops of mud huts used by the shepherd boys she had seen as she was driven to the film location that morning. Everywhere they had been, there was always someone with something to sell.

It was all perfectly easy...and if she got lost she had a compass in her bag. She could join the professor within hours and it would be much safer than staying at the house with that awful Brent Harwood.

Chapter Five

'What do you mean—you have no idea where she is?' Pasha stared across the room at the other man, barely able to contain his fury. 'Or is it that you do not wish her to speak to me? What have you done to her? You'd better start praying it isn't anything I might not like.'

'I've told you, I don't know where she is—and don't much care. She took one of our cars and just drove off last night.'

'And you made no attempt to go after her or discover where she had gone?' Pasha's hands curled into tight balls at his side as he fought to control himself, a vein throbbing at his temple. He wanted to break the other man's neck. 'Have you any idea how dangerous it is for a woman to go off alone out here? This isn't the city...'

He could see by the expression of indifference on Harwood's face that he didn't care what might have happened to Chloe Randall, and the hatred settled into a hard knot inside him. It took all his considerable will power to refrain from attacking him, but he mastered his anger. He would deal with Harwood at a later date.

'You will regret this,' he said coldly, 'if anything has happened to Miss Randall.'

Pasha stepped towards him and the colour was stripped from Harwood's face. 'I know you blame me for Lysette's death,' he said. 'But I wasn't responsible—and the child wasn't mine.'

'You knew about the child?' Pasha reached out and grabbed him by the throat, his powerful hands pressing against Harwood's windpipe so that he choked and gasped for breath. However, he knew exactly the amount of pressure he was exerting, and his victim was in no real danger, though rendered completely impotent by the hold Pasha had on him. 'You had better tell me what you know!'

'For God's sake! You're choking me…' Harwood spluttered. 'Let me go and I'll tell you what I know.'

Pasha relaxed his grip, then gave him a violent push which sent him stumbling backwards into a sideboard. Harwood choked and heaved, eyeing him nervously as he struggled to recover his breath.

'Murdering devil,' he croaked and retreated a few steps as Pasha's eyes sparked with temper. His expression was sullen, fearful. 'Yes, I admit I wanted Lysette, and I would have gone to bed with her if she had been willing—but someone else got there first. She was beautiful and I wasn't the only one who noticed. I don't know who he was, but I do know he was rich—and he wasn't American. I think he might have been one of your people.'

'An Arab?' Pasha's eyes narrowed. 'You're lying. We don't abuse our women like that. A woman of good family is always treated with respect.'

'I don't know about your customs—but Lysette came to me in tears when she discovered she was having a child, wanted me to help her get rid of it. But I warned her it was risky and refused,' Harwood said. 'She told me this man had seduced her and promised to marry her…there was some tale about his having done it to bring shame on you.' Harwood's eyes darkened with hostility. 'If you want my opinion, she crashed that car on purpose. She was afraid of what you would say when you found out she'd been dishonoured. If anyone killed her, it was you!'

Pasha's anger was like a boiling cauldron inside him. It had festered for months, and had erupted without warning. How dare the fool stand there and lie that way? And it was all lies. Harwood had invented the story to cover his own guilt.

'You are a liar,' he muttered, controlling his temper with difficulty. 'Lysette knew I loved her. She knew I would help her.'

'She was afraid you would disown her. Think about it—what would you have thought in her place?'

Pasha turned away, his own thoughts in turmoil. It was all lies. Had to be lies! Lysette couldn't have been that afraid of him. One day he would discover the truth, and then Harwood would pay—but for now there were other things that needed his attention.

With a tremendous effort, he banished the red mist of fury from his mind. After Sashimi had told him where Chloe had gone, Pasha had known he must follow her. He could not risk another young woman's life being ruined by that devil Harwood, but when he'd seen Chloe in that ridiculous costume he had been annoyed with her. He had walked away in disgust, intending to warn the professor of the danger she was running rather than speak to her directly, in case he lost his temper and said things to her he might regret afterwards.

The discovery that the professor had gone off into the desert had made Pasha realise that Chloe was even more vulnerable than he had thought, and he had returned to try and speak with her that morning. Now he discovered that she had taken a car and driven off alone.

Pasha's mouth settled into a grim line, his eyes dark with an intense emotion he hardly understood himself. Clearly Chloe had found out what kind of a man Harwood was for herself!

What had that devil done to her? Pasha reflected that he ought to have killed him while he had the chance—but he wasn't a murderer. He might order an execution once a man's guilt was proven, but that was justice—the justice of his people. Had he still lived in the old way, such things were law—an eye for an eye. It was the justice of men since primeval times. But cold-blooded murder was something else.

Where best to look for Chloe? Pasha was frowning as he got into the car he had borrowed from a cousin and headed off towards the village. There was only one inn. Surely he would find her there?

Chloe squinted down the road ahead of her. Her eyes were tired and she wasn't sure of what she was seeing. She had been driving for most of the night, following the road through the desert—or what she now realised was merely the edge of the miles and miles of arid country ahead of her. At first she had passed small clusters of mud-bricked houses, which she knew were Berber settlements. She had heard the faint sounds of sheep bells or the grunt of a camel, and known there were people living in those little houses.

But it was hours since she'd seen a building of any kind, and the road had got worse and worse, becoming just a narrow bumpy track. Now, suddenly, it had disappeared completely. There was just sand out there, flat for almost as far as the eye could see and then rising to what was either a ridge of rock or a sand dune, but too far away for her to be sure.

Would the car wheels get bogged down in that sand? she asked herself, and common sense told her that of course they would. It would be folly to try and go any further into the desert. She simply had no idea which direction to take. Besides, she wasn't going to get far on foot without either water or supplies. And she hadn't been able to buy any petrol. She glanced at the gauge and noticed that it still seemed to be half full—surely that couldn't be right? She gave it a little tap and it shot all the way up to full again and stayed there.

Oh, no! It must be faulty. A sense of panic filled her as she realised she had no idea how much was left in the tank. It was just as well she couldn't take the car any further into the desert.

How on earth did people travel over terrain like that? Chloe stopped the car and got out to look. She took an experimental few steps forward into the sand and discovered that she sunk into it almost to her ankles. Remembering the tales she'd been told of scorpions and sidewinders, she stepped back hastily on to the road.

What did she do now? She could see a purple smudge on the far horizon that might or might not be the fort or an oasis, but there was no way she could get there alone. Her panic had left her now and only stubbornness had kept her driving for the past hour or so. She knew she had been foolish to attempt to follow the professor alone. She ought to have gone to the inn and waited until Charles Hicks came back— or hired a car to take her back to Marrakesh.

Yes, of course she could do that! Why on earth hadn't she thought of it the previous night? That's what she would do, Chloe decided. She would drive back to the village and inquire the best way of getting back to Amelia and the safety of civilisation…

She looked at the car. She wasn't sure she could turn it around on this narrow track without getting stuck in the sand, which she now realised had been closing in on her for some distance. Looking back, she saw that it would be impossible to turn for quite a while. It had been dark for much of the time she had been driving, and she hadn't realised how awesome and bare the surrounding terrain really was.

Chloe had left the engine running when she got out, just in case she couldn't start it when she got back in. It was still turning over nicely as she put the gears into reverse and began to edge her way back over the track.

It was slow going, because she wasn't as confident in reverse, and she was nervous of running off the road. If she managed to get herself bogged down in the sand, she would have a long way to walk.

Pasha frowned as he left the inn. A few minutes' conversation with the owner had established that Chloe had not been there. So where was she? Had Harwood lied to him? Was she back at the house?

About to return there and force the truth out of the American, he began to walk back to his car when a child darted out and caught at his sleeve.

'You look for English lady in car?'

'Yes—do you know where she is?' The young lad nodded and Pasha took a handful of coins from his pocket, depositing them into his grubby hand. 'Tell me!'

'She went there last night.' The child pointed towards the desert. 'She took the road that leads nowhere.'

Pasha cursed inwardly. The foolish girl! What on earth did she imagine she was doing? Did she think the camp the film crew had set up was the way things really were out here? That there was a road she could just drive along all the way...to the fort?

He shook his head in disbelief. Surely she hadn't tried to find Professor Hicks! The fort was a day's flight, several days by camel train, which was the only form of transport that could cope with the harsh terrain of the desert. And even then she would need experienced guides...she couldn't be that foolish!

But of course she could, he realised. She imagined it was all just the way these ridiculous films portrayed it. She probably thought she could just stop a passing Sheikh and ask for directions. It would have been amusing if it were not so very terrifying. Pasha was shocked to discover that he cared very much what happened to Chloe out there in the desert.

He had to find her, and there was only one way to be sure of having even a fifty/fifty chance of success. It was a good thing that his cousin, Mohammed Ibn Ali, happened to be around...

* * *

Chloe had been able to turn the car and was driving the right way again when the engine suddenly died on her. She stared at the dashboard in dismay, wondering what on earth had gone wrong, and then groaned as she saw that the petrol gauge was registering empty.

'Oh, damn you!' She thumped the wheel in frustration. 'Don't do this to me.'

Now what was she going to do? She knew she was still a long way from the village. She hadn't even reached the first of the Berber huts yet or she might have been able to get help there.

'I'll walk, that's what I'll do,' Chloe said the words aloud because the stillness was beginning to get to her. She had been aware of a growing thirst for a while now, and it was beginning to get a lot warmer. 'It can't be much further now.'

She didn't need to walk as far as the village, she thought. Once she could find someone—a shepherd boy or a man with camels—she would be able to ask for help. She got out of the car, slamming the door but resisting the temptation to kick it in frustration. It was her own fault. She hadn't even considered how she would be able to buy more petrol in the desert.

'I am an idiot,' she told herself. 'A first-class idiot!'

Of course she hadn't been thinking about anything except how to get away from Brent Harwood, and that had been the reaction of a naïve girl. For goodness sake! All she need have done was lock her door! Instead, she had fled into the night on a wild goose chase.

'And where did that get you, Chloe Randall? In a mess, that's where.'

It was comforting to listen to the sound of her own

voice. She started walking down the road, but realised after a few steps that she wasn't going to get far in the stupid high heels she was wearing. She took them off, carrying them for a while and then throwing them into the sand in disgust.

'Stupid things,' she muttered, but she knew it was Chloe Randall who was stupid. She hadn't even brought a supply of water with her. 'Damn! Damn him! Damn…'

It made her feel better to swear, but it didn't make the walking any easier. Her feet felt hot now that she had no shoes, and the drifts of sand scattered here and there on the road got between her toes. The sun was burning down on her, and she didn't have a hat—or anything to cover her arms.

'Fool…fool…fool!' she cursed herself, licking her dry lips. She had never realised it was possible to feel this thirsty. And she was beginning to feel odd. 'Keep going, Chloe!' she muttered aloud. 'It's only another two or three hours…'

She concentrated on the road ahead, but the wind was beginning to blow the sand about and she had to put up a hand to shield her eyes. The road was disappearing as sand swirled across it… For a moment Chloe panicked. Supposing she lost her way? But, no, she could still see the road further on. It was just the wind playing tricks on her.

All she had to do was to keep on walking straight ahead…

Half the morning had gone before Pasha was ready to go and look for Chloe. He had been tempted to drive straight out into the desert after her, but knew that that would only result in a loss of precious time.

He glanced at his cousin Mohammed as he climbed into the passenger seat of the light aircraft Pasha had flown down from Marrakesh the previous day.

'There's no need for you to come,' he began, but the other man held up his hand.

'My place is with you, cousin. This girl is important to you—therefore all my resources are yours while you search for her. My men are on the ground, and we shall make a search by air ourselves. Two pairs of eyes are better than one.'

Pasha nodded, knowing that his cousin spoke the truth. Although they were cousins, they had never been as close or as friendly as Pasha was with Ahmad. He did not know why, but perhaps it was because Mohammed clung to the old ways and did not approve of Pasha choosing to live in the Western world.

However, Mohammed had met all of his requests with an apparent eagerness to be of assistance, and Pasha was glad of his help. If Chloe had been sensible, she would have turned back when she realised the road just disappeared into the desert, and with luck they might find her very quickly.

He had tried to discover how much petrol was in the tank of the car Chloe had taken, and his calculations told him that she might not have enough to make it back to the village. What would she do then? Had she got the sense to wait in the car for help to arrive— or would she imagine that no one would search for her?

Since there would probably not have been a search until Professor Hicks returned from his expedition, had Pasha not been there, Chloe would most likely have chosen to leave the car and walk. He had no idea what she had been wearing, but he would bet on her not having had a sun hat with her—which meant she wouldn't be able to walk far. So they ought to find her somewhere on that road...unless she had become disorientated and begun to go round and round in circles, as travellers lost in the desert sometimes did.

Pasha concentrated his mind on the dangers of dehydration and sunstroke, not daring to think about the other perils that could befall a young woman alone in the desert...

Chloe's head was aching and she couldn't see very well. She wasn't sure whether it was the wind blowing the sand about or whether her eyes were playing her up—but she couldn't seem to see the road any more. Everything was becoming a blur and she was feeling terrible.

'Keep going,' she muttered aloud, licking her lips. Her mouth was so dry...so dry and all she wanted was a drink of water. 'Where is that damned road?'

It was getting difficult to put one foot in front of the other now. Her feet hurt so much it was painful to walk...the sand was burning the bottom of her feet and her arms felt sore, as did her face. She would have terrible sunburn when she got back to the village.

She wondered whether she ought to try and use her compass, and then she realised that she had no longer got her shoulder bag. She must have dropped it somewhere.

She didn't want to lose that bag! It had all her money in it. She was sure she had brought it out of the car with her...or had she? She couldn't remember.

Her head was beginning to spin as she looked back

over her shoulder. If she'd dropped her bag, she ought
to go back for it...but what was that? Something was
coming towards her out of the sun. She put up her
hands to try and protect her eyes so that she could
see more clearly. It was an animal...a camel...a man
on a camel was riding towards her.

She waved to him, shouting in a voice so hoarse
that she knew it came out as no more than a whisper.
But the man had seen her. Yes, he was making his
camel squat in the sand...he was getting down and
coming towards her.

Chloe's head was spinning. The man was dressed
in the robes of a Bedouin...just like the extras had
been wearing at the film location. She took a few
steps towards him, then gave a sigh and crumpled into
a heap just as he reached her.

She heard him say a few words in a language she
could not understand and then he bent over her. Chloe
stared up into a dark ugly face. He didn't look a bit
like Rudolph Valentino, and when he grinned at her
she saw that his teeth were blackened and rotten, and
he had a big gap in the front where several were missing. It gave him a villainous look and she was suddenly terrified.

She gave a little shriek as his hand reached out to
her, and then fainted.

'You will not find her now,' Mohammed said. 'The
light is fading, Pasha. It is a pity she did not stay with
the car...'

They had found the car easily, Pasha spotting it
from the air. His heart had raced with excitement,
believing they had found her, but after landing on the
hard surface of the road to investigate further, dis-

covered only the shoulder bag lying inside on the passenger seat where Chloe had thrown it the previous evening. He had known despair then, for the desert was a treacherous place for a young woman alone.

After a brief search of the immediate area, he had taken the plane back into the air, determined to find her. But although they retraced the road time after time, they saw no sign of her ever having been there. Pasha had been extending his search the whole time, flying in ever increasing circles and criss-crossing the same territory in the hope of seeing something that would give him a clue.

'She cannot have just vanished into thin air,' he said and frowned. 'But you are right, Mohammed— we shall not find her once it is dark. We must return to the village and see if there is news of her. If not, I shall organise another search at first light.'

'I do not think she could survive another night in the desert,' his cousin told him. 'She had no water…it was a very foolish thing this woman did, my cousin.'

'Impulsive and foolhardy,' Pasha agreed. 'But she did not understand how cruel the desert can be. She imagined it would all be like the settlements around the village, and must have thought she would be able to buy whatever she needed for her journey.'

'How can this be?' Mohammed frowned. 'Are these infidels such fools as to visit our deserts without guides?'

Pasha did not answer immediately. Sometimes he forgot the prejudices and hostility that others amongst his people felt towards the West. Prince Hassan and his friends were very pro-British, but many resented the influence of any Westerners in their lives.

'She is merely a woman,' he answered at last with

a shrug. 'Women need the strong hand of a man to protect them, Mohammed.'

'It is true,' his cousin agreed. 'Do not trouble yourself further, Pasha. If it is written that the woman shall die here, you must accept it.'

Pasha made no reply. His religious beliefs were his own, and he would not argue them with his cousin. Besides, he was hoping that there would be some news when he returned to the village.

He had made arrangements for searches to be made on the ground, and he could only hope that the guides and trackers he had paid would have had more luck than he'd had in the air.

'Water…' Chloe moaned as her eyelids flickered. 'Please…water…'

A woman bent over her, holding a little metal cup to her lips and allowing her a few sips. She drank greedily and begged for more, but the cup was withdrawn.

'No more…' the woman replied. Chloe had spoken in English, but the reply was in French. 'Too much is not good…little by little…'

Chloe tried to thank her but her tongue was too swollen and the words would not come out as more than an indistinct mumble. She was conscious of pain everywhere. Her face, arms, neck and feet felt as if someone had poured scalding water over them, and she felt light-headed and sick.

'Please…I'm ill,' she whispered. 'Get help…'

She had tried to speak in French, but she knew that her words were a jumbled-up nonsense. She couldn't think properly. All she knew was that she felt dreadfully ill.

'Help me…' she whispered as the tears trickled down her cheeks. 'Help me…'

She did not know to whom she was making her plea for help, but as she drifted away into unconsciousness again a face came to her mind. If only he would come to her. But why should he? He must think her a foolish girl and unworthy of his notice.

'One of my people has found something.' Mohammed brought Pasha the shoes and showed them to him. 'She must have thrown them away because she could not walk in them.'

'Then she did try to walk back to the village,' Pasha said. 'Tomorrow I shall go back into the desert…' He broke off as there was a commotion outside the door, and then one of Mohammed's guards came to tell him that a man wished to see him. 'Let him come in.'

'He is not of our tribe, my lord. He stinks of camel dung.'

'Bring him to me if he has news,' Pasha said. The insult was usual when a member of another tribe intruded into jealously guarded territory. Mohammed had set up his camp just beyond that of the film location, and his guards stood at the entrance to his tent, in which Pasha was a guest for the night. 'I shall hear what he has to say.'

'Enter, you son of a she-dog,' the guard muttered at the man who waited outside. 'Mind your manners with His Highness or I'll kick your skinny—'

'Come forward, friend,' Pasha invited, cutting off the insults in mid-flow. 'Tell me your news and you shall be paid.'

'May the blessings of Allah be upon you, lord,' the

man replied and flung himself to his knees before Pasha. 'I have heard of your greatness and the generosity you bestow on those who serve you.'

'Yes, yes,' Pasha said, controlling his impatience as best he could. 'Have you news of her—the woman I seek?'

'I found her half-dead, my lord—she is at my encampment being cared for by the women. Word had reached us that you searched for an English woman and I sent my men out to look for her, knowing that you would be generous to those who found the woman…' His eyes narrowed craftily.

'You shall be well paid for your services,' Pasha said. 'I have given my word—but tell me, is she very sick?'

'Had I not come upon her she would undoubtedly have died. But I spared no effort to track and help the woman you desired found.' The man's eyes gleamed with greed as he tried to impress upon Pasha the value of what he had done. 'But it was the will of Allah that I found her. May the blessings of Allah be upon your house, my lord…'

'Yes, yes, thank you,' Pasha replied. 'And upon yours—where can I find Miss Randall? How far is your camp?'

'It has taken me half a day's journey to reach you, lord.'

'Then if we set out now…'

'You cannot go now,' Mohammed said. 'If it is the will of Allah that she lives you will find her still alive tomorrow, Pasha. This man must rest and eat. The morning will be soon enough…'

Pasha felt the frustration eating at his guts, but he knew that Mohammed's counsel was good. It would be better to let the man rest, and the camel needed food and water. He would also need camels himself, and servants to bring all the baggage he might require when he found Chloe. If he took the plane, there was no guarantee that he would be able to land safely or take off again.

This man's women were tending Chloe, and they would know how to deal with her hurts, probably as well as the hospital staff he would have rushed her to if he could—perhaps better. He would take modern medicines with him, which might help if she needed treatment the Bedouin people could not provide.

'As you say,' he replied. 'She is in the hands of Allah—it will be better to wait until the morning.' He looked at the messenger. 'You will be paid when I have seen the woman.' He named a sum which seemed to almost overcome Chloe's rescuer, who was obviously not a wealthy man.

'May the blessings of Allah be upon your house.' He salaamed and bowed, walking backwards out of the tent.

After the man had gone, and Mohammed had left to give instructions as to where the stranger should be housed for the night, Pasha paced the tent impatiently.

He was not content to leave the fate of Chloe Randall in the hands of Allah or anyone else—but he knew that he could do nothing more for the moment. Except pray. It was a long time since he had prayed. Since Lysette's death he had not been sure that God existed at all except in the minds of those who believed.

'Grant me this,' he found himself making a bargain with his own gods—the gods of honesty, justice and duty by which he lived. 'Grant me her life and I shall try to be a better man.'

Chloe woke again and it was night. She cried out and someone came to her, lifting her as she sipped at the water again. It hurt when they touched her, but then someone smeared something on her arms and it eased her a little.

'Thank you,' she whispered. 'Thank you…please help me…'

She was drifting back into that nightmarish place of pain and thirst, the fever taking her into a world of strange dreams where she was not sure what was real and what was false.

The pain was always there in the background each time she woke, but gradually she became aware of a change. She thought that someone else came to her, bending over her and whispering words of comfort. She was given something that seemed to ease her pain, but it made her sink into an even deeper state of unconsciousness so that she was not even aware of being tended.

The terrible thirst had somehow gone, and her body no longer felt as sore as it had, but she could not seem to shake off this drowsiness…a state of being drugged… Somewhere at the back of Chloe's mind was a fear that she had been drugged and imprisoned against her will, and she sat up, crying out in terror.

'Lie still, you foolish girl,' a gentle, reassuring voice told her and she instinctively obeyed. 'No one is trying to harm you. You have been very ill, but I am here now. I shall take care of you and you will soon be well. There is nothing to fear while I am with you.'

Insensibly, the voice calmed her and she drifted into sleep once more.

It was light when she woke again, and looked about her as she struggled to remember where she was.

'Water…may I have some water, please?'

For the first time the words came out clearly. Chloe was aware that her body no longer felt as sore and painful as it had, and her tongue seemed to have shrunk to its normal size again. She tried to sit up, but a wave of dizziness swept over her and she fell back against a pile of soft cushions again.

The cushions smelled of something nice—a fresh perfume like roses. It was not the same as the smell she had noticed when she first came to herself, which had been unpleasant. But where was she? Looking round she saw that she seemed to be in a large tent… Suddenly, Chloe remembered. She had been in the desert when someone came riding towards her on a camel.

She remembered that she had been frightened by the look of him, and she thought she had fainted from terror—or perhaps she had simply passed out from heat exhaustion.

A man had entered the tent and was approaching her couch. He was dressed in flowing white robes and wore the headdress of the Bedouin people. Was it the man who had found her? Her nerves fluttered and she felt a moment of fear. What did he want of her? Would he accept money for helping her or…? Her heart raced, and then she saw his face and she stared at him in disbelieving wonder.

'You came…' she whispered and wondered if she was dreaming. 'How—how did you know where to find me?'

'My cousin had the word put out that I was looking for you. The man who found you was not of my cousin's family, but he came to me and told me…and I came to you as soon as I could.' He smiled at her in a way that set Chloe's pulses racing wildly. His dark eyes were so intense, so full of fire that it set her tingling. 'How do you feel now?'

'Better,' she said feeling foolishly shy as she saw his expression. He looked as if he were struggling with some deep emotion—almost as though he might devour her at any moment. 'I was so thirsty, but I am better now, thank you. Someone has been looking after me…' She stared at him, a flush in her cheeks. 'Was…was it you?'

'Some of the time. I brought medical aids with me that are not readily available here in the desert. You were in such pain, but the drugs eased you.'

'I was so foolish,' Chloe said. 'I thought I could drive to the fort in a few hours…' She blushed as she saw that the expression in his eyes had changed now, becoming slightly amused, indulgent and yet critical—almost as if she were a naughty child. 'I had realised my folly and intended to return to the village and get someone to drive me back to Marrakesh.'

'And what made you feel so desperate that you sought to escape that night?' he asked, his eyes going cold suddenly. 'What did that swine do to you?'

'He—he made suggestions I didn't care for, that's all,' she said and lowered her eyes, unable to meet his gaze. 'He was going to make me the next Mary Pickford—but he wanted certain things in return and he grabbed me…' She faltered, then looked at him. 'I was foolish. I realise that all I needed to do was lock my door, but—'

'You panicked and ran?' Pasha nodded as if he understood. 'Perhaps it was the first time a man had made those suggestions to you?'

'He wasn't very nice,' Chloe said. 'The things he said made me feel sick inside. I hit him and he was furious. I just wanted to get away from him, and I didn't realise the fort wasn't nearby.'

'By air, perhaps,' Pasha said. 'Professor Hicks gave you a sketch from imagination, Chloe—that drawing in your bag is nothing like the kind of map you would need to find the place. Besides, you would have needed experienced guides, camels and a supply of water to last several days. You also needed the proper kind of clothes.'

'Yes, I realise all that now,' Chloe said. She fluttered her hands nervously on the covers, which were cool linen and smelled of a light, fresh perfume. 'You must think I'm such a fool!'

'You have been naïve,' he replied. 'But you are not the first European to underestimate the desert. You knew nothing of its dangers—or of how to protect yourself. I blame Professor Hicks for giving you the impression that it was less than a day's journey from the village—and for leaving you alone with that man. He should be ashamed of what he did—and I shall tell him so when I see him.'

'No—please…' Chloe begged. 'It wasn't really his fault. I should have thought more carefully. I suppose I've always been a little impulsive.' She put out her hand to touch his as he handed her a little cup of water. 'I don't know how I can ever thank you for what you have done for me.'

'There is no need of thanks. I had my own reasons for distrusting Harwood, and it was fortunate that I was able to raise the alarm. Otherwise…' He shrugged. 'But as my people say, it was the will of Allah that you live.'

'The man who found me and the women who cared for me when I was first brought here…'

He smiled as she faltered, understanding what she was trying to say. 'They have been paid and departed two days ago.'

'Then this tent…' She looked about her again, becoming aware that it was rather attractive, and furnished with rich carpets on the floor, chests of wood bound with brass, brass lamps, little wooden tables and another couch piled with colourful cushions. 'This is yours?'

'No—though it is similar to one that I sometimes use. This was borrowed from my cousin Mohammed Ibn Ali, who has many such in his possession. His men are guarding our camp, and his women have been tending you these past five days. Since you were too ill to be moved, we brought these comforts to you.'

'Have I been ill that long?' She stared at him, swallowing hard. Her throat felt tight and she found it a little difficult to breathe normally. 'The professor will be wondering where I am!'

'He has been told that you are being cared for, and that you will be returning to Marrakesh with me when you are well enough to travel.'

'Oh.' Chloe was not sure what to say. He had not suggested that she travel with him, merely informing her that it would be so. Her stomach clenched as she looked at him, and she licked her lips with the tip of her tongue, feeling oddly shy. 'Thank you. I think I must have been a great deal of trouble to you?'

'There is an ancient law that says when you save a life you are responsible for that person. I could do no less than see you safely back where you belong, Chloe.'

'You…you are very kind…'

'No.' He frowned at her. 'Never confuse what is done because it is right or necessary with kindness. I am not kind, Chloe. When you know me better you will discover that when I do something, I do it for a reason.'

'Oh.' She was at a loss to understand him. What was he saying? She did not think he wanted payment, and would not have dared to offer money. So what was his reason for having taken charge of her life?

He smiled and shook his head. 'Do not concern yourself, Chloe. All will become clear to you in time. I shall leave you now. The women will come to you and make you comfortable—and perhaps later this afternoon you may feel able to get up for a little while.'

Chloe stared after him as he left the tent. He had suggested that she would learn his purpose in time and that she would understand when she knew him better.

That strange intense look was back in his eyes, making her tingle once more. Why did he look at her so? Her flesh seemed to burn from the heat of that look, and her throat felt constricted, her mouth dry.

What did he mean? Was she going to know him better? Was he saying that he liked her—that she was special to him? Suddenly, her heart was thumping with excitement and she realised that she would very much like to spend more time with this man.

Chapter Six

After Pasha had left her, two women came to the tent. They gave her food and water, and she discovered that she was hungry. The women encouraged her, smiling and chattering in a language she could not understand. She was sad that there was no way to communicate with them, but her attempts to speak to them in French met with only a shake of the head. However, they were very friendly, and after a few minutes they began to make themselves clear by signing.

They had brought a jug of water and a gleaming copper bowl, indicating that she should wash her face. There were also soft towels, a kind of perfumed liquid soap—and clothes.

Chloe was shown several different outfits, from which they seemed to be indicating she might take her choice. The skirts were long and full, the tunics loose and from what she could see meant to be worn over the skirt, and then belted at the waist with a plaited tie. She saw that they had also brought a head-dress, which would protect her head from the fierce heat of the sun, and a band of what looked like gold medallions to wear around her forehead.

She chose a red skirt and a white tunic, which looked as if they might fit her, and the women nodded approvingly as they showed her a dark gold belt, which seemed to go with the other things.

Looking at her arms as she washed herself in the cool water, Chloe noticed that there were unsightly patches where the skin had peeled away, and was glad that the tunic had wide, flared sleeves. When she was dressed, she glanced at herself in a hand mirror they held for her and exclaimed in horror as she saw the blotches on her face. She looked terrible!

One of the women gave her a little pot of grease, miming the action of rubbing it on her skin and smiling. She was obviously trying to tell her that the cream would repair the damage in time, and Chloe accepted it gratefully.

She wasn't a vain girl, and usually spent the minimum of time fussing with herself, but it was rather disturbing to see her skin looking so patchy.

Chloe smiled, telling them that she understood and put a little of the grease on her face. It smelled of roses and felt light and cooling to the skin.

She was conscious that she didn't look her best when she went outside, and could only hope that her complexion would recover its natural texture and colouring in time.

She paused as she saw Pasha standing with another man of similar height and build, not liking to approach them—but then Pasha noticed her.

He smiled and came towards her. 'The costume suits you better than the one you were wearing for that foolish film. Are you feeling well enough to be introduced to my cousin?'

'Yes, of course. I must thank him for his hospitality.'

Chloe felt oddly shy as she was led forward and introduced to Mohammed Ibn Ali. His dark eyes went over her in what she felt was a critical way, and although he greeted her courteously, he did not smile or offer to shake her hand. She felt that he disapproved of her, and there was none of the warmth or friendliness that she had met with in Ahmad Al-Hadra's home.

Chloe felt extremely uncomfortable. He was a very stern man and she feared she had aroused his dislike. 'I wish to thank you for your help. I fear I have caused a great deal of trouble, sir.'

He inclined his head in assent. 'This is true—but it was written. These things have their purpose.'

Chloe was not sure how to reply. She felt a sense of relief when his critical gaze was removed, sensing that she had been measured and found wanting. It seemed that he was about to take his leave and move on further into the desert, though, as Pasha explained to her later, a few of the men and women were to remain with them.

'They stay to look after us until you are well enough to return to the village,' Pasha told her. 'We must travel part of the way by camel, though a landing area has been prepared and my plane will be waiting for us when we reach the first Berber settlement.'

'You have done so much for me—' Chloe broke off, her voice torn with emotion. She knew that she would have died alone in the desert but for him, and her gratitude almost overcame her. Her eyes misted with tears, which she struggled to subdue. 'I feel foolish and I cannot begin to tell you—'

'You were foolish to agree to appear in that ridiculous film,' he said and frowned at her. 'That costume you were wearing was both inaccurate and scandalous.'

'Oh, but…' Chloe was about to explain that she'd had no choice, but something made her change her mind. Why was he being so arrogant over such a silly thing? She was grateful for all that he had done, but she really could not allow him to dictate to her. 'I do not like Brent Harwood, but that doesn't mean his film would have been ridiculous. Besides, those films give pleasure to a lot of people.'

'We shall never agree on that subject,' he said, a glint of amusement in his eyes. She had the strangest notion that he was provoking her deliberately, trying to make her annoyed with him. Could it be that he did not want her to express her gratitude? 'But we shall agree to disagree. Shall we take a little walk together?'

Chloe nodded. They were encamped at what was obviously a small oasis, and there were trees near the water hole. As she moved closer she could see that some of them had fruit growing on them.

'Dates,' Pasha told her as he saw her interest. 'But not as you would know them at home.'

'I imagine these are unripe,' Chloe said. 'But it surprises me that anything grows in this place—or that any life is sustained in that desert out there.' She shuddered as she looked at the vast expanse that seemed to stretch as far as the eye could see.

'A mere twenty percent of this area is fit for sustaining any kind of crop,' he said. 'Those who choose to live here depend on their sheep and goats, and fruit like this—but water is scarce and precious. The Bedouin were fierce warriors in the old days. Today only a few remain true to the old ways, the others find different ways to live.'

'Like your cousin in Marrakesh—and you?'

Pasha nodded. 'I have many relatives in this part of the world; they are scattered all over the region, here and in Algiers, and Syria—and in the Persian Gulf. Only Mohammed Ibn Ali clings stubbornly to the old ways.'

'He did not approve of me,' Chloe said. 'Was it because you were put to so much trouble to look for me?'

'That and other things. You are not of his faith.' Pasha saw her frown. 'Some of my people accept that we must make friends with the Western world, accept those things that we cannot approve—others resist the change that must come.'

'I see…at least I think I do.' Chloe sighed and smothered a yawn. 'Forgive me.' She swayed slightly towards him. 'I am feeling a little odd…' Pasha put his arm about her, steadying her. Chloe leaned against him, glad of his support.

'You are still weak. You should rest.'

'Oh, not yet,' Chloe begged. It felt so good to be near him—why did it feel so good? Was it just the comfort of his strong body or something more? 'Let me stay here with you a little longer. I do so want to know you better.'

'Do you, Chloe?' His dark eyes were intent, his mouth somehow softer than usual. His look and his voice were making her feel odd. 'That is good, for it is what I want also.'

He gave her a hungry look that made her tremble. She remembered the magic of that dance on board ship, and for the first time began to understand what she had discovered in his arms. This was the passion she had seen portrayed on the cinema screen—but for real! A feeling of intense excitement mixed with a hint of danger ran through her. This was real! She was beneath desert stars with her own Sheikh and he was about to kiss her…perhaps to make love to her…

Her heart was pounding wildly, her limbs seeming to be on fire as she swayed slightly towards him. This strange and wonderful sensation was sweeping her away, making her lose all control, and she sensed that he was feeling it too. He wanted this as much as she did! She could see it in his eyes. And then he reached out for her, his face working with some strong emotion that she could only suppose was desire.

Her lips parted in a tiny sigh as he drew her closer. She wondered if he could feel the frantic beating of her heart, as his strong arm tightened its hold on her, and he lowered his head to kiss her oh so softly on the mouth. A feeling of exquisite pleasure flowed through Chloe. There was nothing frightening or demanding in his kiss, just a sweetness that made her respond eagerly to his caress, her body melting into his as she was filled with a strange sensation she had never known before.

'You are intoxicating,' he murmured against her ear, his body hard and lean beneath the desert robes seeming to burn her. She was melting in the heat of his passion, unable to resist whatever he wished of her. 'Do you know what you do to me?'

'I—I do not know…'

'You make me want to touch every last piece of

your body, to taste you and—' Pasha broke off with
a harsh laugh as she gazed up at him in wonder, her
eyes wide and endearingly innocent.

'Pasha? I...'

Pasha laughed as he saw her expression. 'You look
like a startled fawn,' he said, his tone amused, indulgent. He let her go as his mood changed abruptly. 'Is
it so surprising that I should want to make love to
you, Chloe?'

'I was surprised because it was so nice,' she said
honestly. She was confused by his change of tone,
unsure of how to respond. Why had he drawn back
so suddenly? Had she done something wrong? She
did not know how to behave when a man made love
to her—even though she very much wanted this one
to make love to her. 'I don't know why you should
want to kiss me. I'm not beautiful—and I must look
awful at the moment with my face like this.' She
touched the rough patches on her cheeks.

'You have looked better,' Pasha said, a gentle concern dawning in his eyes. 'But you are lovely, Chloe.
Your smile, your manner, your eyes.' He touched her
cheek with gentle fingers. 'Nothing can change those
things, and these blemishes on your skin will fade.
Now that the peeling has begun, the healing will follow. When we are in my house in the mountains of
Spain you will rest and grow well again.'

'Your home?' Chloe was startled. She gazed up at
him, trying to see into his mind and failing. What was
he suggesting? Her heart began to pound frantically.
'But I can't...I mean...it is kind of you, but...it
wouldn't be right.'

'You are afraid that I might try to seduce you or
imprison you in my harem?'

'Oh, no! Of course not...' She faltered as she saw the gleam of wicked laughter in his eyes. 'But you have already done so much and my work...'

'I believe Professor Hicks will spare you to me.' His smile was gentle and teasing now rather than wicked. 'Shall I ask Sashimi to come with us—for your modesty's sake?'

Chloe could not meet his gaze. 'I—I don't know what to say. I am not sure why you should want me to—' She caught a flash of fire in his eyes. 'Oh...' A flush rose up from deep inside her, sweeping up her neck and into her face.

'I am not Brent Harwood,' he told her. 'But I do believe that some things are meant to be, Chloe.' He smiled and traced the line of her cheek to her throat with his fingertip. 'Will you not trust me, Chloe?'

Should she? He had told her once that he was promised to someone, and it had caused her some jealousy. Yet for some while now she had not quite believed in the absent fiancée.

'Yes...I mean...I thought you were engaged to be married—or was that just something you made up to keep other women at a distance?'

'I see you have penetrated my subterfuge. It was a convenient lie,' he said with a rueful look. 'There is no one important in my life. It is sometimes helpful to have an absent fiancée. Will you forgive me for this small deception? I did not know you then, and the lie was thoughtless.'

'Oh...yes,' she said, feeling oddly light-headed. At that moment, she thought she could forgive him anything if he truly cared for her...if only she didn't feel so very unwell. 'I—I feel a little faint. Perhaps I should go and lie down.'

A smile tugged at the corners of his mouth. 'Have I frightened you, my poor Chloe? Do you want to run away to the safety of your friends?'

'I…no!' she said decisively. 'No, I want to know you better, Pasha, but I really do feel a little odd.'

He swore as she gave a gasp and swayed unsteadily, bending down to scoop her up in his arms as her knees buckled. Chloe's head was swimming as he carried her into the tent and deposited her gently on the couch. She was clearly not completely recovered from her ordeal as yet, but it had felt so right in his arms.

He made her feel safe, and he had saved her life, for she was certain that no one would have looked for her if he had not been concerned for her well-being.

Perhaps it was foolish to let him take complete charge of her life, but she felt that she was being compelled by an unseen force. Perhaps Sashimi was right. Perhaps it was written in the stars…

They lingered for three days in the desert, and each day Chloe grew a little stronger. She walked with Pasha every day, and sat with him in the evenings by the campfire, listening to the singing that often entertained them at night. He taught her a few words of his people's language so that she could thank the woman who helped her, and he also told her stories of his people's history.

'They have lived beneath the desert skies for centuries,' he said to her once. 'But now they must learn to live in the new modern world that this century brings. Things must change. The new oil wealth,

which is coming in the future, will bring new
friends—and enemies.'

Chloe looked at him, sensing some deep emotion
she could not begin to understand, some hidden
meaning to his words, but she did not question him.
He would tell her all that he wished her to know.
They had met as strangers such a short time ago, and
yet it was as if she had been waiting all her life for
this moment.

Chloe did not completely understand her feelings
for Pasha. Perhaps it was true love—but how could
she be sure when she had never experienced anything
like it before? She only knew that something strange
and wonderful had happened to her here in the desert.
Common sense told her that she should ask him to
take her back to her friends now, before it was too
late—but perhaps it was already too late.

She would not have walked away from him if she
could, and she was not afraid of this feeling between
them, that seemed to grow stronger with each hour
that passed. Pasha was careful not to frighten her, but
she sensed a growing urgency in him and knew that
he was holding himself on a tight leash so as not to
frighten her. His kisses were warm and deep, arousing
feelings she could not control—and it was she who
clung to him when he would have let her go, her lips
that begged for more.

When on the evening of the third day he told her
that they would leave the next morning she was sorry.

'I could stay here like this forever.' She sighed.

'No, I do not think so, my Chloe,' he said and
looked amused. 'For a while the romance of it would
appeal, but then you would grow tired of the life. You
would miss the freedom you have in the West, and

the benefits of the modern world. Besides, I have much I want to share with you. We shall go first to Marrakesh to speak with your friends, and then to Spain…after that, who knows?'

Chloe had marvelled at how easily Pasha controlled the small Avro aircraft he flew himself, but then it seemed that there was nothing he could not do. Travelling with him was a revelation. Everything was well ordered and there were no delays, no frustrations. It seemed that he clicked his fingers and people hurried to obey. He carried an aura of authority with him, and she discovered for the first time what it was like to be treated like a princess.

Their stay in Marrakesh was brief. Chloe was taken in a large expensive car to the house where the professor and Amelia were still staying, waiting for her. They were pleased and relieved to see her back safely, but when she explained what had happened, Charles Hicks was horrified.

'I never gave it a thought,' he told her. 'Forgive me, Chloe. I was misled by that man. I thought him a decent fellow, and imagined you would be perfectly safe and happy until I returned.'

'I should have come straight back to Amelia,' Chloe said. 'It wasn't your fault, Charles. I was foolish and went off without thinking—but fortunately for me, Pasha found me.' She gave a little shiver as she recalled her nightmare ordeal and thought of what might have happened if he had not.

'That is Mr Armand,' Amelia said and nodded. 'He spoke to me the day after you left and told me he intended to fly down and make sure you were all right. It was very fortunate that he did…'

Chloe had forgotten that her friends knew Pasha as Philip Armand. 'Yes, it was lucky for me. I think I should have died that day if he had not paid guides to search for me.'

'And now you say you are going to stay with him at his house in Spain?' The professor looked at her uncertainly. 'I am not sure that I can agree to that, Chloe. Your father entrusted you to my care...'

'I am twenty-two,' Chloe reminded him. 'I don't need Daddy's permission or anyone else's to stay with someone I admire and trust. Besides, if he had not helped me, I might never have gone home at all.'

'Yes, I do see that, and I realise that it is partly my fault.' He looked slightly ashamed. 'But I still feel responsible...'

'Oh, no, I am not blaming you,' Chloe said, 'and I am sorry if you think I am letting you down, but I have to go.'

'You are in love with him,' Amelia said, looking at her oddly. 'In that case, I think you should go with him, Chloe. A woman should always follow the dictates of her heart—regardless of whether or not it is wise.'

'Thank you.' Chloe went to her and kissed her cheek. 'Thank you for understanding—but I thought you might.'

Amelia nodded. 'Be happy and make the most of whatever the gods give you,' she said. 'That may be unconventional advice, Chloe, but if you waste your chance it may never come again.'

'I shall write to Daddy and tell him where I am,' Chloe said. 'I want to thank you both for a wonderful trip—I've seen and experienced so many things I would never have known about if it had not been for you, Charles. And you have made it so much easier for me, Amelia. I am sorry if you were worried about me, but please don't worry any more. I couldn't be happier—and Pasha takes great care of me.'

'Yes, I am certain he will,' Amelia said, surprising Chloe with her positive support. 'Please write to me sometimes, Chloe. I should like to know how things turn out for you.'

'Yes, of course I shall.'

The professor had remained silent, and she knew he disapproved of the way she was behaving. No doubt he thought her a foolish girl who had no idea of what she was doing, or the pitfalls that might await her in the future.

But that was not the case. Chloe was well aware that she was being reckless, that there were vast differences between her beliefs and Pasha's—and that these could lead to trouble between them in the future.

Pasha had said nothing of love or of marriage, but how could she expect that when they hardly knew one another? He had asked her to be his guest for a while, and she had accepted his invitation. She did not even know that he cared for her, although the look in his eyes seemed to say that he did; when he kissed her, she was sure of it and of her love for him.

She was taking a huge leap of faith into the future by accompanying him to his home, but to have turned away now would have left her wondering for the rest of her life. And she suspected it might have broken her heart.

'So, you will stay with Pasha, yes?' Sashimi looked at her and smiled. 'I told you when you came here that day that it was written in the stars—and has it not proved so?'

'Yes, you did,' Chloe agreed. 'If you and Ahmad had not been so hospitable that day, I should not have written to you and then...'

'You would have died,' Sashimi agreed. 'But it was the will of Allah that you should live and there must be a purpose for you. When the time comes it will be revealed.'

'Is that what you believe?' Chloe asked. 'It makes life seem so simple when you look at things that way, but if we all thought the same would anything get done? Should we not all sit around and wait for a purpose to be revealed?'

'You do not understand,' Sashimi said, looking at her rather oddly. 'But you will. Now, come and see the things Pasha has ordered for you. He said that you must have suitable clothes for your journey, and asked me to buy what I thought would suit you. I hope you will like what I have chosen.'

Chloe was led into the bedroom provided for her use while they stayed with Pasha's cousin. She gasped as she saw the various dresses, skirts, blouses and embroidered jackets waiting for her. The bed itself was strewn with filmy underclothes, and all manner of pretty trifles—so much that Chloe thought these things could not all be for her.

'But he couldn't have meant you to buy all this,' she said. 'I thought just a few things. My own suitcases are waiting for me in Cetua.'

'I believe Pasha will think I have not bought as much as he would like,' Sashimi said and gave a soft husky laugh. 'My husband's cousin is a very rich man, Chloe—much richer than we are. He will expect you to wear beautiful things…' She picked up a wonderful dress in a deep kingfisher blue and held it against Chloe. 'Yes, I thought this colour would suit you. Try it on.'

Chloe removed the crumpled skirt and blouse she had been wearing, and slipped on the dress, which was made of a soft, silky material that clung lovingly to her figure, then turned to look at herself in the full-length mirror. Even without doing her hair or adding a pair of the pretty sandals Sashimi had chosen for her, she could see that it would make her look very different from her usual appearance in the conservative greens and sludgy browns she often chose because they were practical.

'I would never have dared to buy something like this,' she said, smoothing her hands over the long slim waist and twirling so that the calf-length skirt swirled about her legs. It made her look slim and elegant…another woman entirely.

'I did not choose the short skirts I know are fashionable in your country, because we do not think them modest enough,' Sashimi told her hesitantly. 'But you could have them shortened if you wish?'

'Oh, no, I like this just as it is,' Chloe replied. 'May I wear it now?'

'You may wear whatever you please,' Sashimi told her. 'They are all yours. Choose what you want to wear for your journey tomorrow, and the rest will be packed for you. I shall leave you now, and you may join us on the patio when you are ready.'

Left alone, Chloe held up several of the dresses against herself. There were so many of them, and they were all so much more beautiful than anything she had ever worn before.

She selected a dress she thought would be suitable for travelling and laid that aside, then she took off the dress she was wearing and slipped on some of the delicate underwear, before putting the dress on again and selecting a pair of pretty gold leather sandals. A comb through her hair, a dab of perfume behind her ears and a pretty scarf wound around her throat, and she was ready.

She saw the look of pleasure in Pasha's eyes when she went out to join the others, and smiled at him to show that she was happy and pleased with his gift.

'You look beautiful,' he told her later when they were alone in the gardens. 'But then I always knew you would be dressed in the right things.'

'I've never been able to buy things like these,' Chloe said, a faint blush in her cheeks as she saw the burning look in his eyes. 'I ought not to accept them, but I couldn't resist. I love them, thank you so much for buying them for me.'

'They are nothing,' he said. 'I want to give you much more, Chloe. Believe me, this is merely the beginning.'

Her heart was beating frantically. Surely he must mean that he loved her? He would not buy her gifts like these if he did not care for her a great deal... would he?

Chloe was pleasantly surprised when she saw the house in Spain. Set on the hillside looking out over the Mediterranean, it was long and low, and painted white, very much like the houses she had stayed in while she was a guest in Morocco, but it wasn't huge. There were only three bedrooms, and two reception rooms, besides the bathrooms and kitchen, which were modern and light. The pale grey lacquered furniture had a very Italian look, and the suites were leather, the floors a gleaming pink and grey marble. She had expected a Moorish influence, but it wasn't like that at all, more like a house she would expect to find on the Riviera in France or Italy.

Pasha looked amused when she voiced her pleasure and surprise. 'I have other houses that would probably be more what you imagined,' he told her. 'They are where I entertain guests who expect a certain formality, but this is where I relax. I have never brought a guest here before, except Lysette and Mariam…'

'Mariam.' Chloe wrinkled her brow. 'Am I right in thinking you once spoke of her as your father's second wife?'

'Yes, Mariam is my stepmother. She lives in America—has done so since my father was killed.'

'Yes…' Chloe nodded. 'And who is Lysette?' She was shocked to see the colour leave his face and a look so bleak that it frightened her enter his eyes. 'Oh, I am sorry. I should not have asked…'

'You had the right to ask, I spoke of her,' Pasha said, and took her hand, leading her out into the gardens where to her delight Chloe discovered that there was a tiled patio and green lawns, and at the far end a path leading down to a tiny cove. She was aware that he was gathering his strength, and that what he was about to say was very important to him. 'Lysette was Mariam's daughter. She was very beautiful—a sweet, shy girl, much like you in some ways, but in others very different. Lysette was not as brave as you, Chloe. She had been very protected and sheltered, and perhaps that is why it happened.'

Chloe wanted to ask what had happened, but the words stuck in her throat. She knew that Pasha would tell her in his own time, and after a pause he turned to her and she saw that there was great sadness in his face.

'She died in a car crash a few months ago,' he said. 'The doctors told me she was carrying a child—but she had no husband. I believe that she may have been killed to prevent her causing trouble for someone, that the accident was not what it seemed.'

'Oh, no!' Chloe's hand flew to her mouth. 'Pasha, that's terrible! If you are right and she was murdered…'

'Yes, that is what I believe,' he agreed. He smiled and reached out to touch her cheek. 'Do you remember when I laughed at you and you chided me for it?'

'Yes.' Her eyes were wide and serious as she looked at him. 'You told me that you had not wanted to laugh for a long time.'

'Until I met you, I felt that I might never want to laugh again,' he said, his eyes intent on her face. The look in them was so full of meaning, of desire, that Chloe swallowed hard, her mouth suddenly dry as her heart began to pump with excitement. 'That was because of what happened to Lysette. I loved her. She was my sister and very dear to me, and when I lost her I felt that the light had gone out of my life. You have brought that light back to me, Chloe. You make me feel that there is something worth living for again.'

'Oh, Pasha…' Chloe leaned towards him, her heart racing wildly. How could she doubt that he loved her now? Her whole being was thrilling to his words, to the look in his eyes and the feeling of being wanted, of being loved. She moved closer to him, her arms going up about his neck as he reached for her, fingers straying into his hair, and caressing the back of his neck, arching into his body as he kissed her. This was so right, so wonderfully right. She knew that she wanted what was about to happen between them, that she had been waiting for this moment since he first kissed her in the desert. 'Oh, Pasha, I love you. I do love you so much.'

He bent down to scoop her up as he had the day she had almost fainted, carrying her into the house, to the bedroom she knew instinctively was his own, and laying her down on the bed. She lay gazing up at him as he bent over her and kissed her tenderly, sweetly on the lips, his fingers just grazing her cheek, following the line of her throat to the hollow where he planted a tiny teasing kiss.

'You are sure this is what you want?' he asked, his voice husky with desire, with his burning need, and yet giving her the chance to withdraw if she wished. 'You do not want to run away from me?'

'Never,' she vowed. 'I want to stay with you always, Pasha. You saved my life, and I belong to you. I want to be yours…in all the ways that a woman can belong to a man, I want to be yours.'

'Be certain, my little one,' he murmured as he nibbled at her earlobe. 'Be very certain before you give yourself to me, because once you are mine I would never ever let you go from me.'

'I shall never want to leave you,' she promised, arching her body to meet his as he lay down and clasped her to him, his hands smoothing down her sides, over her hips and cupping her buttocks as he pressed her against him so that she could feel the hardness of his desire for her pressing into her. 'Why should I ever leave you when you are all that I want of life?'

'I just wanted you to know,' he murmured huskily. 'I would never let you go…I want you, need you so much…'

Chloe was thrilling to his words, and to the caresses her willing body was receiving. She trembled beneath his stroking hands, quivering as he parted her legs, seeking out that tender secret place between them that no man had ever touched before. He was bringing her tinglingly alive, teaching her the meaning of love, as she had never understood it, raising her to a state of physical awareness that had her writhing with pleasure beneath him.

His kisses and his tongue played on her as a man might play on the fine strings of a violin, making her moan and gasp as the intense feelings rose to a crescendo of pleasure. Now he was thrusting into her, and briefly there was pain, a sharp pain that made her cry out in protest, but he covered her mouth with his own, and she was drowning in the joy that only he could give her, wanting him to go on.

She was being carried with him to some high peak that she had never seen, and then she was falling, falling into the exquisite pleasure that his relentless loving caused to wash over her in waves, again and again until she wept for joy. Never, never had she dreamed that anything this wonderful could happen to her, and when it was all over she clung to him as if she would never let him go.

He stroked her and soothed her, wiping her tears and kissing the tender places of her body until she was laughing and gazing up at him in anticipation.

'No, no, my darling,' he said and laughed at her. 'Not again so soon. I am merely a man—not a god. You must wait for a while, my angel, until I have recovered my strength. You have taken it all, and I must eat and relax with you in the sunshine.'

Pasha took her hand, and when she would have reached for her clothes he shook his head, pulling her with him out into the sun. Then, laughing wickedly, he picked her up and ran with her down the little pathway to the cove. She laughingly screamed and struggled but he held her, wading out into the sea and then dropping her into the cool salty water, plunging in after her.

Chloe spluttered indignantly as they came up. She wriggled away from him, splashing water into his face.

'How did you know I could swim?' she demanded. 'I might have drowned.'

'Not while I am near,' he said and grabbed her, intending to duck her under the water again. She gave a little shout and wriggled away, going under the water to swim to a large, protruding rock to avoid him, then she hauled herself out and shook the water from her eyes. She crossed her arms over her breasts, feeling a little shy. 'No,' he said. 'Don't cover yourself. I like to see you like that.'

'Someone might come,' she said, blushing as she realised that his eyes were upon her. 'I've never been swimming in the nude before.'

'No one will come,' he said and came out of the water to join her. His body was hard and lean, rippling with health and strength, his skin a light olive shade that was very attractive in a man of his stature. He might claim to be merely a man, but he had the form and beauty of the ancient Greek gods. She knew that to touch him and have him touch her was something that would always give her pleasure. 'You are beautiful, Chloe. Do you believe me now when I tell you that?'

She nodded shyly. 'I believe that you think I am—and that is all I want.' She reached out to stroke his arm, feeling the smoothness of his skin and the faint prickle of the light covering of hair.

His eyes went over her as she shivered. 'I don't want you to turn cold, but you should be proud of your body, my Chloe. You have lovely breasts and a waist many women would die for.'

'No one ever told me that before.'

'I hope no one has ever seen you this way before.' He pretended to glare at her, but she knew he was only teasing her. The fire in his eyes crackled and burned, making her gasp and tremble inside. He must know that he had been her first and only lover. 'I should kill anyone who had—or tried to in the future.'

Chloe laughed. 'Oh, don't be silly, Pasha. Of course you wouldn't...' She turned away, but he caught her, his fingers digging into her flesh as he pulled her back to him. She saw that his expression was no longer teasing, but deadly serious. 'What...why are you looking at me like that?'

'Don't take my words lightly,' he warned. 'I say what I mean, Chloe. You are mine—mine alone. No other man will ever touch you. Do you hear me?'

A shiver ran down her spine as she gazed into his eyes—eyes that were suddenly cold and menacing. Why was he saying these things? Surely he must know it wasn't necessary?

'But I wouldn't betray you with another man,' she

said. 'You must know that, Pasha? You must know that I have never given myself to another man?'

'I know there was no one before me,' he grated harshly. 'I am merely telling you that there must never be anyone else after me.'

'You did not need to tell me,' she said and pulled away from him, feeling a little hurt. Why should he imagine that she was so light or false in her affections?

She dived into the sea and swam swiftly back to shore, running up the pathway to the gardens and then into the house, pulling on a warm towelling robe she found hanging near the door to dry herself, then went in search of the kitchen to look for food.

She had been surprised to discover that there was a refrigerator, but she ought not to have been. Pasha seemed to have everything he wanted, nothing was barred to him. She imagined that his money could buy him anything he required. That thought rankled a little—did he imagine he had bought her?

That scene on the rock had cast a little shadow over the day, she thought, as she opened the cupboards and took out bread and tomatoes, and a soft goat's cheese from the refrigerator.

She turned to him as he entered behind her. 'I am not sure…is this all right for you? I don't know quite what you are allowed to eat. I think Muslims have something about not drinking wine…'

'What makes you imagine that I am a Muslim?'

Chloe looked up, startled. 'I don't know. I just assumed you would be. Sashimi…Mohammed…I thought you must be.'

'My mother's people are all Christians. When I came to England, I learned their ways—and I liked them. I adopted their faith some years ago, though it is not widely known outside my immediate family. I do not speak of it, because of political implications. Sashimi does not know, although I believe Mohammed may. I have told Ahmad, of course. He is like a brother to me.'

'I see.' Chloe was surprised. 'I am sorry. I did not think…'

'Did you imagine I had brought you here to seduce you and make you my mistress?' Pasha asked, and he was smiling now, that harsh look gone from his face. 'And you still gave yourself to me, Chloe? Were you prepared to become a Muslim if I had asked it of you?'

'I don't know,' she admitted honestly. 'I came with you because I couldn't help myself. I knew I loved you the first time you kissed me, Pasha, and I wanted the chance to be with you, to know you better. You asked me to trust you and I did.'

'But you would have taken whatever I chose to give?' He reached out to touch her as she nodded wordlessly. 'Then you do love me—and I was a brute just now. Forgive me? I am a jealous man, Chloe, and I have a terrible temper. My passions are intense, sometimes so fierce that they frighten me. I think myself a civilised man, but there is a part of me that throws back to my warrior ancestors. I shall try to control it, but I do not think I could bear to lose you.'

'But why should you lose me?' she said and moved closer to him, offering her lips. 'I do not give my heart or myself lightly, Pasha. I want us to be together always.'

'So when will you marry me?' he asked and kissed her. 'That is why I brought you here to Spain rather than to one of my other homes, Chloe. We can be married here by the English church…there are many English who settle here in this wonderful climate.'

'Oh, Pasha…' Her face was brilliant with love and happiness as she took a step closer to him, lifting her head so that his lips met hers in a sweet, gentle kiss. 'Whenever you want me to, of course. You must know that I am yours… I shall always be yours.'

'Of course you will,' he murmured huskily. 'I am merely a jealous fool…'

Chapter Seven

Chloe stirred as she felt Pasha jerk violently beside her in the bed. She heard him muttering indistinctly, and realised that he was in the throes of a bad dream. Sitting up, she bent over him, hearing him mutter a name. She thought it might have been a woman's name but she wasn't sure. Perhaps he was having a nightmare about his half-sister, she thought, wondering whether she ought to wake him.

She sat watching him for a few moments as he tossed restlessly on the pillows, but then he seemed to settle back into a sound sleep. It would be a pity to wake him if the dream had passed, Chloe decided, and left him sleeping as she slipped from the bed. She reached for a dressing robe, but didn't bother about shoes, padding bare-footed across the cool marble tiles.

Outside, there was already a kindly warmth in the air, although the sun hadn't really risen as yet, but it was very still and promised to be a hot day. She walked over the grass to the edge of the gardens, which looked out over the rocky cliff to the sea below; it moved lazily, its waters deep blue and rest-less—as restless as Pasha had been in his dream.

It was so beautiful here! Chloe stood watching the movement of the waves, letting the peace and the sheer beauty of her surroundings work their usual magic on her.

She was so happy in this place. She had never ex-pected to live anywhere this perfect, and she wished that they could stay here forever. Pasha had told her that they would come as often as possible, but that he had to return to England as soon as they were married.

'Are you content to be married quietly here?' he'd asked the previous evening as they lay together in the bed they had shared for the past two weeks. 'Or do you want to go home and plan a big wedding?'

'I think it would be best if we were married before we go back,' Chloe said. 'I don't need anyone's per-mission, but my father and grandmother are a little old-fashioned…'

'As is my mother's father,' Pasha agreed. 'That is why I felt it better to present everyone with a *fait accompli*…'

Pasha had told Chloe a little about the English side of his family, but apart from a few cryptic words about his uncle, Prince Hassan, being an important figure politically, he had refused to talk about that side of his life.

'I cannot be entirely English, nor am I entirely free to do as I please,' he told her. 'But none of that need interfere with us, Chloe. You will be my wife, and I shall cherish and protect you. I am sure that you will like my grandfather and my English family—the rest need not concern you.'

Chloe had realised that he did not want to talk

about certain aspects of his life, and she had accepted it. She already knew that his moods could change abruptly and with no warning, and she was aware that he could sometimes be very intense. But he was gentle and considerate with her, and she had been lavished with both love and gifts during their brief time together.

She was so lucky! Chloe could hardly believe that anyone like Pasha could have chosen someone as dull and ordinary as her. He must have met so many beautiful, sophisticated women!

She turned as she heard Pasha's voice calling to her. He came to the door as she walked back towards the house, and she caught her breath as she saw that he was wearing only a towel wrapped around his waist. His skin looked damp, little pearls of moisture clustering on the fine growth of hair on his chest, and her stomach clenched with sudden desire. His body, the strength and power of it, excited her much more than she could ever have expected. She loved to touch him, to stroke and please him intimately in the manner he pleased her, and the joy of being made love to by him was something that lingered always in her mind.

'I woke and you weren't there,' he said, his eyes smouldering with latent heat as he looked at her. 'What are you doing out here?'

'I was just looking at the sea,' she said. 'It is so beautiful here, Pasha.'

'You are beautiful,' he said, reaching out for her. His voice was husky with desire as he pulled her close into him, his mouth nuzzling against her neck as she arched into his body, thrilling to the scent and feel of him. She was aware of the hardness of his sex beneath the towel, throbbing against her, making her feel weak with need. 'Have I told you recently that I adore you?'

'Not for several hours,' she teased.

She was beginning to feel confident in this game they played, to know she could please him, to be aware of when he wanted her—and he wanted her now. She could feel the burning heat of his arousal, and her body melted into his longingly. She turned her head so that their lips met.

His kiss dominated even as it caressed. He was a careful, considerate lover, but she was always aware of his power and strength. Had he used that on her she would have been crushed beneath him, but however urgent his need, he was always patient, always aware of her response, waiting patiently for her to reach her climax. She knew that he took as much satisfaction from her pleasure in their loving as his own.

'Then perhaps I had better show you how much I love you?' he suggested with a wicked lift of his brows.

'Yes, please…'

Chloe laughed and whipped the towel from around his waist, challenging him to follow as she ran into the house. Of course he took up her challenge and caught her, scooping her up in his arms and carrying her to their bed. He bent over her, untying the cord of her robe and beginning to kiss every inch of her body, starting with the rosy peaks of her breasts, licking at her delicately with his tongue, and working his way down to the quivering centre of her sexuality.

Chloe arched her back towards him as his tongue lavished her, making her jerk and moan with pleasure.

Her fingers worked in his hair as she gasped, pleading with him mutely to come to her. When he slid into her, filling her, she was warm and moist for him. They moved together, slowly, deliberately, and then with mounting urgency, Chloe screaming his name as she felt the most exquisite sensation she had ever known. It was almost as if something deep inside her reached out to take hold of him, bringing him even deeper inside her, and the pleasure washing over her in waves made her body spasm again and again.

Afterward, they lay together, limbs entwined as Pasha idly stroked her back, his fingers tracing the hollow of its arch. 'Only another week before you are my wife,' he murmured throatily. He bent over her to flick a strand of hair from her eyes, a slight frown creasing his forehead. 'It is a pity Amelia and the professor cannot be with us, but although I managed to get word to them, they have gone off on one of their treks again and it would be impossible for them to get here in time. The professor sent a small gift for you and a letter to say that he was happy we were to marry. I was keeping it as a surprise for you.' He hesitated. 'Of course, we could put the date back, if that is what you want?' He raised his brows and she shook her head. 'It cannot be soon enough for me. I would have arranged it earlier, but the Reverend Thomas was determined to observe all the rules.'

'He wanted us to be sure before we committed ourselves,' Chloe teased. She felt languid and content wrapped in his embrace, all passion spent for the moment. 'I think he was shocked that we were living together, especially as we had known each other such a short time.'

'I have waited all my life for you…'

'I feel the same way, but it doesn't matter. I already feel that I am your wife, Pasha.' There was not one small piece of her that he had not already made his own!

'Where do you want to go today? Shall we ride, stay here and be lazy, or visit the market?'

'Let's go to the market,' Chloe said. 'I love to shop with you. It makes me laugh to watch the way you never pay what the traders ask.'

'They expect it,' he said. 'It is a matter of honour on both sides. They ask too much, and they enjoy the tussle of reaching the right price as much as I do.'

Chloe smiled and snuggled into his side. Her hand moved over his flat stomach, finding the source of her pleasure to stroke and caress. 'Or we could just stay here like this…'

'You are insatiable, woman,' he mocked, and threw back the thin sheet that covered them. 'Get up and have a swim while I make us something to eat.'

The back seat of Pasha's car was filled with baskets of fruit and fresh vegetables when they arrived back later that day. Chloe was feeling happy and relaxed as she carried two of the heavy baskets into the house.

It had been fun walking around the colourful market in the warm sunshine, and she had enjoyed the haggling as much as Pasha. She had bought him a soft Moroccan leather belt, and he had bought her a fine gold bangle engraved with Arabic signs which he told her were a message of love, which he had promised to explain later.

The woman Pasha employed had been in while they were out to clean the house, and a meal had been prepared for them—rice, fish and salad. All Chloe had to do was bring it to the table.

She spent some time unpacking their baskets, then decided to ask Pasha whether he wanted to eat inside or out. On a warm evening like this it was pleasant to take their food outside and have it on the patio.

Pasha should have been in by now. It usually took him only a moment to lock the gates and put the car away into the cool of the garage at the side. She went to the back door to call him, halting in surprise as she saw that he was talking to two men. Before she could decide what to do, the men turned and walked away.

Something seemed familiar about one of them, and she frowned as she tried to remember where she had seen him before, but the memory eluded her. She didn't think that either of the men were Spanish locals; they had looked as if they might be Arabs. Of course there had been a Moorish influence in this part of Spain for years, and some of the local people could be mistaken for Arabs—but these two had looked as if they would be more at home in the city.

'Who were they?' she asked anxiously as Pasha came to her. 'What did they want?'

'Nothing important,' he replied. 'They work for me sometimes—it was business. I was giving final instructions about something.'

Chloe nodded. This was the part of Pasha's life that he did not wish to tell her about. She felt a little shut out, wishing that he would share his thoughts with her. She wasn't a child to be protected from everything but the pleasant things in life, but she didn't really know him very well yet and she wasn't confident enough to insist that she be told what kind of business the men were involved in.

She had an odd prickling sensation at the nape of her neck, and something told her that she might not like what Pasha had to say if he did tell her. There was, she sensed, a darker side to his nature, and she was a little afraid to inquire too deeply in case she did not care for what she discovered.

'Why so thoughtful?' he asked, and she shook her head.

'I was going to ask if you wanted to eat outside this evening.'

'We'll eat later,' he said and reached for her. 'At the moment it's you I want, not food.'

Chloe's doubts faded as he took her into his arms, his mouth seeking hers, urgent and needy. Desire flared between them, hot and hungry. As he scooped her up in his arms, she gave herself up to the anticipated pleasure of his loving.

What did his business matter? What did anything matter but this feeling between them?

Chloe was surprised at how many people had come to see her being married. Pasha was relaxed and content, seeming proud of his new wife as he introduced her to the guests. Most were Spanish people who lived in the area, though there was also an English couple who lived nearby.

She looked for the men who had come to the house on business, but there was no sign of them. Clearly Pasha did not mix business with personal pleasure. She was still trying to place them, but although the memory was there at the back of her mind, she could not quite capture it. No matter, it would come to her in time.

* * *

'Sorry about springing that on you; I know it was awkward for you, not knowing anyone,' Pasha said after their guests had gone. 'But I thought we'd better invite a few people round. Your family might doubt that I had actually married you if we'd done it in complete isolation.'

'I enjoyed meeting your friends,' she said. 'Mr Milligan was rather sweet…' She saw the flash of fire in his eyes and reached up to kiss him, her fragrant body arching into his provocatively. She felt his instant reaction and laughed up at him. 'You don't have to look like that—the only man I shall ever want is you.'

'Just make sure you remember you are mine, Mrs Armand,' he said, his voice grating harshly with desire. 'And in case you are wondering, I changed my name by deed poll when I applied for my British passport. Yes, you are legally my wife.'

'I never doubted it,' she said. 'But why do you find it necessary to have two names, Pasha? What is it that you need to hide?'

He frowned at her, letting her go and stepping back. 'What makes you think I have anything to hide? It is just more convenient, that's all.'

'More convenient for what?' she asked, determined to break down this barrier of silence. 'Don't you think you could tell me at least a part of it, Pasha? I am your wife, and I think I've proved that you can trust me not to reveal anything you tell me.'

'I have already told you that it is necessary for me to use another name at times, especially when travelling,' he said, his eyes narrowed, slightly wary. 'And you know that my uncle is important politically.'

'In what way?'

'He owns land that is very rich in oil,' Pasha said. 'Between them, my father and my uncle were in possession of a vast tract of valuable land. I inherited my father's land along with the title of Sheikh, which merely means the head of the family. It is more like a feudal baron than a great lord or prince, and a Sheikh's political power comes from his wealth and standing in other ways.

'My land is already a British protectorate, and I receive a certain amount of money for the leases while various people set up a company for producing oil. In time it will be worth a great deal of money, and I shall be paid revenues on whatever is produced in perpetuity—but my uncle is the ruler of a small state and he has so far refused British protection. It is his right to do so, of course, but it makes him vulnerable. There is a great deal of unease in the area at the moment, and an attempt was made on his life a short time ago. Because he has to be so careful, I often negotiate on his behalf and for that reason I sometimes need to be able to travel under another name.'

'Oh.' Chloe was conscious of relief. She wasn't sure what she had been worrying about, but a tiny doubt had been nagging at the back of her mind, and she was glad to have it dispelled. 'I see…thank you for telling me.'

'Are you satisfied now?' he asked, and there was a glint in his eyes, as though it had annoyed him because she had asked. He did not like being questioned, that much was clear. 'You say you love me, Chloe. You should trust me. Believe me, I would never do anything that might harm you. You are too important to me.'

'As long as you don't do anything too dangerous.' She reached up to touch his cheek, and as she did so something clicked in her mind. 'You never did tell me what you discovered about those men I heard in the garden—' She broke off and stared at him as memory flooded back. 'But they were the men who were here the other morning! You were talking to them outside…'

'What are you talking about?' Pasha's eyes narrowed, his expression becoming withdrawn, cold. She sensed anger and something more. Guilt perhaps? 'For goodness sake, Chloe, you have a very fertile imagination. It comes from watching all those silly films I suppose. Now what are you imagining?'

'I heard them talking,' she said and something inside her resented the way he was looking at her, and his constant reference to the fact that she admired certain films. 'That night in the hotel gardens. And then I saw them. One of them looked at me as if he thought I was a threat to him, but his friend told him to forget it. Most of what they said was a mystery to me, because they spoke in a language I did not understand—but they mentioned your name, and they talked about someone being killed. I know they did, Pasha, because just that little bit was in French. One of them made a mistake, because I understood that he was talking about having a man killed!'

'So you jumped to the conclusion that they were trying to murder me?' He smiled oddly, something flickering in his eyes. 'Well, I am sorry to disappoint you, my darling—but they were certainly not planning to assassinate anyone. At least, not if they were the men who came here the other morning. I told you, they work for me…'

'But what do they do?' she asked. 'What kind of work, Pasha?'

'That is my business, Chloe,' he said and the smile had gone. His expression chilled her and she knew she was treading on dangerous ground. 'What is this—an inquisition? This is supposed to be our wedding night, remember? I don't know what ideas you've got in that head of yours, but I wish you would stop looking at me as if—' He broke and walked away from her, going outside.

Chloe saw him walking across the grass. She was tempted to go after him and say she was sorry, to make up their argument, but something held her back. She hadn't meant anything wrong. It was just that she had been a little anxious, in case the men were plotting to harm Pasha while pretending to be loyal. He had reacted as if she were accusing him of some crime.

Chloe felt the coldness spearing through her, sending little chills all over her body. No! She must be mad to think of such a thing. Pasha was right to accuse her of letting her imagination run away with her. It was not possible…he would never…but what did she really know of him? He had told her nothing of that dark, closed side of him, which she had sensed from the beginning.

Chloe felt the sickness swirl in her stomach. How could she think such a terrible thing of the man she had married that day? Pasha was her husband, and she loved him. He was gentle and kind and…there *was* a darker, secret side that he would not allow her to see. She could not deny its existence, much as she might have liked to pretend that it was not there.

She knew she could never rest until she had cleared

this terrible suspicion from her mind, and she followed him outside to where he stood looking out at the ocean. The sun was setting, falling into the sea like a huge orange ball about to sink beneath the restless water. There was something about that sky that made Chloe shiver—a kind of foreboding filled her.

'Is that what they do for you, Pasha?' she asked. 'Kill people—is that why you need to hide your identity?'

He turned to look at her then, and she was shocked by what she saw in his eyes. 'Why did you have to be there that night?' he asked and the bitter words shocked her. 'Why did you have to have such an inquisitive mind?'

'Pasha…' Her heart was beating wildly and she felt slightly sick. Was he admitting that her accusations were true? 'Please tell me I'm imagining all this!'

'Would you believe me?' he asked, and looked at her. 'If I said that I had never found it necessary to order the execution of a man—would you trust me and forget what you've seen?'

'I…' She swallowed hard. 'I want to believe it. I don't want to believe this…this ugliness is there inside you.'

'Don't you?' He seized her by the arms, his fingers digging into her flesh. He held her pressed close against him, his breath hot on her face. 'Well, my darling, inquisitive wife, I'm afraid I can't set your mind at rest. I can't tell you that I haven't ordered the execution of a man who kills for money, because I can't lie to you, not when you look at me like that, Chloe. I would have preferred that you never had to know about the other side of my life, but since you insisted I shall tell you—'

'No!' she cried, shocked and sickened by this revelation. 'I don't want to hear this! I can't listen…'

She turned and ran back towards the house, her heart thumping. It was too horrible to believe—Pasha was little better than a murderer! No matter what he said, what excuse he found to explain his actions, the fact remained.

She was horrified, and bewildered. How could the man she loved do such terrible things? It was beyond her comprehension, beyond her understanding. All she knew was that it made her feel revulsion and disgust, that at this moment she wished she had never met Pasha.

She couldn't stay here another moment. She had to get away—away from him, from this ugliness he had been hiding from her. Her mind was in turmoil, and she could think of nothing but the horror of what he had just said to her.

She couldn't live with him, couldn't continue to let him make love to her. At least not until she had come to terms with what he had told her. She had to leave him…

Still feeling as if her mind was whirling out of control, she began to gather the few things she would need, shoving them into her large shoulder bag. She would go home to her father. She needed time to be alone, to think about this.

'Chloe!' Pasha had come into the bedroom behind her. 'What do you think you are doing?'

'I'm packing some things.'

'I can see that,' he said. 'But your cases have already been sent on ahead. Why are you in such a hurry to pack the last few things?' She wouldn't look at him, and he came to take her by the shoulders, swinging her round to look at him. She felt the anger pulsating in him, sensed that he was barely holding it in check. His fingers bit deeply into her flesh, making her whimper in fright. He looked capable of doing anything. 'You were going to run away, weren't you? Like you did last time…'

Chloe raised her head, looking up at him defiantly. 'I need to be alone for a while.'

'No!' he cried. 'I won't let you leave me. I can't…'

'Why? Because I know too much?' Her eyes widened in sudden shock. 'Is that why you married me, Pasha? So that you could control me? So that I could never go into a courtroom and accuse you of being involved in a murder?'

For a moment she thought he might kill her. He was so angry, so furious that she had dared to defy him.

'You little fool,' he said. 'If you think that…but no matter. Chloe, you are my wife. You belong to me, and I don't let go of what I own.'

'You don't own me!' she cried. 'I can divorce you—'

'Just try it,' he said, and his eyes narrowed to icy slits. 'I warned you, Chloe, and now I'm telling you again. I shall never let you go. You are mine and I intend to keep you as my wife—my only wife. We were married in your church, and that means you are committed as much as I am. I can't see your father or your grandmother thinking kindly of you if you go running back the moment you're married, can you?'

Chloe bit her lip. She could just imagine what Lady Margaret would say to her behaviour.

'I'm old enough to do as I please.'

'But you are not free,' Pasha reminded her. His

expression terrified her; his eyes were so cold, his face implacable. 'I've told you I won't let you go and I meant it.'

'Supposing I leave you anyway?'

'Then I shall fetch you back,' he said. 'Force me and I'll take you to a place where you can't just run off when you please. My father's *casbah* is a remote fort in the Atlas Mountains. You would have little chance of making it back to civilisation on your own from there, Chloe. Remember what happened the last time?'

His reference to her ordeal in the desert made her angry for a moment. He was smiling—oh, he was heartless! How could he smile after what she had endured? Then she saw that though the smile in his eyes seemed to tease, beneath it was a genuine concern for her and despite herself she felt the pull of his charm, the longing for him to kiss her and make love to her beginning deep at the pit of her stomach. For a moment she thought that he would scoop her up and throw her to the bed, that he would force her to respond to his demands and she trembled. For how long could she resist?

'Don't look at me like that,' she said and swung away from him. Surprisingly he let her go. 'Just let me leave, Pasha. It will be better for both of us.'

'No. I've told you, that is out of the question.'

'So what are we going to do?'

'We are married,' he told her. 'That means we stay together, whether you like it or not. I shall take you to meet my family, and you will take me to your home as we'd planned.'

'And after that?' Chloe asked him. She had herself in control now, the moment of weakness passed.

'Don't imagine I'm going to be a wife to you, Pasha. You can force me to stay with you for a while—but that doesn't mean I'm going to let you make love to me.'

'Indeed?' He moved closer, and his masculine strength was very evident as he towered over her. Once again she sensed he was close to breaking, that only an effort of will prevented him from using his superior strength to compel her to obey. 'Supposing I'm not willing to take no for an answer?'

Chloe gave a little yelp of fear and stepped back. She looked at him, her eyes wide with distress. 'You—you wouldn't force me?'

For a moment as he looked at her, nostrils flared, eyes dark with some emotion that she imagined was anger, she thought that it was exactly what he meant to do, but then he turned away, walking to a little coffee table and opening the cigarette box. She watched in fascination as he took one of the exotic flat tubes and lit it; they were Turkish cigarettes and it was only the second time since they had been here that she had seen Pasha light one.

'I didn't think you smoked,' she said for want of something else to say.

'I don't often.' He turned his gaze on her and she was shocked by the coldness in his black eyes. 'So we are agreed then. You won't try to leave me, and you will go through the motions of being happily married, providing I don't touch you intimately.'

Chloe swallowed hard. She felt the full force of his dominance and knew she could not deny him. 'It doesn't look as if I've much choice, does it?'

'No. Neither of us have,' he said. 'I refuse to be made a fool of in public, Chloe. If you whisper a word of this to anyone you will be sorry—and that includes your family and that scatty friend of yours.'

'Justine isn't scatty,' Chloe said. 'She's just impulsive and full of fun… She didn't mean to spill that drink over you. If you hadn't been standing so close to us, it wouldn't have happened.'

'A lot of things might not have happened then,' Pasha said and there was a bitter note in his voice.

'No. I am very sorry,' Chloe said in a small voice.

She wasn't sure why she was apologising, after all, he was the one to blame, the one who had lied and deceived her—and yet she felt as if she had done something terrible, as if she had destroyed something beautiful, irreplaceable.

'Yes, I expect you are,' Pasha replied. 'I am going out for a while. You will be all right here alone?'

'Yes…yes, of course,' she said, her eyes stinging with the tears she was refusing to shed.

The weeping didn't start until Pasha had walked out and she heard his car starting up outside. She sank down on one of the luxurious sofas, and buried her head in her hands as a storm of grief overcame her. It had all been so sudden, and she felt bereft, as if she had lost a part of herself.

For the past three weeks she had spent every moment, both waking and sleeping, with Pasha and it was unbearably lonely without him. What was she going to do? Should she just walk out of the house and try to find somewhere to stay until she could get on a ship going home? Pasha had arranged a private plane to take them first to Paris for a couple of days and then to England.

She had enough money in her bag to buy her a ticket on a ship, but what was the point? Pasha would come after her. He would find her either before she managed to get on the ship or when she left it. His arrogance in leaving her alone told her that he was quite confident that she couldn't escape him.

It would be foolish to try too soon, Chloe realised. If she wanted to have a chance of making her escape work, she would have to wait until Pasha was less suspicious. Besides, she owed him something for saving her life. It would seem very strange if she left him immediately after they were married—and she couldn't tell anyone the truth.

Chloe acknowledged that when she did eventually leave Pasha she would have to invent an excuse for the break-up of her marriage. She could never tell anyone the real reason why she had turned away from him, because that would be a terrible betrayal of confidence.

Pasha had not wanted to tell her anything about the darker side of his life. Chloe had forced it out of him, and in the end he had told her it all—or sufficient to shock her into saying the things she had. She wished with all her heart that she could go back, that she need not know. She did not want to know that Pasha had committed murder—if not with his own hands, by ordering the death of his uncle's political enemies.

Chloe wasn't so naïve that she didn't know these things were done. She had read between the lines in the newspapers often enough to realise that governments found it necessary to turn a blind eye when a political assassination took place and perhaps it was necessary at times.

But she didn't want to be married to someone who could contemplate taking a life without turning a hair. She had never suspected that Pasha was involved in such things, and she was sure that she would never have fallen in love with him if she had.

But did it make him a different person? Chloe's thoughts were whirling in utter confusion as she fought to come to terms with the distress and horror her discovery had brought her.

She couldn't still be in love with him, she couldn't! It wasn't possible to love someone—not when you knew he was very different from the man you had imagined.

Chloe left the house and walked down to the edge of the cliff. She stood watching the restless sea. It hurt terribly to know that Pasha wasn't the man she had believed him, but she was determined to fight her feelings of despair.

She would go through the motions of being a happy bride as he had demanded, and then, one day when he was away on business, she would simply disappear.

Running down to the beach, Chloe took a quick swim in the sea, then returned to the house. All this luxury! Where did Pasha's money come from? Was he paid blood money for arranging a man's death?

She shivered with distaste, and thought of all the presents he had given her. Suddenly they felt tainted, and she wished she could throw them back at him, that she could make him see how evil what he was doing really was.

But they were a part of being his wife, and for the moment she had to go along with the bargain he had forced on her. She had to let his family and hers believe she was thrilled to be Pasha's wife.

She brushed her hair, slipped into a nightgown and went to bed in the spare bedroom, but she didn't lock the door. If Pasha came to her, if he forced her, she would leave him the first chance she got and not care whether it caused him to lose face or not!

Pasha looked at the empty bed in the room they had shared only the previous night, and his expression was bleak. He cursed himself for throwing the truth at her so abruptly. He was a damned fool! He should either have lied to her...or explained properly.

Pride had made him react as he had—his damnable pride! How could he have hurt her? He had seen the horror in those innocent eyes, the way they widened in disbelief and then darkened with disgust and the way she had shrunk from his touch.

His Chloe. The beautiful, innocent girl he had adored had gone in that instant. He knew that he had destroyed something wonderful. Even if he forced her to stay with him, which he had every intention of doing, even then, he could never bring back that naïve, trusting look to her lovely face.

She thought that she wasn't pretty, but she had a deep inner loveliness that he had sensed would blossom into real beauty with time. When they met she had been so young for her age, still almost a schoolgirl in her attitudes to life and love. It had delighted him to teach her what being a woman was all about, and she had responded with such honesty, such natural delight that he had fallen deeper and deeper in love with her.

And now, because of his pride, that had all gone. He could try to win her back, and he fully intended to do so. There was no way he was going to let her leave him; even if she never came to him with love in her eyes again, he couldn't let her go.

For one thing, she would never be entirely safe without his protection. Pasha had too many enemies. He knew that his wife would need to be protected wherever she went, because there was always the chance that someone might try to kill her as revenge against him.

He lit another cigarette as he went outside and sat on the patio, staring at the sky as the dawn started to break beyond the mountains. Perhaps he had been unfair to Chloe, bringing her here and seducing her...marrying her.

He had grown used to living with the threat of assassination. He had been fifteen when the first attempt was made on his life, and only the quick thinking of one of the teachers at his school had saved him that time. There had been other attempts since, but he'd dealt with them himself.

It was after that first attempt that his uncle had decided it would be best for Pasha to change his name, so that he would be free to live without the constant fear of the assassin's knife.

Pasha had vowed as a child that he would be revenged on the man who had killed his father, but it had taken all this time to find and trace that man— and it had only happened after the attempt on his uncle's life.

It had come as a shock to learn that one of Hassan's own people had been involved in the plot to kill him...a cousin who believed that with the prince dead he might be able to snatch power, and the wealth that went with that power.

That man had to die. He had been judged guilty in a court of law in Hassan's own state, but he had eluded the punishment and escaped. Hassan had asked Pasha to find him and arrange for his execution.

'The British will not help us in this,' the prince had told him. 'But they will turn their eyes away. You must do this for me, Pasha—and for your father.'

Pasha had known he had no choice but to accept his uncle's request. He too had wanted justice, and he knew that there was only one way to get it. For years the culprit had eluded all attempts to discover his identity, and he had almost succeeded in killing the prince—and after that he would have come after Pasha.

He had not expected to feel any guilt, and nor should he, for his cause was just. Abdullah must die, none of Hassan's family would be safe until he was dead, but it was harder to order an execution than Pasha had expected, and he had left Morocco without giving the final order, even though he knew the assassin had been traced to his hiding place.

Pasha frowned as he went back inside the house. He tried the door of the bedroom where Chloe was sleeping and found that it wasn't locked. Turning the handle softly, he went inside and stood staring down at her as she slept. God, she looked beautiful that way, her hair spread on the pillow, her face relaxed in sleep. He wanted her, his need so hard that he could hardly keep from going to her, waking her...

How could he bear it if she never looked at him with love in her eyes again? He ought to let her go, but he could not...he didn't ever want to be without her.

Chapter Eight

Chloe had found the travelling and the brief stay in Paris difficult to bear. Pasha had been as considerate of her comfort as she could have wished, but he was cool and distant, and she felt the memory of their quarrel as a constant ache inside her.

In Paris he had insisted on taking her to Coco Chanel's salon, where her measurements were taken and several of the very fashionable two-piece ensembles were ordered. Despite her mixed feelings about Pasha and the source of his wealth, Chloe was unable to remain aloof as she was shown the latest designs and she loved the chic suits that Pasha ordered for her, as well as the perfume and various accessories.

'They are beautiful,' she told him when they left later that afternoon, stepping out into the heat of the streets. Her head was aching slightly, and for a moment she felt a little dizzy, but soon recovered. 'Thank you for buying them for me, but it was completely unnecessary. Sashimi had already chosen more clothes than I need.'

'They were adequate for the house in Spain,' Pasha told her. His dark eyes went over her assessingly, but held no warmth. 'But slightly old-fashioned, didn't you feel? Sashimi chose what she would wear—but you are a very different woman. You have no reason to hide your legs, Chloe—they are beautiful and should be admired. As my wife and living often in London and New York, you will need something more fashionable. I expect you to do me credit, and the clothes were bought as much for my benefit as your own.'

Chloe digested this in silence. She hadn't really been sure of his plans, and she was beginning to real-ise she knew hardly anything about the man she had married. She had simply plunged headlong into a pas-sionate affair without counting the consequences, and now she was caught—a prisoner in a gilded cage, from which there seemed no hope of escape.

But she would escape when she was ready, Chloe decided. She could not leave Pasha while he was so watchful, but he was bound to relax his guard in time. Besides, it was strange how lethargic she had felt these last few days. She wasn't sure what had made her feel so tired, but thought it must be leaving the freshness of the mountain air for the heat of the city.

It was summer and Paris had been very hot ever since they arrived. In fact she had felt dizzy a couple of times in the famous fashion designer's salon. She hadn't mentioned it to Pasha, because she was still uncertain of how to behave towards him. What did he expect her to say to him?

He had told her that he required her to act as if she were a happy bride, but that was going to be more difficult than Chloe had imagined. How could she pretend that everything was wonderful when she felt so awful?

* * *

It was only after they had flown into the airport in London, and were heading for Sir Henry Rendlesham's country house in Hampshire, that Chloe realised quite a bit of what she was feeling was actually physical. She felt dizzy and sick, and she had to ask Pasha to stop the car for a moment.

'What's wrong, Chloe?' he asked, looking at her in concern as he saw how pale she was.

'I—I'm sorry, but I feel unwell…' She wrenched open the car and clawed out as soon as he had stopped, vomiting into the grass verge. She was sick a couple of times, accepting Pasha's handkerchief with a grateful look. 'I'm very sorry. I've been feeling a little unwell for the last two days, but I thought it was just tiredness or a change of climate. It was so hot in Paris.'

'Was it?' His brows arched. She hadn't complained of heat when they were in the desert, nor on the very hot days they had shopped in the Spanish market. She had seemed to thrive in it, especially in Spain. 'Have you considered that it may not be the heat, Chloe?'

'Something I ate?' She glanced at him as she finished wiping her mouth and hesitated over what to do with the handkerchief.

He smiled oddly. 'I think you had better keep that just in case,' he said and held the car door for her. 'I was thinking that you might perhaps be carrying a child.'

'A child…' Chloe felt the oddest sensation. A mixture of pain and pleasure shot through her as she realised that he might be right, that she might already have his child inside her. They had made love freely and passionately for three weeks and, although she hadn't given it a thought until now, it was five weeks since she'd seen her monthly flow. She was so shocked that she blurted her next words out without thinking, 'But that's…terrible.'

Pasha had been looking at her with seeming pleasure, but now the smile vanished and his expression became cold again.

'Is it terrible, Chloe? I had thought you the type of woman who would enjoy having children.'

'Of course I would, but—' She broke off and blushed as he looked at her. What was she about to say—that she wanted children but not his? That would be a wicked thing to say to anyone, and she discovered that no matter what he had done she didn't want to hurt him like that. She was confused, hurt and angry, but she didn't particularly want to strike back. All she wanted was for this ache inside her to go away. 'It would have been wonderful if…if things had been different.'

'You mean if you hadn't married a murderer?' Pasha closed the door of the car as she got in and went round the other side. Chloe snatched a quick glance at his profile, and looked away again as she saw the pulse beating at his temple. She had tried not to hurt him, but she had only succeeded in making him angry.

'Please, don't let's quarrel,' she said. 'I really don't feel well enough, Pasha.'

'I am sorry,' he said, his eyes on the road ahead. 'I'm sorry you wish you hadn't married me, but I'm afraid this makes it even more impossible for you to leave me.'

'Why?' She risked another look, and saw that his hands were white as they clenched the steering wheel. 'I am perfectly capable of bringing up a child alone.'

'Unfortunately, I cannot allow you to do that,' he said. 'You don't understand the dangers. Alone, both you and the child would be vulnerable, especially if that child is a boy.'

'What do you mean vulnerable?' Chloe felt slivers of ice trickle down her spine.

'My son stands to inherit all I inherited from my father,' Pasha said without looking at her. 'That means certain people may try to get rid of him—and you.'

'No!' Chloe felt the fear clutch at her. Instinctively, she placed a protective hand over her stomach, and in that moment she knew that she did want her unborn child despite everything that had happened between her and Pasha. 'That's frightening, Pasha. But what makes you think someone might try to kill us?'

'Because at least three attempts have been made to assassinate me,' he replied, his expression unmoved as he kept his eyes on the road ahead. 'It is something I have lived with since my father was killed, but I was wrong to expose you to that danger, Chloe. If I wanted to marry I should have chosen a different kind of woman, one who didn't mind that her independence might have to be curbed for her own safety.'

Chloe didn't know how to answer him. Her mind was still reeling from the shock of discovering first that she might be carrying his child, and second that both her life and the life of that child might be at risk.

'You should at least have told me,' she said at last.

'Yes, I should,' he agreed but didn't look at her. 'I am sorry, but there really isn't much I can do about it now.'

'You could divorce me. I could change my name— go away somewhere.'

'No. No, I couldn't do that.'

'You mean you won't!'

'That's right, I won't.'

Chloe felt the anger rise inside her. She doubted that her life would be in danger if she left him at all. Perhaps it was something he had invented to make her fearful of going off alone while his back was turned. Well, she didn't believe him, and she was going to leave the first chance she got—but not just yet. Not until she was feeling a little better.

'Welcome home, Pasha—and Chloe. I think I have your name right, my dear?' Sir Henry smiled at her. He was a charming, white-haired man, tall and lean and still attractive though well into his seventies. 'Well, this is a delightful surprise. I can tell you that we were beginning to despair of Pasha ever finding the right person...but now I can see that he was very right to wait. He couldn't have chosen better.'

Chloe blushed as she felt the warmth of his approval. She hadn't expected to be greeted with such pleasure, and she found herself responding naturally.

'Thank you, Sir Henry. It is nice to be here, and I am pleased to meet you.'

'Henry,' he said. 'Please call me Henry, my dear. Come in, come in. Your rooms have been prepared for you. The whole household is buzzing with excitement—we were all so thrilled when Pasha telephoned and told us the news!'

Chloe smiled at him, allowing him to draw her into the house, which was a lovely old rambling place with roses growing up the grey stone walls and tiny leaded panes to the windows.

'What a beautiful house,' she said as he took her

into a comfortable sitting room. It was furnished in cool shades of greens and blues, and just right for a hot summer day. She sank into one of the rather shabby but very relaxing armchairs with a little sigh of relief. 'I didn't expect anything like this. Pasha hasn't told me much at all about his family.'

'Well, I dare say there isn't much to tell,' Sir Henry said. 'Helen was my only daughter. My son died in infancy.' He paused, clearly distressed but fighting an old sorrow. 'I had two brothers and a sister, but there's only Dora left now. She lives with me, but she is visiting her son at the moment and she will be most upset to learn that she missed you. But perhaps you can be persuaded to stay for a while until she returns? I expect her back at the end of next week.' He looked inquiringly at Pasha.

'I am sorry that won't be possible at the moment, sir,' Pasha said. 'We haven't been to see Chloe's father yet. We would like to stay with you for a couple of days this time, but I am sure Chloe can be persuaded to come back again soon…can't you, darling? I may need to go abroad again shortly, and I am sure you would rather be here than alone in my London apartment, wouldn't you, my love?'

Chloe wondered what was in his mind. Was he thinking that it would be harder for her to run away from him if she stayed with his family?

'Yes, I think I would,' she said and sipped the refreshing cup of tea Sir Henry's housekeeper had brought for her. 'I didn't know you had planned another trip, Pasha? Where are you going this time?'

'To see my uncle,' he told her. 'It's just a business thing, darling. I think you would be better staying here. Especially if…' He glanced at his grandfather.

'We aren't certain yet, sir, but we think Chloe may be with child.'

Chloe blushed a fiery red as Sir Henry looked at her. He must be aware that they had been married only a few days, and she expected to see a frown of censure. Instead of that, she saw surprise and then genuine delight dawn over the elderly man's face.

'That is wonderful news,' he said. 'Congratulations to both of you and I would very much like it if you would consider having the baby here, Chloe. I know some of you young things like to go into hospital for the birth these days, but we could arrange to have a nurse staying here—and also a very good doctor I happen to know would attend you during the whole of your pregnancy.'

'I'm not sure,' Pasha said. 'Supposing there are complications?'

'I think it's a lovely idea,' Chloe said and reached across to touch Sir Henry's hand. 'In fact, I would like to come down and visit you often. I much prefer the country to the town. I believe I did tell you that, didn't I, Pasha?'

His eyes narrowed suspiciously. 'Perhaps, I'm not sure. We shall get down as often as we can, of course, and as I've already said, you should consider coming here while I'm away. Henry and Dora will look after you.'

'Yes, indeed we shall,' Sir Henry said and chuckled, delighted at the prospect of seeing more of her. 'I am so glad you enjoy the country, Chloe. Pasha doesn't visit us anywhere near enough. I know he's a busy man, but I'm always telling him he shouldn't work so hard.'

'A business doesn't run itself, sir.'

'No, no, of course not—and you've done extremely well,' Sir Henry said approvingly. He looked at Chloe. 'I dare say he hasn't told you how clever he is? No, I thought he wouldn't—likes to hide his light under a bush, does my grandson. He invented some contraption when he was at college. It's all part of this new technical stuff. I don't understand it myself, though I enjoy listening to the wireless. Pasha tells me there will be a machine that shows us pictures of what's happening miles away one day—and not like the cinema, my dear—he's talking about the moment it happens. Imagine that, pictures from miles away as an event is taking place! It all sounds a bit far-fetched to me, but Pasha says it will come and he must know what's he's talking about. The boffins in the Government think he's the bees' knees, you know—and he's made an awful lot of money...'

'I am sure Chloe doesn't want to know any of this.'

'Oh, but I do,' she contradicted. 'I think I am going to enjoy talking to Henry about you, Pasha. He will tell me all the things you haven't.' She smiled at him, forgetting for a moment that she was angry with him, forgetting that he wasn't the man she thought she had married, and feeling as she had when he had first taken her to Spain. 'Yes, I shall definitely come and stay with you while Pasha is away, Henry.'

'Thank you for being pleasant to Henry,' Pasha said to her later when they were alone in the suite of very attractive rooms that had been made ready for them. 'He happens to be very fond of me for some reason, and I should hate him to be hurt over all this.'

'I wouldn't dream of hurting him,' Chloe said, feeling indignant. 'I am surprised that you could think it.

You obviously don't know me very well if you imagine that I would deliberately hurt someone like Henry. He's a dear…' She faltered and blushed as he looked at her oddly, his eyebrows arched.

'I am glad you like him,' was all the reply Pasha made, but she knew what lay unsaid between them.

'And I don't know you well either,' she went on, saying what she knew to be true.

'No, you don't,' he agreed, a faint smile flickering at the corners of his mouth. 'Your trouble, Chloe, is that you have a fertile imagination. You do not always make sound judgements.'

'That's unfair,' she replied. 'Just because I happen to like certain films—' She broke off as she saw the look in his eyes, changing the subject and heading off what she knew was coming. 'Just what did you invent, Pasha?'

'It was something to do with computers,' he said and smiled at her. 'So far most successful computers have been analogue, but there's something called electronics that is going to be the big thing of the future. I came up with a small idea that may help to make that sooner rather than later, but it was only the first step in building my business, which is design of all kinds. Not just things I might invent myself, but promoting other people's vision of the future. This century is going to see a whole new world emerging, Chloe, things neither you nor I could even begin to imagine.'

'Oh, I see. And you make a lot of money promoting these designs and inventions?'

'Did you think the money I spent on you was blood money, Chloe?'

Something in his eyes made her look away, because it was a look of hurt rather than anger. She felt guilty, as though she had somehow let him down, but she dismissed the thought as ridiculous. What did he expect her to think after what he had told her? But his expression had changed and now he was angry.

'Well, you can ease your conscience,' he told her coldly. 'I can assure you that nothing you are wearing was paid for by my uncle's money—as a matter of fact, what I do for him is out of loyalty. He has never offered payment and I would not accept it if he did.'

'Then I am sorry that I thought it for a moment,' she said. 'It was wrong of me. Please forgive me. I didn't mean to imply—'

'But it was in your mind,' he said. 'You clearly have a low opinion of my morals. In case you are wondering, I shan't be sleeping in your bed tonight, Chloe. The English aristocracy is extremely civilised. They provide a bed in the dressing room, and that's where I'll be sleeping while we're staying here. I've never needed to force an unwilling woman to sleep with me yet, and I don't intend to start with you.'

Chloe didn't answer. She turned her back on him, her thoughts in turmoil. He was acting as though she was the one in the wrong, but he had told her that he had authorised the execution of a man. How did he expect her to behave? Had he thought she would say, 'Thank you for telling me, but now I'll just forget all about it'?

Chloe kept staring out of the window as she heard Pasha walk into the dressing room. Her eyes were burning with unshed tears, but she blinked them back as she started to change for dinner. She wasn't going to let him see how upset she was. Besides, red eyes were always a giveaway, and she didn't want Henry to guess she had been crying. There was no need for him to be dragged into all this.

He was so thrilled that Pasha had married, and that he could expect to see his great-grandchild within a few months. She couldn't disillusion him immediately. She would have to find a way of letting him down gently, and of course he would want to see his great-grandchild.

Chloe felt a little shock of pleasure as she had time to sit and contemplate the idea that she was carrying a child. She had never thought very much about it before this, because she had always expected to work for some years before marrying, but now she discovered that she was thrilled by the prospect of being a mother.

She wasn't sure what she was going to do about the future; the edges had become blurred by the idea that she might be having Pasha's child. Whereas she had been determined to leave him at the first opportunity, she was now wondering if perhaps the compromise he had suggested would be a better alternative.

Especially if she could spend much of her time here at Meadowsweet House with Henry…

'I shall look forward to seeing you again soon,' Henry told her as she and Pasha took their leave a few days later. 'Take care of yourself, my dear. I shall tell Dora your good news if I may? I know she will be as pleased as I am. You see, we are old-fashioned creatures, and one day Pasha's son will inherit the title and most of what I have.'

'Oh!' Chloe glanced at her husband. 'I didn't realise…'

Sir Henry laughed. 'Don't imagine that amounts to very much, my dear. Pasha isn't interested in titles, even if mine did come down from the Conqueror himself—and my estate is not particularly valuable. Your husband is a wealthy man, and he isn't in the least bothered about anything I might leave, which is why it will go to his first son.'

'I—I see,' Chloe said. 'I understand. That's why you would like the child born here?'

'If you would feel happy about that?'

'May I think about it?'

'Of course.' He smiled at her. 'You mustn't feel pressured. It was merely an old man's whim.'

'I shall think about it,' she promised, and kissed his cheek. 'And I shall come to see you very soon.'

They had been driving for an hour or more, before Chloe told Pasha what was on her mind.

'I've been thinking that I might like to spend most of my time at Henry's.'

'Have you?' A tiny pulse flicked at Pasha's temple, but he gave no sign of any other emotion. 'It may be possible for you to spend some of your time there, but I shall want you with me in London when I am there. I attend quite a few social occasions, and it would look odd if you were never there.'

'Oh…yes, of course. Well, I didn't mean all the time.'

'Didn't you?' He glanced at her, a faint glimmer of amusement in his eyes. 'I rather think you did, Chloe, but I'm afraid you made a bargain and you are going to have to stick to it—or I might break mine.'

'You said you wouldn't force me…'

'There are other ways…'

Chloe swallowed as she heard the hard note in his voice. She had noticed him looking at her hungrily once or twice over the past couple of days, but so far he hadn't attempted to do more than kiss her cheek—and that was in front of Henry. The first time he'd put his arm around her waist in a show of casual affection it had taken all her strength not to jerk away, but after a while she had got used to it.

She'd found herself wishing that they were really the happy couple he was trying to portray.

'I don't know if my father will be quite as happy about the situation as your grandfather,' Chloe said, desperately changing the subject. 'He might not be too pleased that I got married without consulting him.'

'I asked if you were sure about having the wedding in Spain…'

'Yes, I know. I agree it's probably best to present him with a *fait accompli*,' Chloe said. 'But he expected me to use my college education, and he may think I've wasted it.'

'Why? There is absolutely no reason why you shouldn't go on with your work,' Pasha said. 'I might even be able to help you put material together for your book.'

'Yes, I suppose you could,' she said looking at him thoughtfully. 'I've often wanted to translate something from the original.' She looked at him as he drove. 'I can't help wondering…you seem such a mixture, Pasha. You live in the West and you talk of the wonders of the modern world—and yet you still believe in the old ways…'

'I respect the views of others, that is all,' Pasha

said and a muscle in his cheek clenched, as he understood what she was saying. 'And I am loyal to those I owe a duty to.'

'Surely loyalty can be carried too far?'

'You don't know what you are talking about. You have no idea.'

'That's because I can only know what you choose to tell me.'

Chloe stared at him. For a moment she sensed there was a battle going on inside him, and she thought he might be going to tell her more. She hoped there was something he could tell her that would ease the sense of horror his revelations still caused her, but she couldn't think of anything that would do that.

'There is nothing I can tell you that will make you feel better,' he said. 'I did what I had to do, Chloe. Believe me, I wish I hadn't told you.'

'So do I,' she said but it was in such a small voice that she doubted he had heard her, and then in a louder tone, 'You turn right here. We are the last house at the end of the street.'

Her father's house was an old-fashioned town house built on four floors, narrow and slightly shabby since he had lost most of his money in that unfortunate investment. She glanced at Pasha to see what he thought of it, but his face was not reflecting any emotion, his features carved out of stone.

She got out of the car without waiting for him to open the door when they stopped, although she knew that he preferred her to wait. He liked to look after her and his manners were impeccable. Although she wouldn't have admitted it, her heart was racing in anticipation of her father's reception of Pasha. She had a feeling that he would not be as welcoming to her husband as Sir Henry had been to her.

The housekeeper answered the door, looking curiously at them both but showing no emotion whatsoever and Chloe's heart sank. Her father must be very angry with her for them to be greeted this way.

He was standing by the long French windows at the rear of the house, his back towards them as they walked into the parlour. Chloe swallowed hard, and took a step forward.

'Daddy...' she faltered and then stopped as he turned to look at her coldly. 'I want you to meet my husband, Pasha...'

'So he married you, did he?' Mr Randall's expression was granite hard, his eyes registering both anger and disgust. 'I wonder that either of you has the gall to come here. If you imagine I shall accept this marriage and welcome you home, Chloe, you are much mistaken. I do not know what kind of a ceremony you went through...'

Pasha stepped forward, his arm going about Chloe's waist. 'Chloe is my wife,' he said in a clear controlled tone. 'We were married by an English reverend in a Protestant church in Spain. It has been established there for many years, for the use of English people living in that part of the country.'

'Indeed?' The cold eyes turned on him. 'And is that supposed to make everything all right?'

'I can understand your being a little upset,' Pasha began. 'It was unconventional to go off the way we did, but we were in love...'

'Love!' Mr Randall snorted. 'That's rubbish! It was irresponsible and scandalous. Chloe didn't know what she was doing, and it is my intention to contest the marriage.'

'You can't do that, Daddy,' Chloe said. She was trembling, glad of Pasha's arm supporting her. 'You know I didn't need anyone's permission to get married and you don't understand. Pasha saved my life. I fell in love with him, and…'

'Charles Hicks has already told me,' her father said, cutting her off. 'Can you imagine how I felt at hearing my daughter had behaved in such a disgraceful manner? I am ashamed of you! You have behaved foolishly all round, Chloe, wasting your education.' His eyes looked over her with evident distaste for what he saw, and she knew he would prefer her still to be the slightly dowdy, obedient daughter she had been rather than the new, sophisticated, well-dressed woman Pasha had made her.

His words flicked her on the raw. She knew that he had intended them to hurt, and they did. He had never been a truly loving parent, especially since her mother's death, but he had been proud of her achievements at college.

'Yes, perhaps I was foolish to run off into the desert like that,' Chloe agreed. 'But I was lucky. If Pasha hadn't found me I might have died…'

'It might have been better if you had.'

'That is a disgusting thing to say,' Pasha put in before she could speak. 'I must ask you to take that back, sir. You are speaking of my wife and I do not care to have her insulted.'

'Then you should take her away,' Mr Randall said. 'And don't bring her back while she remains your wife. I do not agree with mixed marriages. This is doomed to failure, Chloe.' He turned his fierce glare on her once more. 'Do not imagine you can come running back to me when he throws you over for another wife, or concubine or whatever he calls them.'

'You are being unfair to Pasha, Daddy,' Chloe said quietly. 'Whatever you think of him, and whatever he may choose to do in the future—he would not behave so badly towards me.'

'If that is your attitude, we have nothing more to say to each other,' her father said. 'I ask you both to leave my house, and I do not wish to see either of you again.'

'As you wish, Daddy.' Chloe blinked hard to hold back the tears. His contempt was hard to bear. She had sometimes suffered from his coldness in the past, but somehow she had not expected this bitter attack. 'I am sorry if I hurt you.'

'You let me down. I had high hopes for you, Chloe, and you let me down.'

Chloe turned to Pasha, her face white and strained. 'We had better go,' she said, feeling almost at breaking point. 'I don't think there is any point arguing with him.'

'Yes, of course.' Pasha glanced at her father. 'I believe you will regret this,' he said. 'And that is not a threat—it is a prediction.'

Mr Randall made no reply. Pasha kept his arm about Chloe as he led her from the house. Outside on the pavement, he looked at her in concern. She was very pale, and trembling, obviously very upset. His mouth thinned, his anger against her father barely contained.

'Are you all right?' he asked. 'Do you feel faint?'

'No, I'm fine.' She put on a brave smile. 'Well,

that cuts off one avenue of escape, doesn't it? You won't have to worry that I might run home to Daddy.'

Pasha smiled oddly. 'You may not believe this, but I would give much to have had a different reception for you, even if I did have to fetch you home every so often.'

Chloe laughed. 'You don't give up, do you?'

'No. I shall never give up on you,' he said and something in his eyes made her heart jerk as he looked at her. 'I know you hate me now, Chloe…'

'No,' she said quietly. 'I don't hate you. How could I hate the father of my child? But I don't trust you, Pasha.' She faltered as she saw the flash of pain in his eyes. 'I know that hurts you and I'm sorry, but you lied to me, by omission if not in actual fact. I'm not sure if I can forgive that.'

'At least you don't hate me,' he said, but his eyes were bleak. 'That is something. I'll try to win your trust back, Chloe—just give me a chance.'

Chloe didn't answer. How could she? How could anything change what Pasha was—what he had done?

Chloe looked around the bedroom of Pasha's apartment. She had thought his house in Spain beautiful, but this was the height of luxury, the furniture in the Art Deco style, expensive and the functional fittings extremely modern. The apartment didn't have quite the charm of Sir Henry's house, but it was a very pleasant place to live in town, and looked out over one of the city's central parks.

'We have four bedrooms,' Pasha told her. 'You may take your choice. I hope you are going to be comfortable here, Chloe? I can't say happy, because I know there's little chance of that.'

Chloe thought that she could have been very happy had things been otherwise between them, but then she would have been happy anywhere with him had he not told her the unthinkable—that he was a political assassin. She believed him when he told her that he acted out of a sense of loyalty and duty, but it still didn't help.

'I shall be very comfortable here,' she told him. 'I wish things were different, but I have been thinking, Pasha. I was determined to leave you the moment I got the chance…' She saw the gleam in his eyes, but her head tilted as she faced him bravely. 'I know you might have come to fetch me back, but I would have gone again and in the end you might have decided to let me go…'

'But?' His eyes were intent on her face. 'You are telling me this for a reason.'

'I think I must accept things, at least until after the child is born. I have been sick several times in the mornings and I am almost sure that you were right. I intend to see the doctor that Henry recommended to-morrow, and if he confirms our suspicions, then I promise I shan't try to leave you until after the birth.'

'I have no intention of letting you leave me ever, Chloe. Nothing has changed and it never will. Even if you never let me near you again, I intend that you shall remain my wife. My only wife. I didn't just marry you in the Christian church to please you. It happens to be my own belief and I do not agree with divorce. You accused me of being a mixture of old values and new and in this case you are right. I believe in one man and one woman for life.'

Chloe wet her lips with the tip of her tongue. When he looked at her that way it was as if her heart was being tugged in two. She knew that her body was aroused, and that she wanted him. She wanted him to be the way they had been in Spain, wanted him to scoop her up in his arms and carry her to their bed and make love to her until she begged for release.

How could she feel that way, knowing what he was? How could she love a man who was prepared to order a murder—perhaps more than one?

It was impossible. She couldn't live with herself if she condoned his actions. She couldn't bring herself to do that—and to give him what he wanted would be condoning what he did.

'Then we shall just have to stick to our bargain, shan't we?' she said. 'You say nothing has changed for you, Pasha, well, I feel the same way.'

He inclined his head, accepting her words though his eyes glittered with denial. She knew that he was holding himself on a thin thread and wondered how long he would continue to humour her.

If he decided to make her back down, he could do it. Chloe knew that she would not be able to resist him for long…but if he forced her surrender she would despise herself and hate him.

Did he understand that? Sometimes when he looked at her she thought she saw sadness in his eyes, as if he bitterly regretted the breach between them, but at others he could be so hard, so determined to have his way.

He was two very different men, she decided. The modern, sophisticated gentleman who lived in the West and believed in the technological revolution of the twentieth century—and the man whose ancestors had roamed the caravan routes of the desert, fighting and killing their enemies to preserve what was theirs.

She had no doubt that only the strongest and fittest had survived in that harsh environment, and that the instinct for survival must be a powerful force in him.

Which man was the real one? Or was he simply a mixture of the two?

Chloe could not be sure. Nor was she sure that she loved either one in isolation, but in her heart she knew that she did still love him, whoever he was. She loved him, but she could never live as his wife again.

'When are you going away?' she asked, turning aside from him so that he should not see the conflict going on inside her.

'Not for another two weeks,' he said and his voice sounded so close that it made her jump. She felt the touch of his hands on her shoulders and the desire to have him kiss her spiralled through her. 'Chloe, try to understand. I didn't want to do this…'

'Then why did you?' she asked. 'Why throw the truth at me the way you did?'

'That was pride,' he admitted. 'I was angry that you should doubt me. Hurt that you should think me capable of murder. Abdullah deserves to die, Chloe. It isn't murder, it's justice.'

'I'm not sure that I believe in the death penalty even in a court of law,' she replied, her eyes wide and thoughtful. 'But an assassination! That makes you as bad as the man who killed your father.'

Pasha's hands tightened on her shoulders for a moment. 'He *is* the man who killed my father,' he said. 'And I do believe that he should die.'

Chloe stood as if turned to stone as his hands left her shoulders. She felt icy cold all over, shocked by the bitterness of his voice.

'Why didn't you tell me that before?' she asked after a moment. 'It makes a difference…'

There was no reply and she turned to discover that the room was empty. Pasha had left her alone, and she shuddered as she realised that she had made the breach between them worse.

Why hadn't Pasha told her that the man he had ordered killed was the same one who had assassinated his father? She wasn't sure why it made a difference, but it did. She felt that it was still wrong, but now she understood his motives for doing it. He wasn't acting as a political assassin for gain or anything else—he was answering the call of his heart, seeking revenge for what had been done to him.

It didn't change the facts, she could never condone what he was doing, but she did understand.

Chapter Nine

'What were you planning to do today?' Pasha asked at breakfast some days later. 'I have meetings until eight this evening. I hope you won't be bored?'

'Justine rang me yesterday,' Chloe said. 'She asked if we could meet somewhere for lunch today. I told her she could come here, if that is all right with you?'

'Why shouldn't it be?' His brows rose. 'This is your home, Chloe. You are at perfect liberty to invite your friends or go out with them. I have never said that I intended to keep you a prisoner.'

'You said that you might if I attempted to run away,' she reminded him. 'In your father's *casbah*.'

'Even I sometimes say things I don't mean,' Pasha said with a wry grimace. 'I haven't been there for years, and I don't intend to start now. Besides, you've given me your word that you won't think of leaving until after the child is born.'

'And I shall keep it,' Chloe replied, a faint flush in her cheeks. She had never looked lovelier, her hair freshly washed and hanging loose on her shoulders, her complexion soft, eyes bright and enhanced by the bright emerald colour of the filmy wrap she was wearing. 'I'm not sure about the future, Pasha. I don't want to hurt Henry…or you, but one day this farce has to end. I don't see how either of us can continue like this for the rest of our lives.'

'Chloe—' Pasha began but the telephone rang in the hall and he went to answer it. He was gone for several minutes and she had begun to clear the breakfast things when he returned. 'You don't need to do that—the cleaner will come in later.'

'I don't mind clearing a few dishes,' Chloe said. 'I haven't been used to being waited on, Pasha. I like to feel useful.'

'Just being here is all I ask of you,' he said, his voice a little husky. 'Anyway, you will have a guest in a couple of days…that was Mariam. She arrived in Southampton last evening, and she wants to come and stay with us for a few days. I said that she could—I hope you don't mind?'

'No, of course not,' Chloe said and raised her head to look directly at him. 'We can't keep asking each other if we mind all the time, Pasha. Mariam is your stepmother. You want her to visit and naturally I want to meet her.'

'Do you?' He smiled oddly. 'Very well, Chloe, we'll agree to agree on everything, shall we? I have to leave now or I shall be late for my appointment. Have fun with your friend today. You are all right for money, if you want to go shopping?'

'You opened a generous account for me at your bank,' Chloe said.

'But you haven't spent anything yet.'

'It is early days,' she said and tipped her head on one side. 'Be careful, Pasha. If I start I might not know where to finish.'

She was deliberately provoking him, but he knew it and merely smiled. For a moment he hesitated, and she knew that he was wondering whether he should kiss her on the cheek as he had when they were at Henry's, but she turned away, knowing that it would be too dangerous. If he touched her he would guess how close she was to giving in to the dictates of her heart and body. He would know that she still wanted him desperately.

'I shall see you this evening.'

Chloe did not look round at him as he left. Her heart was beating rapidly, and she felt close to tears. It was so difficult living this way. She wished that she could just walk away and forget all that had happened to her, and yet she knew that that was impossible. She would never forget Pasha whether she stayed or left.

'What a wonderful apartment!' Justine said after Chloe had shown her round. 'You are so lucky, Chloe. It's like a dream come true...' She helped herself to one of the expensive chocolates on the little glass-topped table. 'Do you remember when we were talking about you finding a handsome lover when you were preparing for that trip? I never really thought it would happen...but it did. Tell me, is he as fabulous as he looks in his photo?'

'You met him on the ship—you knocked his drink over him, remember?'

'I was too embarrassed to look at him,' Justine said. 'But he seems nice in this picture...at least he looks happy. I don't suppose he is the kind of man you would term nice. But he certainly is attractive!'

Chloe felt a pang of regret. Pasha wasn't happy now.

'Well, that was taken the day before we got married,' she said. 'I'm not a very good photographer, but it isn't bad.'

'Haven't you got any wedding pictures?'

'No…we didn't think about it,' Chloe said, fabricating an excuse. She couldn't tell Justine that her husband had an aversion to employing a professional photographer, because there were parts of his life he preferred to keep secret, like the fact that he had dealings with assassins! 'It's a pity really, but it was just a small casual affair—not like yours will be.'

'That's if I ever find anyone…' Justine pulled a wry face as she crossed her long legs. 'I've been to several parties, but I haven't really seen anyone I like. Mummy has her eye on a baronet, but he hasn't shown much interest as yet. Besides, I would much rather marry an exciting man like—' She broke off and looked at Chloe as a bell rang loudly. 'That sounds as if someone is at your door. Were you expecting visitors?'

'No—at least, not for a couple of days,' Chloe said. 'Pasha's stepmother is coming to stay, but I'm not sure who that could be. I haven't met his English friends yet. We are thinking about giving a party soon.'

She got up and went out into the hall, opening the door hesitantly, but then she gave a cry of surprise and pleasure. 'Sashimi! Ahmad—how lovely to see you both. I had no idea you were coming to London.'

'We thought we would surprise you,' Sashimi said. 'I hope we haven't arrived at a bad moment, Chloe?'

'No, no, of course not,' she said at once. 'Please,

do come in. I have a friend here…Justine, this is Sashimi and Ahmad. Ahmad is Pasha's cousin, and I
stayed with them for a few days in Morocco.'

Justine had been sitting cross-legged on the floor,
and showing an awful lot of silk-clad thighs, but she
got up to shake hands with the new arrivals, looking
a little flustered.

'It is nice to meet you,' Sashimi said. 'But we must
not disturb you, Chloe. We came only on the chance
that you might be here and we do not want to intrude.'

'But you aren't,' Chloe said. 'I am delighted to see
you. Won't you sit down and have some tea or something different?'

'We shall stay only a few minutes,' Sashimi said.
'But we are here in London for a week or so. I do
hope I can persuade you to come out with me sometimes, Chloe?'

'Yes, I should love to,' Chloe said. 'But I'm not
quite sure. Mariam is coming to visit, and I shall be
looking after her for a few days—but after that…' She
hesitated. 'How long are you staying? I know Pasha
will want to see you. You must come to dinner…
when Mariam is here perhaps?'

'That would be delightful,' Sashimi said, but Ahmad did not reply.

Chloe made some iced tea with mint the way she
knew they liked it, and they stayed for perhaps half
an hour before taking their leave.

Justine looked at her curiously after they had gone.
'She seems very friendly,' she observed. 'But he's a
bit reserved, isn't he? Good looking, but a little on
the cold side.'

'Was he?' Chloe was surprised. 'He was very

friendly when we were in Morocco. I can't imagine why he was reserved today.'

'Perhaps he didn't like my being here?'

'Why should he object?' Chloe was puzzled. She thought about it, and decided that Justine was right, Ahmad had been quiet throughout the visit, although Sashimi had been the same as always.

'Perhaps he had something on his mind,' she said. 'Pasha is like that sometimes…when he has a problem…'

'Well, I liked her,' Justine said. 'But I should be careful of him if I were you, Chloe. He was looking at you oddly once or twice.'

'Oh, Justine!' Chloe cried and laughed. 'I am sure you are wrong. Ahmad always welcomes everyone to his home, and he spoils Sashimi ridiculously. I'm sure he wouldn't look at another woman—why should he?'

'I don't know,' Justine admitted. 'I'm not even sure what those looks meant, but I should be a little careful if I were you.'

Chloe smiled and shook her head. She suspected that perhaps Ahmad had found Justine's clothes and manners just a little too modern for his taste, and that was why he hadn't said very much.

'So…' she said, to divert her friend's mind. 'How long are you going to be in London?'

'Oh, at least another three weeks,' Justine replied and wrinkled her nose. 'May I have one of those Turkish cigarettes? I rather like them.' She took one from the silver box on the table and lit up, blowing a smoke ring. 'Mummy is determined that I shall get a proposal before we go home, but I really can't see it myself.'

Chloe laughed. 'Surely there's plenty of time? There's no point in marrying unless you fall in love.'

'Is that what happened to you?' Justine asked and Chloe felt the pain twist inside her as she nodded. 'The real "until death do us part" stuff? I think that's wonderful, Chloe. I hope you realise how lucky you are? I know I shall have to settle for the first man who asks!'

'Of course you won't,' Chloe said, but Justine's words were tearing her apart. 'You'll find someone special in time.'

'I would give anything to have your chances,' Justine said. 'It's so romantic—the way he searched the desert for you, and then carried you off to his *casbah*... It's better than a film, because it's true and you really love each other.'

'It was a house in Spain,' Chloe said with a faint smile. 'I haven't been to his father's *casbah* yet and nor has Pasha, at least not for years.'

'It is still romantic,' Justine said with a sigh. 'Nothing like that ever happens to me...'

Chloe wondered what Justine would think if she told her the truth, but of course she couldn't. It was too shocking, too disturbing.

'You are just so lucky, Chloe.'

'Yes,' she said. 'I suppose I am...'

Chloe told Pasha about Sashimi's visit that evening when he returned home. He nodded, looking slightly surprised by the news that his cousin was in London.

'I didn't know they were thinking of visiting London,' he said. 'It's odd that Ahmad didn't mention it when I spoke to him last.'

'Perhaps it was a spur-of-the-moment thing,' Chloe

suggested. 'Perhaps Sashimi wanted a shopping trip or something. You know how she loves to buy clothes.'

'Perhaps,' Pasha agreed and looked at her thoughtfully. 'She usually prefers Paris, though...'

'Well, the clothes are fabulous there,' Chloe agreed. 'But there are some nice things in the London shops too.'

'Did you go anywhere with your friend?'

'No, we just stayed here and talked,' Chloe said. 'We thought of going to a matinée at the cinema but there was nothing on that we particularly wanted to see.'

'You mean you didn't want to watch *The Sheikh* again?'

Pasha's eyes glinted with amusement as she shook her head.

'I've seen it a number of times.' She lifted her head defiantly. 'But I shall certainly go to his new one when that comes out...'

'Yes, of course you will—you and millions of other women,' Pasha said, arching his brows at her. 'Why will you allow yourselves to be fooled by such nonsense?'

'Oh, you are impossible!' Chloe said. 'It isn't that we believe it all—just that it is very romantic and fun.' She saw his teasing glance and pulled a face at him. 'I believe you say things like that just to make me cross with you.'

'But of course,' he agreed, looking amused. 'I like to see the way your eyes light up, Chloe. You are a very exciting, desirable woman, especially when you are angry...'

He took a step towards her, causing her heart to

race wildly. She caught her breath as he leaned towards her, brushing his lips lightly over hers.

'Pasha…' she began, her eyes dark with distress as she looked at him. 'You promised…'

'I promised I wouldn't force you,' he said. 'But you said this morning that we cannot go on forever the way we are.'

'Pasha…' Chloe turned away, shivering. Could he see how close she was to breaking point? Could he tell that she longed to be with him as they had been in Spain, that she longed to be in his arms, a part of him once more?

He touched the back of her neck, sending spirals of a fierce desire winging through her, but he didn't attempt to take her into his arms or make love to her. She tensed, fighting the urge to fling herself into his arms and beg him to love her.

'Don't worry, Chloe,' he said, a bitter note in his voice as he misunderstood the reason for her tension. 'I'm not going to ravish you. I'm not such a beast as to force myself on you. You may have a poor opinion of my morals but…'

'Of course I haven't,' she said, whirling round to look at him. 'I do understand why you are doing this, Pasha, but I hate it. I hate what it will do to you. There is a darkness inside you…and it is that secret side of your life that is keeping us apart.'

'Yes, I know that you cannot live with what I told you,' he said and the smile had died from his eyes. 'I realise that it shocked and horrified you and I am sorry. The order was given, and there is nothing I can do, nor would I if I could. You have to understand that this man murdered my father…he had attempts made on my life and that of my uncle. None of us is safe until he is dead…and that includes you.' Pasha's expression was cold as he looked at her. 'I have to protect those I care for—if that means you hate me, then so be it.'

He stared at her for a moment longer, then groaned, reaching out to pull her into his arms. She made no protest as he bent his head and kissed her, her body thrilling to the touch of his lips even though her mind was denying him and what he had just said to her. The heat of his arousal was burning her, setting her on fire and she smothered a groan. She felt herself melting into him, her resistance gone, as she looked up at him, her mouth soft and loose with desire. God, how she wanted him, wanted to feel him inside her, filling her, bringing her to a glorious release. She wanted to touch him, wanted to seek out the throbbing source of his passion and take him in her mouth, pleasuring him as he had her in the first days of their loving.

Pasha smiled and touched her face with his finger-tips.

'I shan't make you come to me, Chloe, but I want you to know that nothing has changed as far as I am concerned. I still want you and I always shall…'

And then he turned and walked away from her, going into his own room and shutting the door. Chloe stared at that door. Her instincts told her to go after him. Surely nothing else mattered but this feeling inside her? Surely they could work something out?

Yet even as she longed to be with him, she knew it wasn't possible. Turning, she went into her own room.

Chloe spent the next day shopping for food and getting ready for her visitor. She was looking forward to having Mariam to stay, and Pasha had talked of giving a dinner party while she was with them.

'We'll invite half a dozen couples and a man I know who happens to be around Mariam's age,' he had said to her that morning before he left. 'It will be a chance for you to get to know some of my friends. Perhaps Sashimi and Ahmad will come if we ask them.' He frowned as he looked at her. 'I tried to get in touch with him last night and this morning, but Sashimi said he was out. She sounded a bit odd. I don't know if they are having trouble in their marriage. They haven't been married that long, and I know she has been much indulged by her family…'

'Are you saying that it must be her fault if things are going wrong?' Chloe looked at him hard. Was he blaming her for the breach between them?

'No, of course not—but…' He shrugged his shoulders, obviously deciding not to push the argument further. 'I shall be late this evening. Don't wait dinner for me.'

Chloe nodded. He seemed cool and distant again this morning, even though he had suggested a dinner party, and she thought that perhaps he was angry with her because she had turned away from him the previous evening.

Little did he know that she had spent half the night tossing and turning in her lonely bed!

Chloe was thoughtful as she took a leisurely bath to prepare for that evening. Justine's visit had made her take another look at what had happened to her, forcing her to face her situation. And the kiss Pasha had given her the previous evening had made her realise that she wanted their marriage to be as it had been in the beginning.

Something had to change. She couldn't continue to act as if she felt nothing for Pasha, because her heart and her body told her that she did—and yet she could not condone what he had done.

It was a dilemma she could not solve and she wasn't sure what to do about it. The rest of their lives was a long time, and if Pasha was determined never to let her go…

Could she reach some sort of a compromise in her own mind, find a way to live with that part of Pasha's life that she so disliked? Perhaps she could talk to him this evening, try to discover his true thoughts concerning what he was doing.

The telephone was ringing when she got out of the bath, and she wrapped a towel around herself, padding on bare feet into the hall to answer it.

'Chloe…' Pasha's voice sounded a little odd. 'I'm sorry, but I shan't be home this evening. It may be three or four days before I can get back. I know it's awkward for you. Can you cope with Mariam's visit alone?'

'Yes, of course,' she said and felt an icy tingle at the base of her neck. 'Is something wrong?'

'No. At least, not yet. I've just been told that my uncle is making an unexpected visit to Paris this week. He arrives tomorrow and I have to be there to meet him.'

'Oh…' Chloe's heart was beating so fast that she felt sick. 'What else, Pasha? There's something you aren't telling me.'

'The man we spoke of that night…' Pasha's voice was guarded, but she knew exactly who he meant.

'He eluded my men and we have been warned that he is on his way to Paris.'

'Oh, Pasha.' Chloe's breath caught in her throat. 'Is he…will you be in danger?'

'Perhaps,' he said. 'I am very sorry, Chloe. I can't discuss this on the telephone. I have to go.'

'Pasha…' Her stomach was churning. She wanted desperately to tell him that she loved him, but the words stuck in her throat. 'Please, take care.'

'Yes, of course,' he said. 'And you, Chloe. Don't answer the door to strangers while I'm gone. At least you will have Mariam with you after tomorrow. Until then be very careful. Why don't you ask Justine to come and stay with you? If it weren't for Mariam's visit I would tell you to go down to Henry and stay there until I get back.'

Chloe felt chills running all over her. 'You are frightening me, Pasha. Really, there's no need to worry about me. I shall be perfectly all right.' It was he who would be in danger, but she didn't know how to tell him how she felt about that.

'You are all I care about, Chloe,' he said, and his voice was harsh with emotion. 'Remember that if something happens. Whatever you think of me… remember that I loved you…'

'Pasha…' she whispered. 'I love you…'

But it was too late, the receiver had gone down at the other end, and she had no way of calling him back. She hadn't bothered to inquire where he would be that day, and she knew nothing about his business or even a telephone number where she could contact him.

What a fool she had been! Chloe paced the floor of the apartment, realising that she was going to find the next few days very hard. She wasn't sure what she would do if anything happened to Pasha.

The realisation that he might be killed, and by the man who had assassinated his father, suddenly made her see things from a different perspective. All at once, she could understand why Pasha had been prepared to order Abdullah's execution.

She found herself wishing that someone would find this assassin and kill him before he could harm Pasha. Wild thoughts of taking a gun and shooting him herself filled her mind, and she laughed at her foolish thoughts.

Where were her morals now? She had been so high-minded, declaring that she couldn't live with Pasha because he was capable of ordering the execution of a murderer…and now look at her!

She was frantic with worry over a man she had been determined to leave at the first opportunity. It would be amusing if it were not so tragic.

Chloe spent the next morning rushing around to get the apartment ready for her guest. She went out to the news-stand nearby and bought all the daily papers, and saw there were a few lines to say that Prince Hassan, the ruler of a small but important oil state, was expected in Paris, but there was nothing else. No report of an attempt on his life, or of the arrest of an assassin.

Chloe listened to the news on the wireless that lunchtime, but there was still nothing that might cause her alarm. She began to relax and think that nothing terrible was going to happen.

Perhaps Abdullah had gone into hiding, and would not dare to make any more attempts on the life of the prince or Pasha. Surely he must know that they would be looking for him, that this time he would be killed himself if he attempted to harm the prince? She could only pray that he would not consider it worth the risk.

It was almost three in the afternoon when her visitor arrived bearing an armful of expensive flowers as a gift. Mariam was a woman in her late forties, but still very attractive and extremely smart. She spoke with a slight American accent, and her make up was heavier than Chloe was used to seeing on her friends, but she was a charming woman and Chloe liked her at once.

'I am so pleased to meet you,' Mariam told her and kissed her cheek, rubbing at the red mark her lipstick had made with her fingertips. 'I was afraid Pasha would never forgive himself for letting Lysette down. He seemed to withdraw into himself for a long time, and I thought he might never find happiness.'

'She was your daughter,' Chloe said, after she had shown her visitor into the sitting room. 'Pasha told me about her. I think he loved her very much.'

'He was devoted to her.' Mariam nodded and sat down in one of the comfortable sofas. 'It was because he lost his father that way,' she said. 'It was a terrible time for all of us, Chloe. We all knew that lives might be at risk, especially Pasha's. I wanted him to come to America with me, but his uncle insisted that he be educated in Britain. I suppose it was the right decision, but I've often regretted that we were parted. I was fond of him, and I believe he needed to be loved. Pasha visited whenever he could, of course, but if he had been around more—' She broke off and sighed.

'You feel that Lysette might not have…?'

'Got into trouble with that man?' Mariam nodded. 'She admired Pasha so much, looked up to him, saw him as a cross between a brother and a father, I think. He adored her, but he was very strict with her. I think she would have done anything rather than let him down.'

'Then why…' Chloe hesitated. 'I suppose she was in love with the man.'

'I think he dominated her,' Mariam said and frowned. 'I'm not sure. She wouldn't talk about him, and that wasn't like Lysette. She may have been afraid.'

'What do you mean?' Chloe asked and frowned. 'You don't think she was afraid of Pasha?'

'No, not afraid. She would have hated to let him down, but she knew he would never harm her. It was the other one who frightened her, I think.'

'Did you know who he was?'

'I thought at first it was that film director,' Mariam said. 'He had offered her a part in one of his films and she was very excited about it, but then all at once she changed.'

'How do you mean, changed?'

'She said that it wouldn't be right for her to take part in a film, because she was the daughter of a Sheikh, and that it would bring shame on her family.' Mariam frowned. 'And there were other things…' She sighed and shook her head. 'But there is no point in talking about all that now. It is over and done. Please, tell me about you—and how you came to meet Pasha.'

'We met on a cruise ship,' Chloe said. 'It was all rather strange…'

She explained about the accident that had first

made them notice each other, and then about Brent
Harwood being on the same ship.

'So you see, if he had not tried to…well, I might
never have run away and—'

'Yes, that was odd, especially as Brent Harwood
was involved with Lysette at one time.' Mariam nodded, looking thoughtful. She gave a little shrug of her
thin shoulders, her bones standing out against the silk
of her dress. 'These things are written, my dear. I
believe that with all my heart. If you were meant to
be with Pasha, you would have met somehow…
somewhere.'

'Yes, perhaps,' Chloe said. 'That is what Sashimi
says.'

'Sashimi?' Mariam arched her brows. 'I am afraid
I do not know who you mean.'

'You do not know Ahmad's wife?'

'Ahmad Al-Hadra?' Mariam looked thoughtful as
Chloe nodded. 'I had not realised he was married. He
visited us once, a few weeks before Lysette…' She
paused and her forehead wrinkled. 'I have wondered
if…but no, I do not think so.'

'You are not thinking that Ahmad might have been
involved?' Chloe stared at her in surprise.

Mariam's expression was odd, as if she were trying
to come to terms with her own thoughts. 'It had
crossed my mind, but of course it was just a foolish
fancy.'

'Sashimi is very lovely. I do not think Ahmad
would—'

'No, of course not,' Mariam agreed. 'I am just surprised that he did not mention his wife—but perhaps
he was not married then.'

'No, perhaps not. Pasha said they had not been

married many months—but a marriage would have been arranged long before, wouldn't it?'

'Yes, as a rule,' Mariam said. 'It is often the custom. Pasha's uncle wanted to arrange a marriage for him some years ago, but he refused. He made it clear that he would make his own choice when the time came, as his father did before him.' Mariam smiled. 'My husband was a man of independent thought, Chloe, and I believe his son takes after him in that respect.'

'Yes.' Chloe's lips curved despite herself. She could not imagine Pasha agreeing to having anything arranged for him. 'I would certainly say that Pasha knows what he wants, and nothing will turn him.'

'He is a wonderful man,' Mariam said. 'Generous and considerate, and a great deal of fun to be with— but I am sure I have no need to tell you any of this, Chloe.'

'No,' Chloe said slowly. 'But I would like to hear about him, Mariam. It would be interesting to know more about what he was like as a young boy.'

'Very studious and clever,' Mariam said. 'But he could also play surprising pranks when he chose. He was a very lively boy and full of imagination. He would sometimes tell us the most amazing stories, and they were not always strictly true.'

Chloe smiled. 'That doesn't sound like Pasha. He is always telling me that I let my imagination run away with me!'

'Ah…you must not always take what he says at face value,' Mariam said and gave a tinkling laugh. 'He can be the most dreadful tease, and he comes up with some surprising ideas. The only predictable thing about Pasha is that he is unpredictable.'

Chloe nodded. 'I am so glad that you came to see me,' she said. 'And Pasha will be sorry to have missed you. I do hope you will come again before you return to America?'

'How long will Pasha be away?' Mariam asked. 'I wanted to ask his advice about something.'

'A few days, I am not sure.'

'Then I shall return to you in two weeks' time,' Mariam said. 'I planned to spend two days with you before I fly to Paris. I have to see my doctor there.'

'Oh.' Chloe looked at her anxiously. 'I hope there is nothing seriously wrong?'

'It may be just a false alarm,' Mariam said. 'I have seen a doctor in New York, who thinks I may have a tumour in my stomach and wants to do an operation, but I would like another opinion.'

'That sounds serious,' Chloe said. And for the first time she realised how thin the other woman was—and wondered if perhaps her illness was a reason for the heavy make up. She felt sympathy for her, and wished that there were something she could do for her. 'Is there anything I can do to help you? Anything at all…'

'How sweet of you to ask,' Mariam said and touched her hand. 'You mustn't worry too much, Chloe. At the moment I am quite well, but there may be a problem—and if there is I should like to settle my affairs. I must talk to Pasha. He has always looked after that side of things for me—' She broke off and frowned.

'Perhaps you could contact him in Paris,' Chloe suggested.

'Oh, not if he is with the prince,' Mariam said and pulled a wry face. 'You must know that His Excellency does not approve of me. I went my own way after my husband's death, and refused his protection. Indeed, I advised Pasha to break all ties with him some time ago for his own sake—but of course he refused. Your husband is very loyal, my dear.'

'Yes…yes, I know that,' Chloe said. 'I do hope your trip to Paris will prove worthwhile. I hope you will find that there is nothing seriously wrong.'

'If it is written I shall have many years spared to me yet,' Mariam replied with a little smile and a shrug of her shoulders. 'And if not…I have lived my life as I wished it, Chloe. You must not be sad for me. You are young and you have everything to live for.'

'Yes…' Chloe's eyes stung with tears. Mariam was right, she did have everything to live for. But only if Pasha came back to her safely…

Chapter Ten

Mariam's visit was very quiet. Chloe enjoyed their comfortable conversations together, and she learned a lot about when Pasha had been a boy. Everything she learned made her realise that she loved him more, despite the barriers between them.

However, Chloe soon became aware that her visitor was not as well as she might have been when she took an early morning drink into her. Without her make up, Mariam looked pale and drawn, and Chloe was anxious about her. Her own mother had suffered for some months before she died, though Chloe had been away at school for a lot of the time.

Perhaps because of Mariam's illness, the two became close during the time they spent together, and Chloe was sorry when it was necessary to part from her new friend.

'I wish Pasha had telephoned so that you could have spoken to him,' she said as the car came to take Mariam to the airport. 'I know he would want to help as much as he can.'

'You are a sweet girl, Chloe.' Mariam kissed her warmly. 'I am so glad Pasha has you now. But he is very naughty not to have been in touch with you these past two days, and I shall scold him when I see him.'

'I expect he is busy,' Chloe said and smiled. 'He will contact me when he can.'

She was determined not to show her anxiety in front of Mariam, who had more than enough to worry her, but she was fretting inwardly. Where was Pasha? What was he doing and why hadn't he phoned her?

Sashimi had given her a number to ring, and she telephoned shortly after Mariam had left.

'Oh, I am so glad to hear from you,' Sashimi said. 'I was about to telephone you myself. Ahmad went off somewhere on business, and I have been so bored here alone. Why don't we meet for lunch and spend the afternoon shopping together?'

'Yes, why don't we?' Chloe agreed, feeling that she didn't want to spend the day alone. 'Justine is coming over this evening and we're going to the cinema together, but as long as I'm home by six o'clock, that will give me time to get ready.'

'Oh, you will be home well before then,' Sashimi said. 'Ahmad may be back this evening so I don't want to be too late myself.'

'I'll meet you in an hour's time,' Chloe said. 'Goodbye for now, Sashimi.'

The phone rang the second she replaced it, and she snatched it up, her heart racing.

'Pasha?' she said breathlessly.

'I am sorry to disappoint you, my dear.' Henry chuckled. 'I was just ringing to see how you were, Chloe. Is there any chance of your coming to visit me soon?'

'Yes, of course,' Chloe said. 'And it isn't a disappointment. I love to hear from you. Pasha is away at the moment and I thought it might be him, that's all. But we will come down, Henry. As soon as he gets back we'll arrange something.'

'We shall look forward to that. Dora is eager to meet you. She has done nothing but talk about you since she got back from her son's. I've been getting it in the neck because I didn't keep you here until she came home!'

'Oh, poor you.' Chloe laughed. Henry was such a dear and she enjoyed talking to him.

'I dare say I shall survive, but how are you, my dear?'

'I went to see the doctor you recommended,' Chloe told him. 'He confirmed that I am pregnant.'

'That's wonderful, Chloe dear! I am delighted for you both—and for myself.'

They talked for several minutes, which made Chloe a little late in getting ready for her appointment with Sashimi. She tore round the bedroom, snatching the first dress she came to and leaving her discarded clothes on the bathroom floor.

She had planned to leave a note for Pasha just in case he should return, but now there simply wasn't time.

Sashimi was waiting for her at the restaurant. She looked a little put out and glanced at her watch pointedly as Chloe joined her at the table; the watch was an elegant diamond and white gold wrist bracelet and very expensive. Everything Sashimi wore was obviously the best available, and Chloe thought that Ahmad must be very generous to his lovely young wife, which made her wonder about Sashimi's sullen expression. She didn't look anywhere near as happy as she had seemed in Morocco.

'I was beginning to think you weren't coming…'

'I am sorry,' Chloe apologised. 'Pasha's grandfather telephoned just after I had spoken to you, and we talked for longer than I expected. I didn't want to tell him I had an appointment in case he thought I wanted to get out of talking to him, which I didn't— because he's so pleasant.'

'Well, it doesn't matter now,' Sashimi said, her frown lifting. 'I've ordered Russian caviar, lobster salad and pheasant in a rich sauce. I hope that appeals to you?'

'Good gracious,' Chloe said, shocked at such an extravagant menu. 'Are we celebrating something?'

'I like the best,' Sashimi said carelessly. 'There is no point in eating out unless you make a little splash, is there?'

Sashimi had ordered a vintage champagne to accompany their meal. Chloe was surprised to see that Sashimi drank several glasses of it. She hadn't expected this, but Sashimi seemed to do exactly as she pleased, although she only picked at the expensive food she had ordered.

Chloe thought it was rather a waste, but didn't say anything. She offered to pay her share of the bill, but Sashimi merely signed and said it was an account. She shrugged her elegant shoulders and told Chloe that Ahmad would pay.

This surprised Chloe, because she remembered Sashimi telling her that they were nowhere near as wealthy as Pasha. Yet now Sashimi seemed to have money to throw around.

Chloe was even more surprised when they went

shopping in one of the big shops in Knightsbridge. Whenever she had bought something from there in the past, Chloe had considered it very extravagant and taken her time choosing carefully. Sashimi seemed to buy recklessly, hardly bothering to check the price of the expensive items she bought—handmade leather shoes and bags, and belts all to match. Three silk blouses, and an evening dress that had such a huge price ticket that Chloe winced.

'Does Ahmad give you an allowance?' she asked as Sashimi simply signed for everything, seldom even glancing at the total.

'Oh, no,' she replied uninterestedly. 'He tells me to put everything on his account. He wouldn't give me money in case—' She stopped abruptly as if afraid of saying too much.

'Do you know how much you've spent this afternoon?' Chloe inquired. She herself had bought a pretty silk blouse, which she'd paid for with her own money.

'Who cares?' Sashimi pulled a face. 'Ahmad owes me—and he can afford to pay.'

The other woman's sullen look and her tone shocked Chloe. It was obvious that she was troubled, and Chloe felt concerned for her.

'Are you unhappy?' she asked. 'Is there anything I can do?'

Tears suddenly welled up in Sashimi's eyes. 'I hate him!' she said. 'I wish I had refused to marry him.'

'Oh, Sashimi…' Chloe stared at her in dismay. She had suspected there might be some source of friction between husband and wife, but nothing like this. 'Is there anything I can do to help you?'

'I want to go home,' Sashimi said. 'I don't feel too

well. Will you come with me, Chloe? Please do. I need to talk to you—in private.'

It was clear that Sashimi was distressed, and Chloe didn't think twice.

'Yes, of course,' she said. 'We'll go to your apartment and you can tell me what has happened to upset you like this.'

Chloe remembered that Pasha had thought that Sashimi was merely spoiled and probably sulking because she couldn't get her own way over something. Well, that might be the case, of course, but Chloe felt there was more to this than a mere tiff between Ahmad and Sashimi. Looking at her face as they were driven back to the apartment in a taxi, Chloe thought it must be more serious. Sashimi was pale and on edge, her hands moving restlessly, as though she was nervous. What on earth could have happened to upset her so badly?

Chloe reached across and held her hand comfortingly. 'It can't be so very bad,' she said. 'I am sure Ahmad cares for you. If you've quarrelled you will make it up again.'

'You don't know him,' Sashimi said, then bit her lip and lapsed into silence.

Chloe paid for the taxi as Sashimi opened the door of her apartment block and led the way to the lifts. She was silent as they travelled up to the top floor, and as she fished out her key and opened the door. She dumped her parcels on the floor of the expensively furnished sitting room and left Chloe standing as she went through into one of the other rooms. Perhaps she wanted a few minutes on her own, Chloe thought, and sat down on one of the large, comfortable sofas to wait.

Sashimi did not reappear even after several minutes, and Chloe was about to go and investigate when the hall door opened and Ahmad came in.

'Chloe…' he said, looking at her strangely. His face was strained, and his eyes had a dark, wild look. 'Have you heard? Is that why you came round—to see if I had news?'

'Heard what?' Chloe asked and her heart jumped with fright as she saw his grave expression. 'I haven't heard anything. We've been shopping…'

'And most of this is Sashimi's, of course.' He frowned and then came towards her. Chloe had risen instinctively to her feet. 'I'm sorry, I don't know how to tell you.'

Chloe felt her stomach clench with fear. 'What has happened?' she asked. 'You must tell me, Ahmad, please! Is it Pasha?'

He nodded, his dark eyes intent on her face, their expression frightening her. 'There was an attempt on Prince Hassan's life. Pasha went for the assassin and there was a struggle…' He paused and Chloe's heart took a sickening lurch. 'The gun went off as they fought and…Pasha was injured.'

'No!' Chloe stared at him in shock. Her head was whirling and she felt dizzy. She had been afraid of this, but it was worse than she had feared. It couldn't be happening. Oh, God, please don't let it be happening! Ahmad caught her as she swayed towards him, steadying her. 'Is—is he dead?'

'No, not yet,' Ahmad said and his voice caught with emotion. 'I am so terribly sorry, Chloe.'

'Where is he?' she asked. 'Is he still in Paris?'

'Yes.' Ahmad looked at her sadly. 'I am not sure if we could get there in time…'

Chloe grasped frantically at the straw he was offering her. 'Will you take me to him?' she asked, her eyes wide and dark with fear. 'Will you help me, Ahmad? I must see him. I must…' Her voice caught on a sob.

He seemed to hesitate for a moment, then inclined his head in assent. 'You must leave everything to me. There is no time to return to your apartment, Chloe. We must leave immediately. Sashimi will stay here to arrange for some of your things to be packed.'

Sashimi had come out of her bedroom, having changed her dress. She stood watching them in silence, and then, at a look from her husband, came forward.

'You must go, Chloe,' she urged. 'Don't worry about anything. Give me the key to your apartment. I shall pack a few things for you and follow as soon as I can.'

'Oh, yes…thank you,' Chloe said gratefully. She recalled that Sashimi had been going to tell her something, but that must be forgotten for the moment. Nothing mattered now but that she should reach Pasha in time…in time for what? To say goodbye? Her heart twisted with pain as she took her key from her bag and gave it to Sashimi. 'Could you telephone Justine for me, please? Her number is in the book on the hall table and perhaps you should also let Sir Henry know that…' Her voice broke on a sob. She wanted… needed to see Pasha. Her heart felt as if it were being torn in two.

Oh, God! Why hadn't she told him she loved him before he left for Paris? Perhaps then he would not have been so reckless.

She turned to Ahmad, catching at the lapels of his suit wildly. 'We must leave at once.'

'My car and driver are waiting outside.' Ahmad glanced at his wife. 'You know what to do?'

Chloe was too distraught to notice the further look that passed between them. She could think of nothing but Pasha lying wounded in a French hospital. Ahmad seemed to think that he was dying, but she was praying as she allowed him to hurry her downstairs and out into the waiting car. She was a little surprised when he got into the back of the car with her, but then he reached for her hand and gave it a comforting squeeze.

'I have a plane standing by at a private airfield, Chloe. We shall be there as soon as it is possible. You mustn't despair. Everything is being done for Pasha that can be done. I am sure that we shall get there in time.'

Chloe was pathetically grateful for his kindness. She did not know what she would have done if he had not been in London, how she would have coped with getting a flight to Paris alone.

'You are so good to help me.'

'It was written,' he said, a slightly odd note in his voice. 'Your arrival at my house that day was meant for a purpose, Chloe. All things are as Allah wills them.'

Chloe had closed her eyes. She did not see the fanatical gleam in his own.

Pasha walked into his apartment that evening, sensing already that it was empty. He frowned as he felt a sharp jolt of disappointment. Why should he have expected Chloe to be here waiting for him? She'd made it plain she didn't want to be around him. It wasn't likely that she would welcome him home or fling herself into his arms. Especially when he told her what had happened in Paris. Besides, he had telephoned her earlier to tell her he was flying back, and got no reply.

She wouldn't have broken her promise to stay with him until after the child was born, would she? The pain of that possibility hit him like a hammer blow as he went into her bedroom and glanced round. He saw at once that some of her things were missing.

The wardrobe door was open, and there were several articles on the floor, lying in a heap as if they had been dropped carelessly. Chloe had obviously been in a hurry to leave. Had she guessed somehow that he was on his way back, and decided to go before he could stop her? His heart caught with grief as he saw her key to the apartment tossed carelessly on the dressing table.

She had left him! She had waited until Mariam's visit was over, and then she'd run away from him. He felt as if someone had plunged a knife into him, and it was all he could do to stop himself crying out his agony aloud.

Why had she broken her promise? What had made her run off like this after she had given her word that she would not? Was it that kiss? Did she hate him so much that she would do anything to be free?

Pasha's mind was in turmoil as he heard the doorbell peal several times. He felt a surge of hope. Perhaps Chloe hadn't left him, perhaps she had merely forgotten her key?

He went to the door and wrenched it open, then

stared blankly at the young woman who stood there. She recovered the power of speech before he did.

'You're him, aren't you?' she said. 'Chloe showed me your photograph—and I tipped a drink over you on the ship at Southampton. I was so embarrassed that I didn't really see you then, but I would know you from your photo. Is Chloe here? Has she forgotten that we were going to the pictures this evening?'

'You are Justine,' Pasha said. 'Chloe has often spoken of you as her closest friend. Would you come in for a moment? I've been away for a few days and Chloe isn't here.'

Justine followed him inside. 'I am sure our arrangement was for this evening,' she said with a little frown. 'Mariam was leaving this morning and Chloe asked me to come over, but I had engagements all day…'

'Yes, that's right, Mariam left this morning. I have spoken to her on the telephone in Paris this afternoon,' Pasha said looking thoughtful. 'I cannot understand it. Some of Chloe's things are missing. She didn't say she was going somewhere?'

'No. And it isn't like her not to ring if she was unexpectedly called away,' Justine said. 'She wanted to see the film as much as I did.' She looked at him thoughtfully. 'Would she have gone to see her father?'

'I don't think so,' Pasha replied. 'But she might have gone to stay with Henry. Yes, that is a possibility. Will you excuse me a moment while I telephone?'

Justine nodded agreement. She wandered into the bedroom she knew Chloe used, looking round in surprise. Chloe must have departed in a hurry to leave things in a mess like this—and what was that smell? She had never known Chloe to use a heavy musky perfume like that; it just wasn't her.

She went back into the sitting room as Pasha was replacing the receiver. He was frowning, looking anxious.

'No luck?'

'Henry says she was talking to him earlier. She told him she would ask me to take her down there as soon as I got back.'

'It seems a bit odd,' Justine said and wrinkled her brow. 'This isn't like Chloe. She's usually tidy, and she wouldn't let me down without a good reason. That room looks as if a bomb hit it, and that perfume…it isn't Chloe's. Unless you gave her something exotic.'

'Perfume?' Pasha stared at her for a moment, then went back into Chloe's room. He had been so disturbed by the state of it that he hadn't noticed the first time. Now he could smell it clearly and he knew it at once. 'Sashimi has been here…and recently.'

Justine nodded. 'That's what I thought. I noticed it particularly when we met here a few days ago. I found it too strong. I wouldn't mind betting that Sashimi did this.'

'But why—and where is Chloe? Why hasn't anyone left me a note?' Pasha was thoughtful. 'Do you think she went to stay with Sashimi?'

'Not without ringing me to explain,' Justine said. She hesitated uncomfortably. 'I am sorry if you don't like this, but I warned Chloe to be careful of your cousin. I didn't like the way he looked at her, and I didn't particularly trust him either.'

'What do you mean?' Pasha's eyes were suddenly

narrowed and intent. 'How did he look at Chloe? You must tell me, this could be important, more important than you imagine.'

'It was sort of a leer…and speculation too, as if he were wondering what she would be like in bed.' Justine's cheeks went bright red. 'Oh, that sounds awful. Mummy would be absolutely furious if she heard me. Perhaps I shouldn't have said?'

'I am very glad you did,' he said. 'Thank you, Justine. You've been a big help to me—more so than you may guess.'

'Has something happened?' Justine asked, looking anxious. 'I know it sounds as if I'm letting my imagination run away with me. Chloe would probably say I watch too many romantic films…but I think she may have been abducted.'

'Yes, I'm very much afraid you may be right,' Pasha said and a nerve flicked in his cheek. 'I was aware that I had an enemy—one that I did not know, working in the shadows, but I was looking in the wrong direction. I learned that in Paris earlier today.' He smiled grimly. 'Thank you, Justine. I think you may have saved me a lot of wasted time and anguish.'

'What are you going to do?'

Pasha's eyes were icy cold as he looked at her. 'I'm going to pay Sashimi a little visit.'

'Do you know where to find her?'

'I have a good idea,' Pasha said. 'But if I don't find her this evening, I have a head start on them.'

Chloe was getting restless. They seemed to have been driving for ages. When would they get to the airport? She peered out of the car window into the darkness. They had left London more than an hour ago—how much longer could it take?

'How much further?' she asked. 'Surely we have travelled too far? We could have got to an airport in London much quicker.'

'This is a private airfield. It will be better this way.'

'But why?' Chloe glanced at his profile in the growing dusk, feeling a prickling sensation start at the nape of her neck. Something was wrong. She was suddenly sure that she had been tricked into coming with him. 'Where are you taking me? We aren't going to Paris, are we?'

'We shall be there soon. Pasha is waiting for you.'

'No,' she said, a new decisive tone in her voice. 'I don't believe you. You lied to me, didn't you?'

Ahmad turned to look at her, an unpleasant smile on his lips.

'It was much easier than I anticipated. Sashimi said you would suspect something was wrong immediately. She didn't want to help me, but I bribed her. My wife is addicted to spending money, Chloe. I threatened to close her accounts...that soon brought her to heel.'

Chloe felt chilled as she heard the menace in his voice. So many things were beginning to make sense now. Sashimi was desperately unhappy—that was probably why she spent so much money. And that last shopping spree had been defiant, as if she were buying things she did not want simply to punish her husband.

'Why have you abducted me?' Chloe asked. Surprisingly, she was more angry than frightened as she accepted what had happened to her. Her mind was working busily as she tried to make sense of all this. 'It's to get back at Pasha for something, isn't it?'

'Keep your mouth shut, woman,' he muttered fiercely. 'What I do is my business. I do not discuss it with a woman—any woman.'

Chloe refused to be cowed by his bullying. 'Pasha hasn't been injured, has he? You were lying to me.'

Ahmad glared at her but said nothing.

'And there wasn't an assassination attempt.'

Ahmad's hand shot out, grabbing her by the throat. 'Still your tongue! You tempt me to kill you, but it may be necessary to keep you alive for long enough to lure that traitor Pasha to his death.'

'Pasha is not a traitor!' she said, choking a little as he relaxed his hold and thrust her back into the seat.

'He has betrayed his ancestors by becoming a Christian,' Ahmad said, his face twisted with hatred. 'He makes a mockery of all that he once held sacred and for that he must die. I tried to tell my uncle that he shamed our family, that he was less than the dust beneath his feet and unworthy of favour, but still he prefers Pasha. He will make him his heir and so they both must die.'

'You want the land Pasha inherited?'

'I want it all—the money and the power.' Ahmad looked at her, eyes narrowed. 'Pasha is a fool. He would give it all away.'

'So you plan to kill him.' Chloe said. 'You are in league with Abdullah.'

'Abdullah is dead,' Ahmad said. 'He was a fool. He let hatred rule him, and became careless. He tried to kill the prince and failed. And Pasha killed him. It was true that they wrestled for the gun, but it was Abdullah who died.'

'Oh.' Chloe felt slightly sick as she listened to him spew out his bitter words. It was all so hateful…the killing and the greed that had led to it.

'Pasha is too clever, or perhaps he has been lucky. Three times I have tried to have him killed so that I could take his place as our uncle's heir…and three times he escaped.'

'That was you!' Chloe opened her eyes and gazed at him in horror. 'Pasha thought—'

'That it was Abdullah, of course. I planned it that way, fed the poison into his mind so that he would believe it was the same man who had killed his father.' He smiled horribly. 'As soon as I saw the way Pasha looked at you I knew I had found the key. You are his weakness.' He traced the line of her cheek with his fingertip, making Chloe draw away in disgust. 'Oh, yes, he will walk into my little trap now that I have you. Once before I believed I held him in the palm of my hand, but Lysette was a fool.'

'You were the one who shamed her! It was your child she was carrying…' Chloe felt the horror trickle through her.

Mariam had been right! Chloe was careful not to blurt out her thoughts. This man was ruthless, and Mariam was ill and vulnerable. If he knew she suspected him…a shiver ran through Chloe as she imagined what he might do to anyone who stood in his way. She glanced at his profile, realising that this man was truly evil.

She had thought Pasha ruthless to order the execution of his father's murderer, but now she knew for certain that she had been wrong. Pasha had done what he thought was just in order to save more lives, and it had not been easy for him. She remembered the night he had tossed so restlessly in their bed, and began to understand what it must have cost him. This man would kill without compunction—he would kill for pleasure and greed.

How could she have said such terrible things to Pasha?

She knew now that he had been justified in ordering the arrest and execution of Abdullah. Men like that would stop at nothing to destroy anyone who stood in their way.

Ahmad had been planning to use her against Pasha ever since he realised that she was important to his cousin. He had forced his wife to do as he instructed, using her to lure Chloe back to their apartment that afternoon.

Chloe felt sick inside as she understood that she would be instrumental in bringing about Pasha's death. They had tried to kill him three times without success, but they would succeed this time, because he would come for her.

Chloe knew without the shadow of a doubt that Pasha would give his life for hers. They had only to offer a trade and he would come willingly to the slaughter. He would do whatever they demanded to save her and the child she carried.

But he mustn't. He mustn't! Chloe closed her eyes to hold back the tears that threatened to overcome her.

She wasn't worthy of his sacrifice. She had turned from him, doubted him—and she loved him. She did not want to live if he died trying to save her.

Sashimi opened the door of the apartment and looked at Pasha. He could see the mountains of luggage waiting in the hall, and knew that he had been right in assuming that it would take her a while to pack her things. She would never leave without her belongings.

She gave him a sullen stare, and there was a flicker of malicious pleasure in her eyes. 'I knew you would come,' she said. 'Ahmad thought he was so clever. He thought you would believe that Chloe had left you, and that we should have her safely hidden where you would never think of looking, but I knew you would work it out.'

'You went to my apartment to collect her things.' Pasha frowned. 'Where has he taken her, Sashimi?'

'To a house in the country,' she said. 'He will wait there until I come. He wouldn't leave without me. He's afraid that I might run away from him.'

'Why don't you?'

Sashimi rolled up the sleeve of her expensive dress, showing him the dark bruises on her arm.

'That was just to persuade me to help him,' she said. 'Can you imagine what he would do if I really defied him?'

Pasha frowned as he saw the marks, a sense of revulsion filling him as he realised what his cousin was capable of. 'I had no idea he did this to you. Why do you put up with it? You could go to your father. He is powerful enough to protect you.'

Sashimi's eyes filled with tears. 'My father would send me back to my husband. A husband is allowed to chastise his wife if she is wilful. I have always been wilful. My father spoiled me and he did not choose to beat me, but he would accept that it was Ahmad's right.'

Pasha knew that it was true. He looked at her gravely.

'I would have helped you had you told me.'

'It was not so bad until recently,' Sashimi said. 'Sometimes he spoils me. I loved him when we married, but I did not know him. There is a devil in him, Pasha. He is capable of such evil.'

'I am sorry,' Pasha said, but her words made him anxious for Chloe. 'I must find my wife. Help me now and I promise you will never have to go back to him. I have influence with the prince, and he will tell your father that you are to be taken back and never given to your husband. I must stop him leaving the country with Chloe. It is my only chance.'

'He will keep her alive until he is sure of you,' Sashimi said. 'I told him he should leave England at once, but he would not listen to me. I am merely a woman and cannot know these things.' Her eyes flamed with sudden anger. 'I hope you kill him, Pasha.'

'He will be brought to justice. I promise you that.'

Sashimi nodded, her lovely face harsh. 'He deserves to die. He does not know that I know...but he ruined Lysette. It was his child she was carrying when she crashed her car.'

'What?' Pasha's eyes narrowed. 'How do you know that?'

'I found a letter amongst his things. She had written to him, begging him to marry her and save her from her shame. She was distraught and terrified of telling you. She thought you would do something terrible to Ahmad when you discovered what he had done.'

'I might have killed him had I known then,' Pasha said, his eyes dark with remembered grief.

'I wish you had!'

'Will you take me to this house, Sashimi?'

'You promise that you will protect me? He would kill me if he knew I had betrayed him like this.'

'You have my word.'

Sashimi inclined her head. 'He will kill me anyway one day,' she said. 'I want you to punish him, Pasha—for Lysette and for me.'

Chapter Eleven

They had been driving along an isolated country road for some time when the car finally drew into the gateway of a house. Set back in some trees, it was difficult to see from the road, and Chloe felt the despair wash over her as Ahmad opened the car door and dragged her out. Once they had her prisoner in that house, she would never be able to escape.

She put up a struggle as he hustled her towards the house, kicking and scratching, scratching his cheek enough to draw blood, and biting at him like a wild thing. Then she sensed that someone else was near, and realised it was the man who had driven the car.

'Help me subdue the cat,' Ahmad said, and Chloe felt a pad of some kind put over her face. The strong smell of chloroform choked her and she felt herself swaying as she lost consciousness.

'She is a wild one,' Ahmad said to his companion as he caught her and carried her into the house. 'I would strangle her and have done with it, but Pasha may demand to speak to her before he comes near.' He glared at the other man, feeling the sting of torn flesh where her nails had scored his cheek. 'Give me a hand with her. The sooner she's locked away the better.'

They carried her upstairs and dumped her on a bed. Ahmad stared down at her for a moment before turning away. He might enjoy teaching that little she-devil a lesson before he finally disposed of her, but his main objective was to get Pasha where he could finally destroy him.

He glanced at his watch as he went back downstairs. How long before Sashimi arrived? His wife was becoming too sulky and wilful for his liking, and he might just take his bad temper out on her...

Sashimi glanced at the stern profile of the man driving the car. She hoped she hadn't chosen the wrong side, because Ahmad was going to make her pay if he came out of this on top, but she was determined that she wasn't going back to him whatever happened.

She had already begun to fear his moods when she discovered that letter from Lysette. Some little devil inside her had provoked her into confronting him with it, and that had been her mistake. He had really hurt her that time, and though he had afterwards apologised and promised that it wouldn't happen again, it had. She knew that he would continue to beat her whenever it pleased him, and there was little she could do about it. Her father might try to remonstrate with Ahmad if she complained to him, but he would insist that she return to her husband, unless Pasha supported her.

Supposing Ahmad killed his cousin? Sashimi knew that it was what he hoped to achieve. The black hatred and jealousy had eaten into his soul, and he had destroyed a young woman in the hope of also destroying his cousin, but he had wanted Pasha to go after him so that he killed in self-defence, because otherwise he would not inherit the prince's wealth.

Looking at Pasha's strong hands on the steering wheel, she knew that he was very angry at what had happened to Chloe. She was sure he would kill Ahmad, and she felt a fierce joy inside her. She would be free at last, free to live her life as she chose.

With the money settled on her when she was married, she could live in Paris and she need never be bound by the restrictions that Ahmad had tried to inflict on her, because she would never ever marry again…

Pasha was aware of Sashimi's eyes on him, though not of her thoughts. He was wondering how far he could trust her. Was her apparent willingness to co-operate a part of his cousin's plan to trap him?

He cursed himself as a fool for not realising before that Ahmad was the traitor they had suspected but had not been able to find. He had taken him at face value, believing he was his friend, confiding in him the plans he had for the future of their people—and all the time Ahmad had been plotting against him.

The attempts on his life…but it was Lysette that mattered, the evil that had been done to her deliberately, and now Chloe. Pasha's hands tightened on the wheel as he wondered what was happening to his wife. If she had been hurt…

Pasha's mind shied away from that avenue of thought. He was not sure what he would do if Ahmad had harmed her, and his guilt at having so carelessly involved her in all this cut at him like a sharp knife.

She was innocent, and unused to dealing with men as ruthless as Ahmad—and himself. He had already shocked her and hurt her and now she had been abducted by a man who would kill her once his purpose was served.

But what might he do to her before he killed her?

Pasha could hardly prevent the groan inside him from breaking free, but he knew he had to hide his feelings as much as he could. He believed that Sashimi was frightened of her husband, and that she wanted to leave him, but would she lose her nerve when the time came?

How could he be certain that she would not simply change sides again at the last minute?

Chloe's head ached when she finally came to herself again, and she leaned over the bed as the vomit rushed up in her throat and she had to spill it out on the floor. She felt awful, her head swimming as she tried to stand, and she was forced to fall back on the bed as the faintness swept over her.

Several minutes passed before she began to feel better at last, and this time when she attempted to stand she discovered that she could without falling. The stench of the vomit was unpleasant, and she wanted to get away from it, to get out of this room.

Walking a little unsteadily to the door, she tried it and discovered that it was locked. Damn! Damn them! After tugging at it uselessly for a moment or two, she looked round the room. It was possible to see because there were no curtains at the windows and it was just beginning to get light.

She saw another door to the right of the bed, and went to investigate, finding that her head was beginning to clear and that she felt better. Opening the door, which gave easily this time, she discovered a bathroom. Feeling grateful for that mercy, she used the toilet and then took a towel and went to clear up the mess she had made.

Chloe sat on the edge of the bed and wondered what to do next. She was clearly on the second floor of the house, and it was unlikely that she could escape through the window—so what was left? It seemed that she had no alternative but to sit and wait for someone to come.

Perhaps an hour passed before she heard footsteps outside her room, and then a key in the lock. The door opened slowly and then the man she recognised as Ahmad's driver entered carrying a tray with what looked like a bowl of fruit and a jug of water, and a bread roll. It seemed that she wasn't to be starved, at least for the time being.

'When are you going to let me out?' she demanded. 'Tell Ahmad I want to see him. I want to be let out of here.'

The man looked at her, seeming not to understand, at least he wasn't going to answer even if he did. He wrinkled his nose at the smell, and after depositing the tray on top a chest of drawers, he went over to the window and opened it a little at the top.

It was a sash window, and stiff, but slid down halfway when he tugged at it hard. Chloe thought that she would not have had the strength to move it and drew a breath of fresh air gratefully.

'Thank you,' she said. 'But please—I must speak to Ahmad.'

'Eat.' He gestured at the tray and then went out

again, locking the door after him. Chloe got up and wandered over to the window. She stared out idly for a moment, then stiffened as she saw that there was a kind of flower box outside the window. It was very narrow and some of the stone looked a bit crumbly, but it had an iron railing above it to make sure that the flower pots did not fall…and there was another one on the next window along.

Supposing she could push the bottom of the sash window up, get out and somehow climb on to the next window box…

A shiver ran through her as she looked down. It was a long way to fall, but Ahmad was going to kill her anyway. She thought that it might be a chance worth taking and struggled to push the top window up again so that she could open the bottom.

She struggled with it for several minutes, but it proved to be too stiff for her and she had to give up. It was probably impossible to open the window next door anyway, she thought.

Feeling hungry, she picked up the roll and an apple and took them back to the bed, sitting on the edge to eat. She had finished about half the apple when she heard someone coming, and then the door was opened and Ahmad stood there looking at her.

'I need you,' he said and walked purposefully towards her. 'It's time.'

'Time for what?' Chloe asked, getting to her feet warily.

'Time to make your loving husband aware of the truth,' Ahmad said, glaring at her. 'He should have spent the night thinking that you had run away from him, and he will be ready to hear from you.'

'What do you mean?'

Chloe hung back as he reached out and grabbed her wrist. She tried to resist as he pulled her with him, but he was too strong for her and she was obliged to go with him as he half-dragged her along the landing and down the stairs.

She hung on to the banister at the bottom, fighting him all the way, but he succeeded in prying her from it and pushed her into a large sitting room. 'Where are we?' she asked. 'Where is Sashimi? I thought she was coming…' She broke off as she saw Ahmad's expression of annoyance. He was clearly furious because Sashimi was not here as he had ordered.

Ahmad pushed her into a chair by the windows, and told her to pick up the receiver of the phone next to her. 'Telephone the apartment,' he said. 'Tell him you are being held prisoner, but that you haven't been harmed yet—and then give it to me.'

'And if I refuse?' Chloe said defiantly. 'You can't make me. I know what you want. You want me to lure him down here so that you can kill him.'

'If you don't, I shall kill you—and him. He will die soon whatever you do,' Ahmad said, pushing his face near hers so that she could smell the sweet oils he used on his hair.

'You are going to kill me anyway.'

'But I can make you suffer,' Ahmad warned. 'Do as I tell you, woman, or you will wish you had.'

'No!' Chloe jumped to her feet and started to dash for the door, but he came after her, grabbing her by the waist and wrestling her to the ground. He lay on top of her, grinning down at her, enjoying his triumph as he looked at her. 'Get off me, you brute.'

'Why?' he asked. 'Maybe I'll just teach you a little lesson while I have you where I want you—'

Chloe brought her knee up sharply, making him jerk back and exclaim with pain. He got off her and she scrambled to her feet, but before he could make another grab at her the door opened and a man came in.

Chloe was only half-aware that someone had entered the room behind her. Her eyes were fixed on Ahmad and she was breathing hard, poised for flight. Somehow she had to get out of this house before he managed to force her to make that phone call…

Suddenly, she realised that Ahmad's manner had changed. His eyes were bulging and he was no longer staring at her but at someone behind her. Whirling round, she gave a cry that was half-fear and half-joy when she saw Pasha standing there.

'Get behind me, Chloe,' Pasha ordered and she saw that he was holding an evil-looking pistol in his hand. 'I have a car waiting in the lane. Try to get there before someone else comes in and stops you.'

'Come with me,' she said. 'He wants to kill you, Pasha. He wants the money and the power that will be yours as the prince's heir.'

'I know what he wants and what he is,' Pasha told her. 'Now do as I say!'

Chloe looked back at Ahmad, and saw that he was sweating. She knew that he was afraid now that Pasha was the one in command. He had been exposed, and he believed that his cousin would kill him, as he deserved.

Chloe swallowed hard. She thought she knew what would happen in this room once she had gone, and she was reluctant to leave.

'Have him arrested, Pasha,' she urged. 'He isn't worth it.'

And then she walked from the room. No one had yet come to investigate what was going on, and she thought that Ahmad's driver was probably expecting to hear screams from her and would not take much notice unless his master shouted for help.

She managed to gain the front door, slipping outside without being caught, and then she began to run down the driveway to the lane outside the grounds where Pasha had told her the car was parked.

Pasha was aware that Chloe was reluctant to leave, but, even though he had already dealt with one man, who was now lying bound and gagged, he was not sure how many might be around and could not risk someone coming in on them in case she got caught in the crossfire.

Ahmad licked his lips nervously as he stared into Pasha's cold eyes. 'Why don't you just do it?' he asked. 'What are you waiting for?'

Pasha wondered why he was waiting. He had intended to shoot first and think about it afterwards, but although his finger hovered on the trigger, he hesitated.

'I'm going to have you arrested,' he replied. 'The prince will have you tried and executed—and that's what you deserve. Shooting is too good for you, Ahmad. After what you did to Lysette and Chloe…'

Ahmad sneered at him. 'Haven't got the guts to pull that trigger, have you? You've gone soft, lost your edge.'

'I'll watch you executed with the greatest of pleasure,' Pasha replied, a slight smile on his mouth. 'Chloe was right. You aren't worth soiling my hands on. I'm going to render you unconscious, then I'll tie you up and deliver you to some friends of the prince's. I dare say they may not be quite as gentle with you, and you may suffer at their hands, but that's their business, not mine.'

'Coward!' Ahmad jeered. He was feeling sick as he thought about what would happen to him if Pasha carried out his threat. He would be beaten and tortured to make him confess, to give up the names of any fellow conspirators, and then he would be beheaded. 'Give me a quick death, Pasha.'

'And have your death on my conscience?' Pasha asked. 'Turn round, Ahmad. I'll make this as quick as possible.'

'No! Please. We can work something out…' Ahmad was beginning to plead. His head turned to one side as someone else came into the room, a glimmer of hope in his eyes. 'Sashimi! Get help for me. He's going to—' He broke off as he saw that she too was holding a tiny pistol in her hand. 'Kill him.'

'Oh, no,' she said. 'It isn't Pasha I am going to kill.' And then without a moment's hesitation, she raised her arm, aimed directly at Ahmad's heart and pressed the trigger.

Ahmad's eyes widened in surprise, and then he clutched at his chest, his knees buckling as he sank to the floor and then fell forward on his face.

'Is he dead?' Sashimi asked coolly as Pasha went to bend over him.

Pasha got to his feet and looked at her. 'What did you think you were doing? I was going to knock him unconscious and hand him over to the prince's men.'

'I know that,' she said. 'I heard everything you were saying. It wasn't enough, Pasha. I had to be sure that he couldn't get away from you.'

'Give me the gun,' Pasha said. He had laid his own down, and was holding out his hand. She hesitated, seeming unsure what to do and he frowned. 'Give it to me, unless you want to be arrested for the murder of your husband?'

Sashimi's face went white. She passed him the gun, her own hand beginning to tremble. 'Are you going to hand me over to the English police?'

'It is what I ought to do,' he said. 'But no, I'm not that cruel, Sashimi. Go back to the car now. Chloe should be waiting there for you. Drive back to London. Go directly to my apartment and wait for me to come before you do anything.'

'What…are you going to do?'

'Take care of things here,' Pasha said. 'You are not to breathe one word of this to Chloe—do you understand me? I will not have her endangered by being involved in this. If you do as I tell you, I shall see that you are looked after. Otherwise…'

Sashimi looked into his cold eyes and shivered. 'Yes,' she said submissively. 'I'm sorry. Not for what I did—he deserved to die—but for causing you trouble.'

'His driver is out cold in the kitchen. We'll see what the power of money can achieve, but I have friends who will tie up any loose ends necessary.'

'Thank you.' Sashimi turned away as he began to move about the room, smashing lamps and china. It was obvious that he was making it look as if there had been a fierce struggle here.

She left him to it and went out, meeting Chloe on her way back to the house.

'Pasha wants us to leave quickly,' she told her.

'I've got to drive you back to London and stay with you until he gets home.'

'Pasha told you that?' Chloe stared at her. 'I heard a shot...'

'It was nothing,' Sashimi said, remembering Pasha's promises and his threats. 'Please, I can't tell you any more.'

'No, I don't suppose you can,' Chloe said and the sickness stirred in her stomach. A part of her wanted to go back into the house and demand to know what was going on. Instead she was tamely allowing herself to be sent off with Sashimi as if she were a parcel. She must be mad to trust either of them! Yet somehow she didn't have the will to fight. At the moment she didn't particularly care what happened to her; she just felt drained and empty, her heart heavy.

Oh, why hadn't Pasha listened to her? Why had he killed Ahmad? It wasn't that his cousin didn't deserve to die, of course he did for all the evil things he had either done or tried to do, but now Pasha had blood on his hands.

'We'd better go then—if it is what Pasha wants.'

Chloe was thoughtful as she went back to the car with Sashimi. At the moment she was still too shocked to feel the pain she knew would come later.

She got into the front seat beside Sashimi, allowing her to drive because it seemed as if that was what she wanted, staring at the road as the other woman steered them out of the isolated country lane and began to make her way back towards the main highway.

What was she going to do now? Chloe was conscious of a kind of despair seeping through her. She had come to terms with the fact that Pasha had been prepared to order the execution of his father's assas-

sin, and that he had killed him in the struggle to protect his uncle—but this, this was too cold-blooded for
her to accept.

Pasha had come prepared to kill his cousin, and he
had done so. It was too horrific for her to contemplate,
and she could only cope by pushing it to the back of
her mind.

She wouldn't think about it yet or she would go to
pieces, and she had to be calm to face Pasha when
he came back. She had to be able to talk to him in a
reasonable manner, and tell him why she was leaving
him.

It was useful to have friends in high places, Pasha
thought as he was flown back to London in a light
aircraft. He hadn't told Forbes the truth of course. His
own gun had been wiped clean of his fingerprints and
was now in Ahmad's hands, complete with his own
prints and Forbes's men were on the scene, clearing
up the mess. Soon it would appear that nothing had
happened in that house.

Pasha grimaced as he recalled the half-lies he had
told to cover what Sashimi had done. He would have
much preferred to carry out his own plans, but Sashimi had had other ideas—and he couldn't allow her
to pay for her folly.

Ahmad must have been a brute to her for her to do
that, Pasha reflected. He had given her his word to
protect her, and he would do it to the best of his
ability. She would be given a new identity, which he
would arrange for her and enough money to live life
as she pleased—and he had a good idea what she
would choose to do.

It wasn't his affair. Pasha shrugged. Once this was

over, he didn't care if he never saw her again. All he wanted from now on was a quiet life with Chloe. But how was she going to feel about that?

He would simply have to persuade her that things would be better in future, tell her of his plans to make sure there were changes.

Pasha frowned. He wondered if Sashimi had kept her word not to tell Chloe anything of what had happened in that house. It was much better if she did not know. He did not want her involved in this nastiness any more than she had been already.

His face was grim as he recalled the scene he had interrupted. Had Sashimi not helped him to find her...he had little doubt in his mind that his cousin would have raped her. Ahmad had clearly enjoyed humiliating women.

For a moment Pasha's thoughts went to Lysette. He had been on completely the wrong track there, blaming that film director for what had happened to his half-sister. Now he knew that it was Ahmad, and he tasted bitter gall in his mouth, as he understood exactly why she had been used in that way.

Ahmad had wanted to humiliate him. He had not cared that he was hurting an innocent girl in the process. So Lysette had died because she loved him, Pasha.

She had been afraid of seeing disgust or perhaps disappointment in his eyes, and he knew that had she told him he might not have been able to disguise the way he felt. When he'd had time to come to terms with it, he would of course have done everything he could to help her—he might even have forced Ahmad to marry her. What a disaster that would have been!

Pasha's brow wrinkled as he realised he must have

been at fault in his past behaviour towards Lysette. If she had chosen to die rather than tell him the truth…

Was he such an ogre? Was that why Chloe was so desperate to leave him—because he frightened her?

Pasha's thoughts were blacker than the heavens as the storm began just as they touched down at the airport in London. He ran towards the waiting car, thinking with irony that it was his relationship with the prince that had given him these privileges…privileges that had to be paid for. Sometimes the price was very high, perhaps too high.

Pasha had never used those special privileges for himself before, but he had been forced to do so this time and he found that they left a bad taste in his mouth.

Was this really the kind of life he wanted to live?

Ahmad was dead, but that didn't mean it was all over. There were others who would not balk at using him or Chloe to get their own way, and it would go on.

He couldn't allow that to happen! Pasha's expression darkened as he remembered what had so nearly occurred. Next time he might not arrive in time.

Chloe had to be safeguarded in future. He wasn't sure how he was going to make certain that she wouldn't have to go through the same thing again, but he would find a way. Even if it meant…

Pasha's thoughts veered away from that avenue. He couldn't give her up…he couldn't. And yet he might have to.

The hours passed so slowly. Since they'd arrived back at the apartment, Sashimi appeared to have gone into a kind of trance. Chloe wasn't sure how the other woman had managed to drive them back to London, but having done so she appeared to have abandoned all responsibility. She was just sitting in one of the armchairs, staring into space, not even answering when Chloe spoke to her.

Chloe made coffee. It was hot and strong, and she placed a cup on the little table beside Sashimi, but she ignored it.

'What are we going to do?' Chloe asked. 'Did Pasha say how long he would be?'

Sashimi shook her head. It was as if she were beyond speech, in a state of shock—as well she might be if she had seen her husband shot down in front of her.

'I'm sorry about what happened,' she began.

'I'm not,' Sashimi said. 'I'm glad he's dead.'

She got to her feet as if Chloe's words had brought her to her senses. 'I need to use the bathroom. Excuse me.'

Chloe watched as she walked away. She drank some of her own coffee, but couldn't relax, and got up to pace about the room. Where was Pasha? What was he doing? Would he be in trouble with the police for what he had done?

Chloe felt her stomach clench with nerves. Pasha might be able to get away with this sort of thing abroad, but in England things were different, weren't they?

Supposing he was arrested for murder? Would they hang him?

She felt a pain around her heart and clutched at herself fearfully, wrapping her arms about her chest protectively. She couldn't bear it if that happened.

She loved him…and yet what he had done filled her with horror.

She couldn't bear to think about it. How long before…? Oh, God, she couldn't stand this. She wished that she had refused to leave when Pasha bid her. She couldn't stay here a moment longer. Surely there was something she could do? She stiffened as she heard a key in the lock and then Pasha came in. He was soaked through, and for the first time she realised it was raining heavily outside.

'You are wet,' she said. 'I hadn't realised…'

'The storm broke just as we landed,' he replied, looking at her. She was unnaturally calm, and he thought she must still be in shock. 'I am very sorry for what happened, Chloe. It was my fault for leaving you unprotected like that.'

'You couldn't have known,' Chloe said, licking her lips nervously. She wanted to run to him, to throw herself into his arms and be kissed, but something held her back. Perhaps it was a look in his eyes, or it might have been her own thoughts…the picture of a man lying bleeding, shot in cold blood, that kept coming into her head even though she was trying desperately to block it out. 'Besides, I ought to have been more careful. Justine warned me about Ahmad. I thought it was just her imagination, but she was right.'

'It's thanks to Justine that I caught Sashimi before she left,' Pasha said. He walked across to the sideboard and poured himself a glass of spirits. It was very seldom that he drank anything stronger than wine, but this was a case of need. He was glad to see that his hand did not shake as he poured some of the amber liquid into a glass and sipped it, then tossed the contents back in one go. 'Had I wasted the night wondering where you had gone…'

'I suppose they made it look as if I had left you,' Chloe said. 'Did Sashimi agree to help you or did you—?' She broke off as she saw the blaze in his eyes. 'I mean…'

'I know exactly what you mean,' Pasha said, and a little nerve flicked in his cheek. 'As it happens bribery was enough, but I dare say I might have used force if it was necessary.'

'Oh.' Chloe turned away from him. Why was he looking at her like that, as if she were the one who had something to answer? 'I thought she might have been willing. I believe Ahmad was violent towards her.'

'She showed me the bruises to prove it,' Pasha said. 'I had no idea. If she had told me…'

'Did she tell you about Lysette?'

Pasha inclined his head. 'Yes. Did she tell you or was it…?'

'He told me when I began to realise that he wasn't taking me to the airport. He tricked me, Pasha. He told me that you were dying. I practically begged him to abduct me like the fool I was.'

'How could you have guessed what he was planning?' Pasha frowned at her. Did this mean that she had wanted to see him when she thought he was at death's door? Hope flickered somewhere deep within him.

'I didn't even think twice,' Chloe said. 'I was desperate to see you, to tell you…' The words died on her lips. She had wanted to tell him that she loved him, that she would live with him as his wife again— but how could she say that now?

'What did you want to tell me?' Pasha's eyes narrowed as she shook her head. 'What is the matter, Chloe? Are you thinking that you can't live with a murderer? Because that's what you believe I am, isn't it?'

'I know you had good reason to kill him,' Chloe said slowly, her mouth dry and her stomach tying itself in knots as she stared at him. 'But why wouldn't you listen to me? Why couldn't you just have handed him over to the police?'

'Would that have made a difference?' he asked, wondering why he didn't just tell her the truth. Yet something inside him refused to yield. 'You had already made up your mind about me, hadn't you?'

'Don't look at me like that,' Chloe begged. 'I know that I said terrible things to you—but it was such a shock. It took me a while to come to terms with what you had done—'

'Planned to do,' Pasha told her, his face hard. 'Abdullah got away from my men and went to Paris as I told you. He tried to assassinate the prince but I was mingling with the crowd and he didn't see me. I wrestled with him, Chloe, and the gun went off. He was killed almost instantly.' His eyes flickered with some emotion she could not fathom. 'So I must be a murderer in your eyes already. What difference does one more death make?'

'That was an accident…self-defence,' Chloe cried, her voice rising. 'It makes a world of difference, you must see that, Pasha? What you did was brave and saved your uncle's life. I could never condemn you for that!'

He bowed his head to her, a sneer on his mouth. 'I thank you for those kind words, Chloe. How nice that you are prepared to accept that kind of killing…and what a pity that Ahmad's death cannot be put down to self-defence. Although it will be, of course. Ahmad, it may surprise you to know, was killed by political terrorists, unknown persons whom the English authorities will never be able to trace.'

'Is that why you stayed behind—to arrange it?' Chloe stared at him, feeling relief as well as disappointment. She was glad he was not in danger and yet somehow what he had done seemed to make it even worse. 'Well, at least I shan't have to worry that they will hang you.'

'Oh, no, I don't think you have to bother about that,' Pasha replied, his voice as cold as ice. 'As far as the British are concerned I've simply got rid of one more problem, one more fanatic who would have made trouble for them in the future.'

'Is that how things work?' Chloe was horrified. 'I suppose I should be glad that you have friends in high places.'

'They come in useful at times.'

There was a glint in his eyes that told Chloe he was goading her. Why? Why was he trying to make things worse between them? If he had shown some remorse perhaps…but, no, it was his pride again. His pride had made him fling the truth at her once before, and now it was making him taunt her.

She didn't know him in this mood at all, and she felt a desperate urge to be free of him. 'You know I'm going to leave you after this, don't you?' she said. 'Henry wants me to stay with him, and I think I shall—at least until after the baby is born.'

'Yes, I think that is a very good idea,' Pasha said. 'You will be as safe there as anywhere while I make certain arrangements. This isn't quite over yet, Chloe. Ahmad wasn't the only one who would like to see the prince pulled down.'

'You are agreeing to my staying with Henry?' Chloe was puzzled as she stared at him. Why was he giving in so tamely? 'For a few months—or are you agreeing to let me go?'

'I think it's probably best we part,' Pasha said, his expression telling her nothing. 'Given the way you feel about me, there is really little point in my trying to keep you with me.'

'I love you,' Chloe said, her throat closing with emotion. 'It's just that I can't stand the thought—'

'Why don't you tell her the truth?'

Sashimi's voice came from behind them, making Chloe turn to look at her in surprise.

'I told you to keep quiet,' Pasha warned.

'Why?' Sashimi was smoking a Turkish cigarette, which she had taken from his bedroom. 'You have set me free, Pasha, and I don't ever intend to be told what to do by a man again. I know you can take away your promise to give me money, but Ahmad's money will come to me, because my father saw to that when we married.'

'Sashimi, please…'

Sashimi blew a smoke ring into the air. 'I'm sorry, Pasha, but I think your wife has a right to be told the truth.' She directed her clear gaze at Chloe. 'I can't see why you should care what happened. Ahmad deserved to die for what he did to others, but it wasn't Pasha who fired the shot that killed him.'

'It wasn't Pasha…' Chloe's eyes narrowed as she looked at her. 'Then who…?' Her words died away as she suddenly knew. 'It was you! You killed him!'

'Yes.' Sashimi smiled, apparently unmoved by what she'd done. 'I fired that shot, Chloe. Pasha told me not to tell you, but it doesn't matter now. He has arranged it all nicely, and I've got away with it—so why should I care? Ahmad is dead. I killed him and I'm glad. I told you that you came to us for a purpose, didn't I, Chloe?'

Chloe stared at her as she walked towards the door. How could she kill her husband and show no emotion? She must surely feel it inside!

'Where are you going?' Pasha asked.

'I'm going back to my apartment to pick up the bags you made me leave behind,' she said, 'and then I intend to fly to Paris later this afternoon.'

'The English police may want to question you.'

'Oh, no, I don't think so,' she said. 'I shall be informed of my husband's tragic death, and I shall play the grieving widow to perfection—and then I shall enjoy spending his money.'

Chloe was silent as the door closed behind her, and then she turned to Pasha, swallowing hard.

'I am sorry…sorry I misjudged you.'

'Are you?' He raised his brows and she sensed his anger. It was a deep, cold anger that chilled her to the bone. 'How kind of you to say so, Chloe.'

She was trembling inside, but tried not to let it show. 'Please, Pasha. I know you are angry, but this makes a difference.'

'Does it?' He stared at her and then went over to the drinks tray to replace his empty glass. 'I am tempted to get drunk, but that is so uncivilised, isn't it, Chloe? I am pleased that it makes a difference for you but, you see, it does not for me.'

'What do you mean?' she asked, her heart racing

as he turned to look at her. His expression was so
cold, so harsh, that she felt as if a knife had been
plunged into her heart.

'It means that our marriage is over,' Pasha replied.
'I think that we have said all we have to say to one
another, Chloe. I must apologise for what happened
to you. That was my fault, and I freely admit it. I
should never have married you. I see that now.'

'No! It wasn't your fault!' she cried. 'Please
doesn't be like this, Pasha. Don't hate me.'

'Should I love you?' he asked in a soft tone that
sent shivers through her. 'But you know what that
means, Chloe. It means that you would belong to me
totally and just because Sashimi killed Ahmad before
I could doesn't mean that I won't kill in the future,
does it? I think you should take this chance while you
have it, my dear. Besides, I find that I am no longer
interested.'

Chloe watched as he walked away from her, going
into his bedroom and locking the door. The sound of
his key turning in the lock was like a death knell in
her heart.

She had killed any feeling he'd had for her. It was
over and she had no one to blame but herself...

Chapter Twelve

Pasha insisted on driving Chloe down to the country the next morning. After spending a sleepless night, she had packed her cases, presenting him with a pile of luggage in the hall. He accepted her decision to leave at once without a flicker of emotion.

She had told him that she would be perfectly happy to go on the train, but he would not allow it.

'I can get a taxi from the station. There is really no need for you to come all that way, Pasha.'

'You are still my wife, Chloe, even though we may both wish that was not the case. While you remain so, I shall take care of you and the child.'

Chloe glanced at him and then away quickly. What did he mean? She had thought that their marriage was over and that surely meant a divorce, didn't it? She wasn't sure how she felt about that or anything, the ache in her breast blotting out everything but the desire to weep. However, she was determined not to let him see how miserable she was.

Pasha hardly spoke to her during the journey, other than to make sure she was comfortable. She wondered what Henry would make of this silence between them,

but when they arrived to be greeted with warm smiles
and hugs from Henry's sister Dora, she discovered
that he was as charming as always.

'Oh, but she is lovely,' Dora cried as she put her
arm about Chloe's waist. 'Absolutely lovely. You are
a very lucky man, Pasha, and I hope you appreciate
it.' Her brown eyes twinkled merrily at him. 'And I
am glad to see that you have come for a long stay,
my dear.'

'I am going to be travelling with the prince for a
while,' Pasha said smoothly, leaving Chloe with nothing to say. 'Chloe wanted to come here, and I thought
it was a good idea for you all to get to know one
another. You can blacken my name at your leisure
now, darling Dora.'

'Oh, you wicked boy!' Dora gave him an indulgent
look. He was clearly a favourite with her, and he was
fond of her. 'As if I should do any such thing. Besides, Chloe is far too sensible to listen!'

Of course, that was why he was so easy now that
he was with people he cared about, Chloe thought.
Her husband was such a complex character, and she
was still a long way from knowing him, but she did
know that he had a devil that drove him at times.

He had deliberately provoked her into quarrelling
with him. It was cruel the way he had allowed her to
believe that he had killed Ahmad in cold blood, when
all he had really done was to cover up Sashimi's
crime. That was wrong in itself, Chloe supposed, but
having had some hours to think about it, she realised
that she ought not to have expected anything less of
Pasha. He knew that her husband had mistreated Sashimi, and he had wanted to protect her from the consequences of her actions.

But what was the alternative after all? Would Chloe really have wanted her to be arrested and tried for the murder of her husband, knowing that the punishment would be severe? Asked honestly, the truthful answer was that, although it was morally wrong of Pasha to do what he had, it had been merciful.

Ahmad was a wife beater, and he had seduced Lysette in order to bring shame on her so that she would lure Pasha into a trap. Quite what he had expected to happen she was not sure, but she imagined that Ahmad had hoped to make Pasha so angry that he came after him in a rage. He would then seem to be the aggressor and it would appear that his death had been brought about through his own rash behaviour. It was the act of an evil, vengeful man.

She couldn't really regret what had happened to Ahmad, although it would have been better had Pasha managed to bring him to justice, as she realised now he had probably intended. Had he wanted Ahmad dead, he could have killed him almost immediately.

She had jumped to conclusions because of what he had told her that night in the gardens in Spain, and now she must pay the consequences. Pasha no longer loved or wanted her—and why should he since she had shown herself unworthy?

She had told him that she loved him, had told herself that she loved him, and yet she had not been willing to trust him. What kind of love was that? She was little better than her own father, who had been prepared to grant his love as a reward to a dutiful daughter—and to take it away when she refused to obey him.

Chloe had decided that she would never try to see her father again after he had thrown them out of his house. She had felt hurt and a little bitter that he could behave so unkindly to her, but had she behaved any better towards her husband? A man who had only ever shown her love and kindness.

Chloe was reflective as she watched her husband with his relations, saw their respect and deep affection for him, and his for them. What kind of a fool was she that she hadn't realised his true nature before?

Yes, he might be severe at times, but he was honest and everything he did was well considered and judged. She was the one who had been naïve and foolish to imagine that ruthless men could always be contained by what she thought of as justice. Was she then a child that saw everything as black and white, good or bad? Life could never be that simple, surely? She saw now that there were times when perhaps, however regrettable, the taking of a life saved others.

Chloe had learned a lot very quickly since that nightmare journey with Ahmad, and she wished desperately that she could go back and begin again, that she could have Pasha the way he had been when they were in Spain together. She thought longingly of the way he had spoiled and teased her, and regretted all that she had lost.

But it was too late, much too late. She knew that it was too late when she looked into his eyes, and read the hurt there, saw the reserve that he now had towards her and her heart ached.

She would have to learn to live with what she had lost somehow—but at least she would have his child.

'Please take care of yourself,' Pasha said to her before he left that evening. He had decided against staying with them overnight despite all that his grandfather could say to try and persuade him. 'I am not sure what the future will bring for either of us at this moment, Chloe—but we both need time to think about things. I may be away some months, but I hope to be here when the child is born.'

Chloe dared not look at him as she said, 'Do you want a divorce, Pasha?'

'Not particularly,' he replied, sounding indifferent. 'But if you feel that you wish to marry again, perhaps we may arrange something.'

'No!' she said quickly, perhaps a little too quickly because it made Pasha stare at her oddly. 'No. I have no wish to marry again. I thought you might wish to. Especially if my child happens to be a girl...'

'You think that I wish for a son and heir to inherit the land I had from my father?' A wry smiled touched his mouth. 'Believe me, Chloe. I would not wish to inflict that on your son.'

'What do you mean?' she asked uncertainly.

'Think about it,' he said. 'We shall discuss this again when I return.'

Chloe watched from a landing window as he left, her heart aching. She didn't want him to leave; she wanted him to stay with her and be safe, but she knew she had forfeited the right to ask him to give up that other part of his life—a part of his life she now realised had been a burden to him.

She turned away as his car disappeared out of sight, lifting her head as she went downstairs to sit with Dora and Henry for the rest of the evening. Her life was here with them now, and she must learn to live with this ache in her heart. Pasha had gone and she did not know if he would ever return to her.

* * *

Life was calm and uneventful at Henry's country house. Both he and Dora were kind, comfortable companions, the pace of their existence slow and steady. It was exactly the calm atmosphere she needed to wait for the birth of her child, but Chloe missed her husband unbearably. Always, he had seemed to bring excitement into her life, making her pulses race just by the touch of his hand or a smile.

'It is such a shame that Pasha has so many official duties,' Dora said to her as they were picking deep red chrysanthemums in the garden one autumn afternoon. 'I often think that it would be much better if he did not feel he owed a duty to the prince.'

'Yes,' Chloe agreed wholeheartedly. 'Much better.' She looked at the basket of flowers on her arm. 'Do you think we have enough of these?'

'Oh, no, we might as well pick them all,' Dora said. 'It will make a nice splash of colour all over the house and they will only die once we get the heavy frosts.' She shivered in the chill wind and looked up at the sky, in which storm clouds seemed to be gathering. There was a definite bite in the wind that afternoon as winter threatened 'I wonder how Mariam is getting on. She was having her operation today, wasn't she?'

'Yes.' Chloe glanced anxiously at her wristwatch. 'I think I shall telephone the hospital when we've done the flowers.'

'Why don't you take your basket in now?' Dora suggested. 'I can finish here—and I should like to know how Mariam is.'

'Yes, I shall then,' Chloe said and smiled at her. She had become very fond of Dora in the two and a half months she had spent with her. 'I asked Henry if he thought it would be a good idea for her to convalesce here, and he said we had plenty of room and he would be delighted to have her. Would you mind if I asked her?'

'No, of course not,' Dora said. 'We must pray that the doctors found that the tumour was not malignant.'

'Yes…'

Chloe hurried inside, placing her flowers in the little back room where they would later be arranged into various vases, then went through into the hall. As she did so, she was met by Sir Henry's housekeeper, who told her that there was a telephone call for her in the study.

'I was about to call you, madam,' she said.

'Thank you.'

Chloe quickened her step and went into the comfortable book-lined study, which was inclined to be dark on a grey afternoon like this. She was a little breathless as she picked up the telephone, hoping that it would not be bad news from Paris.

'Chloe!' Justine's excited voice came over the line. 'Oh, I'm so glad I got you. I wanted you to be the first to know outside the family. I'm engaged to a wonderful man!'

'That is good news,' Chloe said. 'I am so pleased for you. But you are a dark horse! You didn't breathe a word of this! Where did you meet him, and how long has this been going on?'

Justine giggled. 'Well, I haven't said anything, because Matthew didn't seem interested and well…you know how it is.'

'Matthew?'

'He's Sir Matthew actually,' Justine said, 'so Mummy is ecstatic as you can imagine. But he isn't stuffy at all, Chloe. He dances the Charleston like a

dream! We are having a little dance next week and I
wondered if you would come up and stay?'

'Yes, of course. I should love to,' Chloe said. 'You
know I wouldn't miss it for the world, although I
shan't be doing much dancing. I'm beginning to feel
a little oddly shaped.'

'Oh, you silly thing,' Justine said. 'I'll bet you look
lovely. Will Pasha be home in time to come with
you?'

Chloe felt a sharp pain in her breast as she answered, trying for carelessness, 'Oh, I very much
doubt it. He is still away with the prince.'

'Oh, well.' Justine sighed. 'I envied you when you
married him, but it must be awfully boring that he's
away so much.'

'Yes, it is,' Chloe agreed, but it wasn't boring. It
was painful and it didn't get any easier with time.

She was thoughtful after she finished talking to her
friend and replaced the receiver. She had hoped that
it might become easier to accept that her marriage was
over as the days, weeks and then months passed, but
it wasn't. In fact, it got worse as she became more
aware of the child growing inside her, and wished that
Pasha were there to share the experience with her.

But of course all that was finished, the closeness
and the loving were gone for good, and the ache in
her heart was a constant reminder of that. Even if he
was here, he would look at her with cold eyes, and
that would be even harder to bear than his absence.

Sighing, she reached for the telephone and began
to call the hospital for news of Mariam. It took her
some time to actually make contact with the doctor
who was treating Mariam, but when she finally did,
the news was mixed.

'We have removed the tumour,' he told her. 'I think that it may have been malignant, but we have managed to get it all and I believe that we may have been able to stop it spreading. Only time will tell—but at least she now has that time.'

'Yes, of course, thank you, doctor.'

Chloe replaced the receiver, feeling a little down. She could only hope that the doctor was right and that Pasha's stepmother did indeed have some time left to her.

But she mustn't let herself dwell on Mariam's illness; there was good news too. Justine was engaged, and she would be going to stay with her for a couple of days the following week.

But it would have been so much better if Pasha had been here too. She thought wistfully of the last time he had kissed her and wished that she could wave a magic wand and turn back the clock.

Pasha glanced at the heavy gold watch he wore on his wrist and sighed. These damned meetings seemed to drag on forever, and he was bored with having to attend them. It had taken weeks of negotiations to get his uncle to the stage where he was willing to sign the treaties with the British government, but at long last it looked as if he might be on the point of signing.

Pasha frowned as he saw the prince rise to his feet. Now what was wrong? He had thought that this was to be the morning for the signatures to go ahead, but it appeared that the prince had changed his mind once more and that would mean endless meetings and discussions to bring him back to the point.

And all Pasha wanted was to be in the country with Chloe. He had tried very hard to shut her out of his

heart and mind these past weeks, telling himself that
he would be a fool to let himself love a woman who
could not bring herself to trust him, but she wouldn't
be shut out. Her image haunted him by day and by
night…especially by night. Sometimes his dreams
were so vivid that he felt she was with him until he
woke to a cold bed and disappointment.

He had hoped that once these meetings were over,
he would finally be able to bow out of politics alto-
gether—to live the life he wanted instead of being at
his uncle's right hand. But it seemed that he would
have to control his own needs and desires once more.

The prince was leaving, and from his expression it
appeared that he was not pleased. Now what had the
British slipped into the treaty? There must be a new
clause, because he had checked everything with
Forbes and gone over it with the prince with a fine
toothcomb.

He was about to follow his uncle from the room
when Forbes put a hand on his shoulder, delaying
him.

'May I have a word with you, Pasha?'

'Yes, of course.' Pasha smothered a sigh. No doubt
Forbes was about to try and persuade him to accept
whatever it was the prince had rejected, but there was
simply no point. It had taken ages for Pasha to talk
his uncle into agreeing to the treaty as it stood and
if…

Even as he hesitated, there was the sound of gunfire
from outside the room, then shouting and screaming.
Pasha looked at Forbes in alarm, both of them starting
off at a run, only to halt in sudden horror as they saw
the scene of carnage that met their eyes in the corridor.

Three men were lying on the floor, having been shot several times. Pasha hurried to his uncle's side, and was greeted by a furious glare from Mohammed Ibn Ali, who had been summoned to the meeting by the prince at the last moment.

'My God!' Pasha stared in horror as he realised that his uncle was amongst the dead. How could this have happened when he had demanded so many security checks before agreeing to the meeting? A surge of grief and revulsion went over him, and he blamed himself for not being there when his uncle needed him. If he had been, there was just a chance that he might have prevented this.

'This is your fault,' Mohammed accused Pasha. 'The prince knew that he should never have agreed to this treaty...and now look what they have done to him.'

'This was the work of extremists,' Pasha said, his eyes narrowed and suspicious. He glanced down at the face of the man he had served faithfully for some years and saw that he was dead. 'Are you hurt, Mohammed?' He put out a hand to touch his cousin, who moved angrily away from him.

'It is a mere scratch.' He shrugged his shoulders, his face harsh. 'Would that they had killed me instead of him!'

Pasha saw that Mohammed was bleeding slightly from a wound in his arm, but that his uncle's bodyguards were both dead. Whoever had done this had been quite determined to kill those closest to the prince, which would have included him had Forbes not delayed him.

'You should go to hospital,' Pasha said to Mohammed. 'Your arm needs attention.'

'Better it should wither than an infidel should touch it,' Mohammed said bitterly. His eyes were dark with anger. 'Do not imagine I do not know why this has been done. He refused to sign, but you are his heir. They know that you will sign in his place.'

With that parting comment, he turned and walked away, brushing aside the officials and police alike as he strode out of the building.

Pasha stared after him, his brow furrowed. He was well aware that at least a part of what his cousin had just said might well be true.

'This is a terrible business,' Forbes said, coming up to him. 'It will set the whole question of a treaty back months, if not years. If they had to get him at last, I wish they had done it anywhere but here.'

'Yes, it is most inconvenient for you,' Pasha said, hiding his anger at the other man's choice of words. 'Will your police allow me to see to things here or will they insist on taking charge?'

'You must leave it to them for the time being,' Forbes said. 'I'll make sure that you are given access as soon as possible and you can make the arrangements for his body to be taken home.'

'Thank you,' Pasha said and inclined his head. 'Now you must excuse me.'

He was seething with anger as he walked away. He had thought that the British were dealing straight with him, but if Mohammed was right...

Sick to his stomach, he thought that the sooner he could wash his hands of this whole business the better he would feel.

Chloe paid the taxi and stood on the pavement clutching her small bag. She hadn't bothered to bring much with her, because she knew that most of her clothes would not fit her well enough. She planned on doing some shopping before she went to Justine's the next day, but for the moment she was going to stay in the apartment.

She had the key in her bag, and was just about to open the door of the apartment when she heard the telephone ringing inside. She went in quickly, picking up the phone even as she wondered who knew she was here. She had told no one but Henry and Dora. She held the receiver to her ear, sounding a little breathless as she answered.

'Yes—Chloe here…'

'Are you all right, my dear?' Henry asked. 'Only when we heard the news we were anxious.'

'I've just arrived,' Chloe said and perched on the chair next to the hall table. 'What news is that?'

'There was an assassination in London today,' Henry said. 'I hope this isn't too shocking for you, but the prince was killed and two of his bodyguards.'

'Pasha…' Chloe's heart raced madly. The colour drained from her face, her eyes wide with shock. 'Was he hurt? Oh, please, don't tell me he was shot, Henry. I couldn't bear it…'

'No, no, my dear. Pasha rang himself to let us know. I told him you were coming up. He says he's fine.'

'Oh, thank God, thank God,' Chloe said. She bent over, head dipping as she fought to get her breath, her back towards the open door of the sitting room. 'I couldn't bear it if he'd been killed, Henry…' She choked back a sob, then, hearing a sound behind her, she whirled round fearfully. 'Pasha!'

Leaving the telephone hanging, she ran towards

him, everything forgotten in her relief at seeing him alive. She was laughing and crying at the same time and as he moved to catch her in his arms, she flung hers about him.

'Pasha…Pasha…' she wept. 'Henry just told me… I am so sorry about your uncle.'

A shadow passed across his face, and she understood that his ties to his uncle had been far deeper than she had imagined. For the first time she knew why as a last resort he had been prepared to order the assassination of a man who had sworn to kill his uncle because he had sincerely believed there was no other way to protect a man he loved! Just as he would protect her with his life if need be.

What conflict that must have caused him, torn between affection, duty and his own conscience. And now the prince had been killed despite all his efforts.

'You mustn't blame yourself, my darling. You did all you could.'

Her words were smothered by his kiss, which was both hungry and demanding, stripping her of the ability to think at all until he released her a moment or so later.

'I am so glad you are safe,' she said, clinging to him as he gazed down into her tear-drenched eyes. 'I love you so much…so much…'

'I love you, Chloe,' he said, and then gave her his teasing smile, that look she had missed so much. 'I think you should hang up on poor Henry properly, don't you?'

'Oh, yes.' Chloe caught back a sob that was almost a laugh. She went over to the phone and caught up the receiver. 'I'm sorry, Henry. Pasha is here.'

'No need to be sorry, my dear,' he told her. 'It's

about time that husband of yours came home and took care of you—and you tell him that from me.'

'Yes, I shall.' Chloe laughed. 'We'll be in touch soon.'

She replaced the receiver carefully this time, and went back to Pasha, who took her in his arms and kissed her again. It was some while before either of them felt like talking.

She was lying in his arms, after his gentle love-making had carried her to the heights, when he began to tell her of what had happened—and what was in his mind for the future.

Chloe eased herself up and looked at him, her eyes serious and still dark with passion. 'Are you sure that is why your uncle was killed—because he would not sign the treaty that would make his land a British protectorate?'

'It's what Mohammed thinks.'

Chloe wrinkled her brow as she recalled the memory. 'He was with you in the desert, and he didn't like me...'

'He doesn't like me very much either,' Pasha said and smiled oddly. 'But at least he doesn't pretend to be a friend to my face and plot behind my back.'

Chloe reached up to touch his face lovingly. 'I missed you so much,' she said. 'So very much. When Henry said—'

'Yes, I know. I heard you,' he said and smiled at her ruefully. 'I've been a stubborn fool, Chloe. I was angry and fearful of what might happen to you, but I shouldn't have left the way I did. I wanted to come back to you weeks ago.'

'Only weeks?' she asked, a look of mischief in her

eyes. 'I wanted you to come back two seconds after you left!'

'I should never have gone,' Pasha said. 'It's my pride, Chloe.'

She touched her fingers to his lips, shaking her head. 'No, Pasha. Your pride is only partly to blame. I was too naïve when we married. I didn't understand and I judged too quickly. I was more at fault than you were.'

'We were both at fault,' he said and smiled oddly. 'I have learned a lot about myself these past weeks, Chloe, and there is one thing I am certain of, apart from the fact that I love you, of course.'

'As long as you learned that,' she said with a contented sigh and nestled against him. 'Oh dear, Philip does come between us a bit, doesn't he?'

'Philip?' Pasha's brows arched in amusement. 'You've decided that he is going to be a boy then?'

Chloe kissed his shoulder, smoothing her fingers through the crisp hair on his chest. He had such a firm, well-muscled body, a product she knew of the sport he had played as a youth, and still kept up. Apparently he excelled at playing the game of tennis, riding over fences in three-day event trials, and swimming. Her stay with Henry and Dora had taught her a great deal about him, but of course she had known about the swimming. Why else would he have had his own house built so close to the sea in Spain? At the time she has just thought of it as an extravagant luxury, but now she knew he had needed it when he had time to relax.

'Well, I should like to have a son just like you.'

'Just like me?' he teased.

'Well, almost like you,' she qualified. 'But I hope

Philip will prefer to stay in this country rather than go haring all over the world.'

'Then he will be just like me,' Pasha said and touched the end of her nose with his fingertip. 'That is what I learned these past weeks, Chloe. I am tired of the way I have been living. It was never what I wanted, but I felt I owed it to my uncle—and to my father's memory.'

'Yes, I can understand that,' Chloe agreed. 'I would rather you never had to be involved in any of that political stuff again.'

'Yes…and somehow I am going to make sure that I'm not,' Pasha said, looking thoughtfully at her. 'I thought I knew the way, Chloe. But now I am not so sure.'

'What do you mean?'

'It is best that you don't know.'

'Please,' she said. 'Don't do that again—don't shut me out, Pasha. Let me share what is worrying you…let me be a part of all of your life, not just some of it.'

He gazed down at her for a moment, and then he inclined his head. 'It wasn't that I wanted to shut you out, Chloe. I wanted to protect you,' he said. 'I wanted to be sure that you were not touched by any of this.'

'I am not a silly little girl any longer,' she said, tilting her head at him. 'I've grown up.'

'Yes, you have,' he said and looked grave. 'You've lost that funny little girl look that I loved—and I did that to you.'

'It wasn't you,' Chloe said. 'It was Ahmad—and life. I would have had to grow up one day, Pasha. I couldn't stay a little girl forever.'

'No, of course you couldn't.' He smiled down at her. 'And though I may miss the little girl look, I would rather have the woman you have become, darling.'

'Thank you.' She blushed as she saw the heat in his eyes, knowing that their loving had been hungry and passionate—perhaps more passionate than ever before, with her more than holding her own. 'I like being her, Pasha. And I love being married to you.'

'Good, because I intend that you shall stay that way,' he said and touched her cheek. 'I hope you didn't believe all that rubbish about letting you go, Chloe? You must know I didn't mean it.'

'That's fine with me.' She snuggled up to him. 'Because I've no intention of leaving you.'

They lay close to one another in silence for a moment or two, and then Chloe looked up at him. 'So what are you going to do, Pasha? You are your uncle's heir, aren't you?'

'Yes.' He sighed. 'I know the British expect me to sign their treaty, and a part of me thinks it's the best thing for all concerned, but there's another part of me that keeps telling me I am betraying my past. Selling out.'

'And you still care about your past, don't you?' Chloe asked. 'It still matters to you despite the fact that you've spent so much time in England these past years. You still feel the call of the desert—of your blood.'

'Yes, I suppose it does,' Pasha agreed. 'I want to be free of it all, the political double-dealing and the power. I hate it, Chloe, and the easy way is to hand it over to the British. On the other hand…' He sighed and seemed troubled.

'You feel that might be betraying your uncle and your father?' Chloe knew that she was right as he nodded. 'Why don't you go back to your past?' she asked. 'Go back to where it all happened, to your father's *casbah,* to the desert.'

'It's odd that you should say that,' he said, holding her pressed close against him, his hand stroking the satin smoothness of her back, following the arch and cupping her buttocks. 'I have been thinking of doing just that recently.'

'It might be that you could find the solution,' Chloe said. 'Until you do, you will never be at peace, Pasha.'

'But I don't want to leave you again.'

'Why should you?' she asked. 'I'm not quite five months pregnant. There's no reason why I shouldn't come with you.' She laughed up at him. 'There's no way I'm letting you go off without me again, whatever it takes.'

Pasha laughed and began to kiss her on the lips once more, his mouth taking its lazy journey down the line of her throat to her breasts. He sucked and teased at the nipples until he had her arching towards him again, willing him to love her, his dark eyes wicked with love and mischief as he looked down at her.

'I was conceived under desert stars,' he said. 'Are you prepared for your son to be born in the desert, my darling?'

'As long as you are there to take care of us both,' she said and giggled as she felt a kicking sensation in her belly. She took his hand and placed it gently on her stomach. 'Can you feel that, Pasha? Can you feel him moving? That is your son telling you he just wants to be near his father.'

Pasha looked at her, wonder in his eyes.

'Are you sure you feel well enough to go travelling?'

'If your mother could have you in the desert, I can have my child there.'

Pasha laughed. 'My mother had far too much sense. She demanded a Western doctor present at the birth, and I shall make sure you have the same, Chloe. But we can fly out to the *casbah* in easy stages, and be back in London long before our son is born.'

Chapter Thirteen

It was dark when their plane landed at the small private airport. Chloe glanced about her but was unable to see very much, except for a few white buildings at the perimeter. They had flown the last stages to the prince's Home State, where Pasha was to attend his uncle's funeral.

Pasha turned to Chloe as they descended from the plane. 'We shall be surrounded by my uncle's people at any moment,' he told her and smiled. 'I am afraid it will be all protocol once that happens, and you may feel a little left out, but don't forget that you are more important than anything else to me.'

'Please don't worry,' Chloe assured him. 'I do understand.'

She saw a man walking towards them and caught Pasha's arm urgently: for some reason an alarm bell was ringing in her head as she saw the man raise his right hand.

'He has a gun!'

Before she could finish Pasha gave a cry of anguish and pushed her away from him. Chloe stumbled and fell as a series of shots rang out. She screamed, fearing that her husband may have been shot, but then she heard his voice as he knelt by her side.

'Forgive me if I hurt you, my dearest,' he said in a voice tight with emotion. 'This is what I have always feared, that an attempt would be made on my life when you were with me.'

'What happened?' Glancing in the direction from where the assassination attempt had been made she saw that men were running everywhere and shouting. Another man lay on the ground, obviously dead. 'They killed him.'

'Yes.' Pasha frowned as he saw her white face and felt her shudder. 'It was the quick action of the reception committee that saved us, Chloe.'

'But you saved me,' she said. 'That first shot…'

She felt sick as she realised that either of them could have been killed. It no longer surprised her that Pasha had been so possessive of her, even going so far as to forbid her to leave him, he knew that her life was as much in danger as his own.

'Forgive me,' he said in a broken voice. 'It won't happen again. I promise you that. I cannot have your life at risk; it is too important to me. I shall and will do something.'

'Oh, Pasha, my love…'

Chloe did not ask what he meant, but she could see by the determined look on his face that he intended to make some sort of a change for the future.

Chloe did not attend the state funeral of Prince Hassan. She was left behind while Pasha did all that was expected of him as his uncle's heir. She knew that he had been besieged with people wanting to talk to him since they arrived in the small Gulf state, but he had managed to spend as much time with her as he could.

'Today belongs to the people,' he told her when he left to attend the lengthy ceremony. 'Forgive me for abandoning you, but I cannot do other than what is expected of me.'

'You must do what is right,' Chloe told him. 'I shall write to Justine and to Mariam while I wait for you to come back.'

They had been able to attend Justine's engagement party, and to see Mariam safely settled at Henry's before they left on their journey to convey the prince's body back to his homeland. It had taken several days to clear all the paperwork despite Pasha hurrying it along as best he could, because the police had been reluctant to release the body. Arrests had been made and there was a diplomatic tussle going on over where the assassins were to be tried. But, in the end Pasha had finalised the details so that the journey home could begin.

However, once the funeral was over, Pasha had told Chloe that he intended to fly his own light aircraft to Morocco, and after a short stay in Marrakesh to take care of some unfinished business, they would go on to his father's *casbah* in the Atlas Mountains.

She had been given splendid rooms in the prince's palace, and his wives had made her welcome, several of them able to talk to her either in English or French. They were all curious about her clothes, and asked her where she had bought them. She saw envious looks on some of their faces as she told them she had visited the salon of Coco Chanel in Paris.

She was asked what would happen now that the prince was dead, but Chloe merely smiled and shook her head. She could not tell them for she did not know yet what Pasha would decide.

He spoke of giving up his political life, and spending more time with her. He had a business to run, and many other interests, and she believed he genuinely wanted to break free—but would he be allowed to do so?

'Not if the prince's advisers have their way,' Pasha told her when he returned late that evening, clearly drained. 'They are worried that the State is vulnerable to being taken over by another ruler if I do not grasp the reins myself.' He frowned and ran his fingers through his hair, looking more tired than she had ever seen him. 'I have to decide what is best, Chloe.'

She instinctively understood that his worried expression was for her, for what effect the assassination attempt might have had on her, on her peace of mind.

'I know you will do whatever is right. You mustn't worry about me, Pasha. I was a foolish child when we married, but now I understand so many things. I know that you must do whatever is necessary.'

'My dearest Chloe. If I should lose you…'

'You won't,' she told him with a loving smile. 'Nothing can part us now.'

'If only I could be sure.'

'Come to bed, my love,' she said, going up to him and putting her arms about him, reaching up to brush her mouth softly over his. The effect was instantaneous, his tiredness falling away as he scooped her up in his arms and carried her to their bed. 'I am so heavy,' she said and laughed at him as he laid her down. 'Soon you will not be able to lift me.'

Her teasing was having its desired effect. Pasha

threw off his worries and began to kiss her, stroking her body until it quivered and trembled and she was ready for him to love her again.

That night Chloe was woken by Pasha's violent thrashing beside her in the bed, and she knew that he was troubled by his dreams. He feared that he was being dragged into a life that he disliked but could not avoid…and there was nothing she could do to help him, except offer him her love and her body.

Only Pasha could decide what he must do.

Chloe felt excited as they circled over the fort so that she could see it completely from the air. It was built of a pinkish stone, as were many of the ruined forts in the mountains, but this was neither ruined nor abandoned.

She could see people moving about below them, looking up at the sky, shading their eyes with their hands to watch as the small aircraft prepared to land on the strip that had been prepared specially for their coming.

As they flew over the mountains, Chloe had seen the children herding goats and sheep, their clothes much as their fathers and grandfathers had worn before them. This might be the twentieth century, but time had stood still here for many years. The land was arid, fit only for the poor living that these people wrested from it, relying mainly on their flocks.

However, when Pasha helped her from the plane and they began to walk towards the fort, the people came out to greet them, shyly at first, and then with mounting enthusiasm as if they were genuinely pleased to see their feudal master.

The children gathered about Chloe, pulling at the long skirts of the dress she had chosen to wear, which reached almost to her ankles and, though of rich materials, was otherwise much as their mothers might wear.

'What are they saying?' she asked Pasha as they chattered and pointed at her, their little faces as cheeky as they were happy.

'They are saying that you carry my child,' he replied, 'and they think it is good that you should be so fruitful so soon.'

Chloe flushed bright red. 'Do they know when we were married? I thought you hadn't been here for years?'

'I paid a brief visit when I was travelling with my uncle,' Pasha said. 'I thought it was time I checked to make sure that they were all managing well, and I was able to make some improvements. A new well down in the valley and other things.'

'Well, they certainly seem pleased to see you.'

'I think it is you they are mostly interested in,' Pasha said. 'It seems they have not forgotten the way my mother tried to help the women when she lived here.'

'She wanted the women to learn a trade, didn't she?' Chloe remembered that his mother had died of blood poisoning after cutting her hand on a piece of rusty metal.

'Apparently, they had a visit from a western merchant some months ago. He was interested in buying cloth the women had been weaving. I'm planning to set up some weaving sheds here so that the women can make a little money for themselves. They may have to be dragged into the twentieth century, Chloe, but I believe they are beginning to see the benefits as well as the evils.'

'With you to help them, I am sure they will,' Chloe said, her eyes warm with love for him. She reached out to touch his hand, and then saw that the children were giggling, clearly watching everything she did with avid interest. 'I shall have to be careful what I do!'

'Oh, they won't mind.' Pasha laughed. 'They believe that it is your influence that has brought them their good fortune. You are a talisman and can do no wrong.'

They stayed at the fort for five days before Pasha decided it was time to move on. Chloe was reluctant to leave the friendly people who had taken her to their hearts, and she waved to the children who stood watching as their plane rose like a huge white bird into the sky.

'I am not surprised that they tug at your heart-strings,' she told Pasha. 'I like your people.'

'And they liked you,' he said, smiling at her tenderly. 'We shall go back there one day, but first I have something I must do.'

'You have arranged a meeting in the desert with Mohammed…' She looked at him doubtfully. 'Is it wise to meet on his territory? Can you trust him, Pasha?'

'As much as I can trust any man,' he replied and frowned at her. 'I do not fear a knife in my back while we are in Mohammed's camp, Chloe. If he wished to murder me it would not be while we are his guests. We were safe while we stayed with Ahmad. It was only later that he tried to harm you.'

Chloe nodding, understanding that it would be against the Bedouin code of honour to offer an insult to a guest.

'Have you heard from Sashimi at all?' she asked him. 'Is she still living in Paris? I gather that is where she went when she left England.'

'She lives there still,' Pasha said. 'I believe that she has lovers, though she vows never to marry again, but she likes men who give her presents, I have heard.'

'Who told you that?'

'Mohammed,' he replied. 'He is angry that she flaunts our ways like that, but he was forbidden to approach her while the prince lived. I have made a similar order.'

'So you protect her.' Chloe smiled at him. 'I was such a fool that day, Pasha. I should have known that you would not kill in cold blood…'

'It is forgotten,' he said and smiled at her, his eyes going over her in concern. 'Are you well, my love? I know there are still some months but I am anxious for you.'

'There is no need, I am perfectly well,' Chloe replied. 'You know that I am, Pasha. It is merely that I grow fat and ugly like a cow.'

'You are beautiful and most un-cowlike,' he said, looking amused.

'That is not what I was told yesterday,' she said. 'One of the women told me that I was like a beautiful sleek cow and that I would give birth to a fine calf.'

Pasha chuckled, his brows rising. 'She believed she was paying you a compliment, Chloe. A cow such as she meant would bring a good price in the market.'

'I dare say,' Chloe said. 'But I had far rather not be sold, if you don't mind.'

'Oh, it all depends how many camels I am offered for you,' he said, a wicked gleam in his eyes. 'I think I shall not take less than ten.'

'If you were not flying this plane, I would strangle you!'

'I must remind you of that tonight,' Pasha murmured. 'When I summon you to my couch. Remember, woman, I am a Sheikh and you are about to be taken to my tent in the desert…'

'I think it's a bit late if you were intending to seduce me,' Chloe said and pulled a face at him as she patted what she liked to think of as her bulge. 'Did you know that they are talking of making *The Son of the Sheikh* now? I shall expect you to take me to see that when it is shown at home.'

Pasha looked at her oddly. 'You never know,' he said. 'I might do more than that, providing you give me the son you promised me, woman.'

'And what does that mean?' she asked, intrigued by his provocative look. 'Just what have you been up to now, Pasha?'

'Something I think you may enjoy,' he said, but would not be drawn further, no matter how she pouted and provoked. 'You will just have to wait and see…'

They had begun to circle lower over the desert. Chloe looked out of the window as the tents began to look real and not just like tiny dots in the acres of sand surrounding them. People were looking up as they approached the landing area, some of them waving.

She held her breath as they touched down. The last time she had been in the desert she had been close to death, and then she had fallen in love.

* * *

Chloe was washing her face in a brightly polished copper bowl when Pasha walked into the tent that evening. They had been three days in the desert and she had hardly seen him in all that time. He and Mohammed had been talking constantly day and night, and Chloe had been relegated to the women's company.

She was well aware that Mohammed did not approve of her being given as much freedom as Pasha normally allowed her, and she had noticed his dark eyes watching her with barely hidden hostility.

It was a surprise then when Pasha told her that she was bidden to a feast that evening.

'My cousin has asked that you sit with him at his right hand,' Pasha told her. 'He wishes you to tell him about the way women live in your world.'

'Are you serious?' Chloe asked, staring at him in surprise. 'I thought that was the last thing he was interested in.'

'My cousin has finally realised that it is time he became a twentieth-century man,' Pasha said, a wicked glint in his eyes. 'I am very pleased to tell you that I believe we have finally reached an agreement, Chloe—and this banquet is to celebrate. Mohammed wishes to show you honour, and I believe you will be surprised by the change in him.'

'That sounds very intriguing.' Her eyes held curiosity as she looked at him, but he merely smiled and shook his head. She pouted at him, but she was too content, too serene, to demand an answer. She was beginning to understand him now, to know that whatever he did would be just. 'You are being mysterious again, but I shall not be drawn. I don't care what you are up to, Pasha. I like being here. There is something special about the desert…it calls to something inside me…' She laughed and looked self-conscious. 'I suppose that sounds foolish?'

'It sounds good to me,' Pasha said. 'I hope that we shall return both to the *casbah* and the desert one day, my love.'

As he turned and went out, Chloe began to look through her clothes. She would have to choose something very special for that evening, for she sensed that it was an important occasion.

Pasha looked at her when she presented herself, his eyes warm and admiring. She had chosen a long flowing gown in a rich royal blue. It had a squared neckline and a high waist caught beneath her breasts with an embroidered band, and the sleeves were long and flared.

Her hair, which was below her shoulders now, and much lighter than it had been when they first met, was swept back and caught with a gold headband that looked very much like any Bedouin woman would wear, but she wore no veil. Her throat was bare and she wore no other jewel except her wedding ring.

'You look beautiful,' Pasha said and took her hand. 'And I love the way you have chosen to show respect and yet be yourself—a woman of the West.'

'Since you told me that Mohammed wishes to know what the women of my world like, I thought it right to show as well as to tell him—should he ask for my advice.'

'Oh, he will ask,' Pasha said. 'You see there are to be big changes in Mohammed's life, and he has realised that he must begin to live in the new world to which he is called.'

'What have you done, Pasha?' Chloe gazed up into his eyes. 'I think I can guess, but you do not wish to tell me yet. Why?'

'Because the announcement is to be made at the feast this evening,' Pasha said. 'It would not be fitting if I told my wife before the other men are informed.'

Chloe nodded her understanding. She could not, of course, expect to be told something this important until it was officially announced, but she had guessed what Pasha had not told her.

A huge tent capable of holding many people had been erected at the edge of the camp, and as Pasha led Chloe towards it she saw that several men had arrived. Important men by the look of it, men who had brought their followers with them, women and children too so that the camp had spread outwards from the oasis into the sand for a long way.

Fires were burning all over the camps, and the smell of roasting meat filled the air, as did the sense of excitement. It was clearly a large feast and the mood of celebration had spread amongst the people; it was as if they all knew that something momentous was about to happen.

Inside the tent, silken cushions were placed everywhere with little lamps and tables. Here there was the scent of sweet oils burning, spices and a heavy musky perfume. At the far end there were three raised couches, where Mohammed was already seated, and Pasha led Chloe towards them.

Mohammed rose as they approached, bowing to her and coming forward to take her hand and lead her to the place of honour on his right-hand side.

'You are welcome, lady,' he said in the most courteous tone she had had from him. 'Please honour me by sitting here and giving me the favour of your conversation. I have much to learn, and my honoured cousin tells me that you are well disposed towards our people.'

'I have found your people friendly and your way of life good,' Chloe said. 'There are many wonders to be found in the modern world, sir, and I believe that we should take the best of them, but the simple ways of the desert people should not be entirely forgotten.'

Mohammed nodded, his eyes seeming to hold amusement. She had not thought it before, but now she began to see something of Pasha in him, and to realise that they were more alike than she had imagined.

'You speak wisely,' he said. 'I believe when we first met I misjudged you, princess, but now I understand why Pasha married you. I believe your influence has been good for him.'

'My husband acts always as he believes right, sir.'

Mohammed nodded again. 'This too is right and we shall hear more of this before the night is over…' He motioned to her to sit down. 'Sit, eat, my lady, and we shall talk.'

Chloe sat on the couch and smiled as she was approached by one of the serving women with a little silver dish, on which were all kinds of delicacies. She took one of the little cakes, which were sticky and soft in the middle and tasted of almonds, nibbling at it as Mohammed began to ask her questions.

Chloe found that he was far more knowledgeable of the ways of the West than she had imagined, and although he clearly did not approve of the fashions women wore these days, which he thought hardly decent, he was very interested to learn that she had been to college and that she was interested in Arabic literature, in particular poetry.

They spoke of Omar Khayyam, the astronomer-poet of Persia, who was born in the eleventh century, the son of a tent maker.

'Your people know of his writings through the translation of the *Rubaiyat* and other works,' Mohammed said. 'But there was far more to the man. He was a great mathematician and he reformed the Muslim calendar.'

'Yes, I have read several of the translations,' Chloe agreed, 'and a life of the poet. But I have also read lesser known poets I think his equal or perhaps even more intriguing.'

They spoke for some time of the poets and of the possibility of some original material that Mohammed possessed that he would be willing to lend her so that Pasha could help her translate it. After that they talked more of what Chloe felt he might do to help the women amongst his people live more enriching lives.

It was not until quite late in the evening, after they had all eaten and been entertained by jugglers and dancers, that the business began.

All at once silence fell as Pasha rose to his feet and addressed the assembled company in his native tongue. He spoke for some minutes, and then sat down again. Mohammed then rose and did the same, and at a signal from him two men brought in two little tables with a very elaborate-looking document on each.

Pasha signed his, and then Mohammed signed and

the documents were exchanged. Only then was there a collective sigh from the company.

Then the men got up and went to Mohammed, bowing before him and kissing the hand he offered. They also bowed and salaamed to Pasha, but did not kiss his hand. Mohammed said something more, and then everyone started to leave the tent. From outside, Chloe could hear the sound of guns being fired.

She looked at Pasha in alarm, but he smiled at her.

'It is a celebration,' he told her. 'The documents we just signed make Mohammed my uncle's heir. He will assume those duties that would otherwise be mine. We have agreed that two-thirds of the oil revenues from his land and mine shall be used for the good of our people. The money will be used to build a modern city that will be as good as anything the Western world can provide, and it will have schools and hospitals for the people.'

'Oh, Pasha…' Chloe looked at him with moist eyes. 'I think that is wonderful…really wonderful…'

'I am glad that you approve,' he said, and stood up. He gave her his hand to help her rise, and then he bowed his head to Mohammed and she did the same. 'I know that you will rule justly and wisely,' Pasha said. 'You have offered me a position such as I held with the prince, but I have refused. I believe that in giving the safe keeping of our land into your hands, I may now retire to live my own life in the way I choose.'

Mohammed nodded, his dark eyes gleaming with satisfaction.

'You have acted with wisdom and generosity, my cousin, and our people shall know of your goodness. Your name shall be honoured amongst us. Go in peace with your woman, and may the blessings of Allah be upon you both.'

Chloe curtsied to him, and then Pasha led her from the tent. She glanced at him when they were outside.

'You have the wisdom of Solomon,' she said. 'Where did that idea come from?'

'I had been thinking of putting my oil revenues into a trust for the people, for in truth it is their land, Chloe. Why should one man have all the riches that come from the earth? It will be a great deal of money one day, and I have enough through my own endeavours. I kept back one-third, and that will be used to improve the lot of my own particular people.'

'The people at your father's *casbah*?'

'Yes.' His eyes looked into hers. 'It sets us free, Chloe. Mohammed is the right man to step into the prince's shoes. I had thought it for a while, but I could not simply hand over to him without some form of treaty between us. I was not prepared to see the wealth that will come from oil squandered. But I was right to believe that Mohammed would agree to use it for the people, and I am content that he will be a just ruler.'

They had not returned to their tent at once, but walked under the stars to the edge of the oasis, away from the noise of the celebrations to the quietness of some sand dunes. And there Pasha took her in his arms, kissing her tenderly on the lips.

'Are you sad that I shall merely be Mr Armand from now on and no longer a powerful Sheikh?' he asked her teasingly.

'You could never be *merely* anything,' Chloe said and laughed as she gazed into his wicked eyes. 'I shall be quite content to have Mr Armand as my husband, but we shall come back to the desert sometimes, Pasha? It is so romantic here beneath the stars.'

'I believe you are more a Bedouin than I am,' Pasha teased her and put his arm about her waist as they both looked up at the dark sky, sprinkled now with a cluster of stars. Behind them the lights of the fires were red against the sky, but here they were alone with the mystery of the desert that had remained unsolved for centuries. 'Yes, my darling. We shall come back sometimes. Like you, I feel the pull of its beauty, especially at night when the heat is not so fierce.'

'So…' Chloe gazed up at him, love and mischief combined in a face that became more beautiful every day. 'Have I at last convinced you that it is romantic to be carried off by a Sheikh?'

Pasha's laughter was warm and throaty. 'I see that I shall never cure you, Chloe. You are a hopeless romantic.'

'You have revealed one of your secrets,' Chloe said, arching her neck as she looked at him provocatively. 'But there is something else…something you mentioned as we were coming here…'

'Ah…' Pasha gave her a teasing look. 'For that you must wait, my darling. When I have my son…then I shall tell you.'

Afterword

Chloe glanced at herself in the mirror. She was wearing a very elegant new gown that Pasha had chosen for her in an expensive New York store earlier that day. They had been in America for three days, having travelled there on a luxurious liner once she was over the birth of their son.

She turned as her husband came into the bedroom.

'Has he settled with Nanny now?' she asked, knowing that he had been with Philip Henry, because he had *that* smile on his face—the smile he always wore after being with their child.

'Yes,' he replied and looked at her. 'You are more beautiful than ever, my darling. Are you looking forward to the party this evening?'

'Yes, of course.' She touched the pearls at her throat. 'You spoil me, Pasha.'

'You are worth it,' he said and put his arms around her waist from behind, looking at her in the mirror. 'I promised you a surprise, didn't I?'

'Ages ago,' she replied. 'I thought you had forgotten.' She swung round to gaze up at him. 'Is it to do with the party?'

'Yes and no.' He had that teasing glint in his eyes again. 'You know that the professor and Amelia are coming.'

'Of course.' Chloe laughed. 'I think what we did pushed Amelia into doing something she ought to have done years ago—she asked him to marry her, you know.'

'And he said yes—sensible man,' Pasha said. 'I was always sorry that we didn't invite them to our wedding, but as you know he had dragged poor Amelia off to some remote fort again.'

'Not so poor—she loves him.' Chloe pulled a face. 'So what is my surprise, or are you going to make me wait forever?'

'I've invited some people from the motion picture business to our party.' Pasha laughed as he saw her face. 'As a matter of fact, we're on the verge of a breakthrough with talking movies.'

'We…?' Chloe frowned. 'I don't understand. What do you mean *we* are on the verge of a breakthrough?'

'I invested in a firm researching the idea some months ago,' Pasha replied. 'Tomorrow I'll take you to see something special, but tonight I have a more important surprise for you.'

Chloe gave him a murderous look. 'Pasha! If your son wasn't sleeping peacefully in the next room I might do you a serious injury.'

Pasha chuckled as he saw her impatient expression. 'I've been told that we might have an extra guest at our party…a certain Mr Valentino…'

'Valentino…' Chloe stared at him in amazement. 'You don't mean it? Coming to our party? Oh, it is a pity Justine couldn't manage to be here. She is mad about him.'

'I thought you were rather partial to him yourself?' Pasha raised his brows.

'He's wonderful in the pictures,' Chloe said, a roguish smile touching her mouth. 'And of course he always looks so romantic and exciting but...' She paused wickedly. 'I have my very own Sheikh now and I don't think any other man could quite measure up to my ideals.'

'Flatterer!' Pasha said but his eyes glowed like hot coals. 'It is just as well you said that, lady wife, because otherwise I might have had to cancel the party and carry you off to my *casbah*...'

* * * * *

Modern Romance™
...seduction and
passion guaranteed

Tender Romance™
...love affairs that
last a lifetime

Sensual Romance™
...sassy, sexy and
seductive

Blaze Romance™
...the temperature's
rising

Medical Romance™
...medical drama on
the pulse

Historical Romance™
...rich, vivid and
passionate

27 new titles every month.

*With all kinds of Romance for
every kind of mood...*

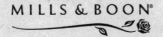

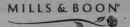

FREE!

2 Books
and a surprise gift!

We would like to take this opportunity to thank you for reading this Mills & Boon® book by offering you the chance to take TWO more specially selected titles from the Historical Romance™ series absolutely FREE! We're also making this offer to introduce you to the benefits of the Reader Service™ —

★ FREE home delivery
★ FREE gifts and competitions
★ FREE monthly Newsletter
★ Books available before they're in the shops
★ Exclusive Reader Service discount

Accepting these FREE books and gift places you under no obligation to buy; you may cancel at any time, even after receiving your free shipment. Simply complete your details below and return the entire page to the address below. **You don't even need a stamp!**

YES! Please send me 2 free Historical Romance books and a surprise gift. I understand that unless you hear from me, I will receive 4 superb new titles every month for just £3.49 each, postage and packing free. I am under no obligation to purchase any books and may cancel my subscription at any time. The free books and gift will be mine to keep in any case.

H3ZEB

Ms/Mrs/Miss/Mr ....Initials.............................
BLOCK CAPITALS PLEASE

Surname...

Address...

....

....Postcode ....

Send this whole page to:
UK: The Reader Service, FREEPOST CN81, Croydon, CR9 3WZ
EIRE: The Reader Service, PO Box 4546, Kilcock, County Kildare (stamp required)

Offer not valid to current Reader Service subscribers to this series. We reserve the right to refuse an application and applicants must be aged 18 years or over. Only one application per household. Terms and prices subject to change without notice. Offer expires 30th May 2003. As a result of this application, you may receive offers from Harlequin Mills & Boon and other carefully selected companies. If you would prefer not to share in this opportunity please write to The Data Manager at the address above.

Mills & Boon® is a registered trademark owned by Harlequin Mills & Boon Limited.
Historical Romance™ is being used as a trademark.